# BANDSLAM:
# THE NOVEL

**Adapted by Aaron Rosenberg**

**Based on the screenplay by Josh A. Cagan and Todd Graff**

PSS!
PRICE STERN SLOAN

PRICE STERN SLOAN
Published by the Penguin Group
Penguin Group (USA) Inc., 375 Hudson Street, New York, New York 10014, USA
Penguin Group (Canada), 90 Eglinton Avenue East, Suite 700, Toronto, Ontario
M4P 2Y3, Canada (a division of Pearson Penguin Canada Inc.)
Penguin Books Ltd., 80 Strand, London WC2R 0RL, England
Penguin Group Ireland, 25 St. Stephen's Green, Dublin 2, Ireland
(a division of Penguin Books Ltd.)
Penguin Group (Australia), 250 Camberwell Road, Camberwell, Victoria 3124, Australia
(a division of Pearson Australia Group Pty. Ltd.)
Penguin Books India Pvt. Ltd., 11 Community Centre, Panchsheel Park,
New Delhi—110 017, India
Penguin Group (NZ), 67 Apollo Drive, Rosedale, North Shore 0632, New Zealand
(a division of Pearson New Zealand Ltd.)
Penguin Books (South Africa) (Pty.) Ltd., 24 Sturdee Avenue,
Rosebank, Johannesburg 2196, South Africa

Penguin Books Ltd., Registered Offices: 80 Strand, London WC2R 0RL, England

Library of Congress Control Number: 2008041681

ISBN 978-0-8431-3484-1                                    10 9 8 7 6 5 4 3 2 1

SUMMIT ENTERTAINMENT AND WALDEN MEDIA PRESENT A GOLDSMITH-THOMAS PRODUCTION "BANDSLAM" ALY MICHALKA VANESSA HUDGENS GAELAN CONNELL SCOTT PORTER AND LISA KUDROW MUSIC SUPERVISORS LINDSAY FELLOWS LINDA COHEN EDITOR JOHN GILBERT, A.C.E. PRODUCTION DESIGNER JEFF KNIPP DIRECTOR OF PHOTOGRAPHY ERIC STEELBERG EXECUTIVE PRODUCERS RON SCHMIDT MARISA YERES PRODUCED BY ELAINE GOLDSMITH-THOMAS STORY BY JOSH A. CAGAN SCREENPLAY BY JOSH A. CAGAN AND TODD GRAFF DIRECTED BY TODD GRAFF

PG PARENTAL GUIDANCE SUGGESTED
SOME MATERIAL MAY NOT BE SUITABLE FOR CHILDREN
SOME THEMATIC ELEMENTS AND MILD LANGUAGE

WALDEN MEDIA    READ THE BOOKS FROM PENGUIN GROUP (USA) INC.    SOUNDTRACK AVAILABLE ON HOLLYWOOD RECORDS

www.BandslamMovie.com

# PROLOGUE

Will Burton looked through the car window as they pulled out of the driveway, then quickly looked away again. Somehow word of their move had gotten out, and several other kids had come to see them off. Many of them held signs saying things like DRIVE CAREFULLY, DEWEY! and KEEP YOUR EYES ON THE ROAD AND BUCKLE UP! And, of course, REMEMBER DENNIS. Other kids just careened along the sidewalk, pretending to crash into each other and laughing.

Will was glad they were leaving Cincinnati.

His mom, Karen, glanced over at him as they turned and left their old house and their farewell behind. "Don't worry," she said, giving him a quick one-armed hug before returning both hands to the wheel. Will nodded and popped in a CD. "Walk and Don't Look Back" started blaring. They both sang along at the top of their lungs.

"Mick Jagger recorded this with Peter Tosh," Will mentioned as the song wound down. "Hear the rhythm track? It's almost ska. It's like reggae but it pops more, and they don't sing about Jah." Then he looked over at his mother, saw her expression, and laughed. "You have no idea what I'm talking about, do you?"

Karen shook her head and pointed to her ear. "Van Gogh's ear for music, remember? But it's nice to see you happy." She smiled at him. "Things will be better in New Jersey. You'll see."

Will glanced at her, wishing once again that he'd inherited some of her blond good looks instead of his own bland features and brown curls. "There's a phrase you don't hear very often," he remarked.

Karen laughed, and Will couldn't help laughing with her. He pulled out his camcorder and started filming the scenery as it sped by. They talked more about music—his favorite subject—and what it would be like in New Jersey, and cars on the road, and whatever else came to mind. Will's comments were as dry and pessimistic as ever, but deep down a part of him hoped she might be right. Maybe things really would be better.

They couldn't get much worse.

# CHAPTER ONE

"You can do this," Karen told Will yet again. They were standing at the bus stop. A boy around Will's age stood a little ways away, next to a girl who was obviously his younger sister. They had barely glanced over at Will and Karen. Will considered that a step up. "This is a new, baggage-free chapter of your life," his mom was insisting. The school bus pulled up, and she grabbed Will for one last hug before he got on. "I'm not worried one little bit."

"Hug's a little desperate for that to ring true," Will pointed out.

Karen pushed him away and pointed at the bus. "World," she stated firmly. "Go conquer."

Will nodded and climbed aboard. The bus driver had the door shut and the bus moving before Will had even reached his chosen seat—the very last bench, conveniently empty. He could see Karen still standing outside, watching, as he dropped into it and switched on his MP3 player. Then the bus pulled away and he was off to his new school.

Martin Van Buren High School. Lodi, New Jersey.

Looking at it, Will wanted to laugh. It was almost a perfect replica of his old school in Cincinnati. With one major difference.

No one knew him here.

Will trudged up the steps, pulling his cell phone out of his pocket before the first ring died down. He knew who it was before he even answered.

"Well?" Karen asked.

"Elvis is entering the building," he replied.

"Unharmed?"

"Completely."

"All right! I told you it would be different here."

Will glanced around again. "Night and day."

"Don't sit in the back, okay?" Karen asked him. "Honey?"

Will ignored that request. "Later, creator," he replied. Then he hung up and stashed the phone before heading inside.

The first half of the day passed without incident. History, trigonometry, literature—Will sat in the back each time. The semester here started a week later than in Cincinnati so he hadn't even missed any school. Which meant that he also hadn't missed the first day "Hello, class!" introductions from each teacher. But at least that meant he wasn't already behind everyone else. A few kids nodded at him when they sat down, and Will nodded back. No one tried to speak to him. No one except the teachers asked his name. And that was just fine by Will.

Entering the cafeteria—actually a cafetorium, half lunchroom and half auditorium—made his pulse race, however. Lunchtime had always been the bane of his existence. But no one noticed him. Will bought his lunch—good to know cafeteria food looked and smelled the same the world over—and looked around. He could spot several familiar cliques already: the jocks, the brains, the band geeks, the art geeks, and the theater geeks.

At the far end, one table was almost empty. Only one girl sat there, and she was hunkered down over a book. Will steered that way. She glanced up as he sat down, giving him a quick once-over, and he studied her as well: black jeans, black T-shirt, long dark hair hanging down like a curtain over her face. After a second, they both looked away.

Will ate in silence. Every so often he glanced at his tablemate. Was she a goth? She didn't look sad enough, and there was a small group of goths over in another corner, anyway. But why all the black, then? He watched, confused, as she pulled a Twizzler out of her bag, bit off the ends, and inserted it into her Coke. Then she used it as a straw. All without looking up from her book.

Clever.

"Happy New Year, Van Buren!" A loud voice broke through the lunchroom buzz.

Will glanced up at the shout. A guy, probably a senior by his appearance, had hopped up onto the stage at the front of the room. He had a cordless microphone in one hand. He was smooth, comfortable, clearly popular. The anti-Will.

"For those of you who don't know me, I'm Scott Donnelly, your student body president." That got cheers and applause. "Thank you!" Scott continued after the noise died down. "Now I have one question for you, Van Buren." He paced the stage. "What is the biggest event of the year?"

"BandSlam!" the entire lunchroom roared in reply.

"I can't hear you!" Scott claimed, cupping one hand by his ear.

"BandSlam!" they shouted again, louder. Many of them were on their feet, stomping and clapping.

"And who's going to take home the gold?"

"Glory Dogs!" the room announced. Will was amazed. He'd never seen anything like this. Was there something in the water?

"That's right," Scott agreed. "So give it up right now for Ben Wheatly and the Glory Dogs!"

The curtains behind him parted to reveal a band. And the crowd went wild. It was just like being at a rock concert—at least, from everything Will had heard about them. Only this time the rock stars in question were fellow high school students.

One of the band members stepped up and took the microphone from Scott. He was tall, good-looking, with rugged features, and brown hair. Clean-cut but not prissy clean—Will immediately thought of a young Bruce Springsteen. He was sure the comparison was deliberate. Judging from the crowd's reaction, this was Ben Wheatly.

Ben took all the applause like he was born to do it. He smiled and waved and clasped hands as other kids ran up to the stage. Then he motioned them to quiet down—and amazingly—they did.

"So last year," he started, and from his clear, clean voice Will could already tell the guy was a good singer, "last year Ben Wheatly and the Glory Dogs made it all the way to the BandSlam finals!" The crowd cheered and he held up a hand. "And we tied Burning Hotels for second place." The cheering turned to boos, but Will could tell they weren't directed at Ben. How could they be? Clearly everyone in Van Buren worshipped him.

"But this year," Ben continued, grinning, "this year's

gonna be different! Because this year there's some new dogs in the pound!" He walked over to the band's bass player. "First up, on bass, let's hear it for downtown Quinton Pearce!" The crowd shouted and clapped.

Will rubbed at his eyes. *Now why*, he wondered, *didn't I get a welcome like that? Oh, right.*

"And on guitar," Ben continued, "transferring all the way from Montclair High, and moving in with his dad, who he hates, just so he can roll with the Dogs, the Sambora to my Bon Jovi, the Miami Steve to my Bruce—the one, the only, Dylan Dyer!" The kid he pointed to pounded out a spine-tingling guitar solo, and Will had to agree with the crowd's assessment. Dyer was amazing.

"Are you with me?" Ben shouted. The crowd went nuts again. "This year the Glory Dogs rule!"

Will could barely think through all the noise. The only other kids not jumping up and down shouting and screaming were a beautiful blond girl off to one side with a mismatched pair of guys—and the girl at Will's table, the one with the Twizzlers and the book. So he turned to her.

"Exactly how big a deal is this BandSlam thing around here?" he asked. Well, shouted.

"Texas-high-school-football big," she replied without looking up. Her voice was flat and dry. "You're new."

"Yeah."

"Let me see your class schedule." She glanced up at him

and stuck out her hand. There was no way Will could reach her from where he was, so he slid down the table until he was across from her. Then he handed it over.

"We have Human Studies together," she commented after scanning the sheet.

"Really?" Will couldn't stop himself. "You're in my grade? You look young."

"I'm gifted," she replied. "What's your name?"

"Will Burton." He gathered his courage. "What's yours?"

She pulled a pen out of her pocket and tore a piece of paper from a notepad in her backpack. Then she scribbled something down and handed it to Will, already standing up and stowing the pen and her book.

He looked at the piece of paper. It said SA5M.

"The five is silent," she told him. Then she walked away.

Will watched her go. She was the most interesting girl he had ever met. He wasn't sure which was stranger, the whole BandSlam thing or the fact that he'd just talked to someone—and a girl, at that. One thing was certain: Karen would be thrilled. He put any other thoughts aside as the bell rang and kids began pouring out of the cafeteria. Just like that they were back to being normal high school students. The blonde he'd noticed before glanced back as she left, and for a second Will thought she might have been staring at him. Nah. This place was weird but not *that* weird. He dumped his tray and joined the crowd, sure he'd somehow moved to the Twilight Zone instead of Lodi, New Jersey. Though maybe they were the same thing.

"Welcome to Human Studies," the woman announced from the front of the room. "I'm Ms. Wittenberg. This semester we're going to talk about what it means to be human, what it means to be part of society. And what it means to be us." She beamed at all of them and Will, sitting in back, rolled his eyes. An idealist. Great. Sa5m was a few seats away, and he caught her eye. She shook her head in agreement.

"Now," Ms. Wittenberg went on, "this semester I want you to pick another student and create a five-minute presentation to tell us who that person really is. Distill each other down to your essences. What lies beneath, hm? You can use photography, poetry, video—get creative, people. By Christmas we're going to know one another in ways we never expected. So buddy up."

She gestured to a large board at the front of the classroom. "I've written each of your names onto a tag," she explained. "When you find a partner, put your tags on the board together. Okay? Go ahead." There was a mad stampede as most of the class charged forward, hoping to get the partner they wanted. Will waited until the rush had died down before getting up. Why hurry? He didn't know anyone here, anyway.

Sa5m was slowly moving to the front as well, and the two of them threaded their way past the rest of the class, who were already moving desks into pairs so they could sit with their new partners. Reaching the board, Will saw that only two tags were left at the bottom, unpaired. His—and Sa5m's.

"Well," Ms. Wittenberg said with a smile, "I'd say it was fate, wouldn't you?"

"Might as well," Will agreed. No point annoying the teacher on the first day. He took his tag and Sa5m took hers—together they moved them up to the "paired" side of the board.

"There, that was painless, wasn't it?" Ms. Wittenberg asked. "Now go sit together and get to work!"

Will shrugged and headed back to his seat. Sa5m followed, detouring to grab her bag. Then she took the seat next to his.

All around them the other students were chattering away. Will caught random snippets of their conversations—they were exchanging names, birthdays, family histories, favorite television shows, and more. Many of them were clearly friends already and were simply talking about concerts they'd seen over the summer or parties they were going to together.

Will glanced over at Sa5m. She was looking around the room as well, and she looked horrified.

"Morons," she said softly.

"Idiots," Will agreed. Then she pulled a book out of her bag and started reading. It looked like the same one she'd had in the cafeteria.

"Um," Will said after a minute and a "get on with it!" glare from Ms. Wittenberg. "So, I guess we're supposed to get to know each other."

Sa5m didn't respond.

He tried again. "What's your favorite color?"

She glanced up at him and laid one hand on the desk in front of her. Will noticed the nails were painted black.

"Guess," she said flatly.

"Pink?"

"This is stupid." She hadn't even cracked a smile.

Up by the front, Ms. Wittenberg cleared her throat. "I hope you're all making a good start," she said, and Will noticed she carefully avoided looking at him and Sa5m. "Because this presentation will count for half of your final grade."

"Half?" Will shook his head and turned back to his "partner." "Look, there's too much pressure here," he told her. "I can't converse on command, can you? Maybe we should, I don't know, hang out after school? We could go somewhere and talk without Ms. Wittenberg glaring at us like a crazed hall monitor. You know, just relax and let stuff bubble up naturally."

"What, like vomit?" Sa5m replied.

"Come on, we have to do something," Will pleaded. "It's half our grade. What do you say?"

"All right, all right," she said after a second. "Enough with the pouting and the puppy dog eyes. After school."

"Great." Will scratched his chin. Now, he wondered, where do kids go around here?

An hour later, Will and Sa5m were sitting on a bench at the local mall. It looked the same as every other mall Will had ever seen—the wide fake-brick walkways, the potted plants, the crisscrossing escalators, the glass skylight ceilings. The place was filled with other kids and the occasional adult. He watched them for a while, dazed by the constant noise and motion.

It didn't seem to affect Sa5m. She was back in her book again.

"You wanna start?" he asked her finally.

"What's your favorite color?" she replied without looking up. Her voice out of school was just as flat.

"Come on," Will urged her. "We have to dig deeper. This counts as half our grade, remember?"

"Fine." She closed the book and looked at him. "Now what?"

Will racked his brain for ideas. "Why don't we take each other to our most favorite spot and our least favorite spot in the whole world?" he suggested finally.

Sa5m thought about that. "Okay."

"Least favorite?" he asked her.

She gestured around them. "Done."

Will nodded fervently. "Done," he agreed. "Most favorite?"

"Can I get back to you on that?" she asked. At least he thought it was a question. Without inflection it was hard to tell.

"Why do you talk like that?" he asked bluntly, both horrified and amazed at his own audacity.

"Like what?" She glared at him through her hair, daring him to reply, but Will wasn't going to back down now.

"Like that," he answered, mimicking her monotone.

"Why do you look like that?" she shot back.

He shrugged. "I just do."

"Same here," she answered. Then she looked away. "I used to stutter," she admitted quietly. "The doctor told me controlling my emotions would help. And it did." She raised her hands to frame her face, as if on display. "See, no stutter."

"There may be a middle ground," Will suggested. He was impressed, though, that she'd given him a real answer. Impressed and pleased.

A group of girls, probably from Van Buren, walked by just then. They were chattering loudly at one another and into their cell phones. Sa5m visibly recoiled from the noise, curling back into herself, and Will sighed. One of the girls had a half-empty frozen yogurt in her hands. She tossed it into the garbage pail beside their bench as she walked past, but she misjudged the distance. The yogurt hit the edge and slid down, leaving a big sticky mess. The girl didn't even glance back.

"Morons," Sa5m muttered. She was back to monotone again.

"Idiots," Will agreed.

"So, how was school?" Karen asked Will after she got home that night.

"Surreal," he admitted. "But not horrible."

Karen smiled. "And the mall?" As Will had suspected, she'd been thrilled when he'd said he was going there with a classmate.

"The same. Plus Sunglass Hut." Will looked up from his computer. "What about you? You like the new job?"

"It's amazing!" she told him. He stared at her. "What?" she demanded after a second. "It's good, really," she insisted.

"Good and amazing are two different things," Will pointed out.

"Yeah, yeah, whatever," she said. "I'm just trying to be a positive role model while I still have some influence over you."

"Too late."

Karen stuck out her tongue at him. "In that case, how about we grab dinner and a movie?" she suggested.

"It's a school night," Will pointed out.

Karen glanced around quickly. "Don't tell your mom," she whispered. She smiled and held up the car keys, jangling them invitingly. Will smiled back but shook his head.

"Fine," Karen said after a second, stuffing the keys back in her pocket. "In that case"—she pulled a video game controller from behind her back and tossed it to him—"we have unfinished business."

"This obsession of yours is unhealthy," Will pointed out. But he followed her into the living room anyway.

# CHAPTER TWO

"Watch out! Runaway train!"

Will froze automatically, his blood running cold. How—? But then a guy went barreling past him down the hall, clutching a football. Oh, right. *Way to go, Burton*, Will chided himself mentally. *Way to think it's all about you.*

The guy threw the ball back to another student, who dodged between two others to run the length of the hall as well. Will recognized the new player. It was Ben Wheatly. He was surprised there weren't groupies all over him.

Ben flew past and Will backed up against the nearest locker to give him plenty of room. So did the few other students in the hall. One wasn't so lucky, however. She was tall and thin, with light brown hair and plain features. She was wearing plain clothes, too, serviceable but not fancy, and lugging a cello case. Will realized he'd seen her at the music geek table at lunch the first day. She looked up now as Ben came charging toward her, and frantically tried to sidestep, but it was too little, too late. They collided, both of them landing on their butts—the football went one way, the cello case another.

"Incomplete!" Ben shouted, laughing as he jumped back to his feet. "Sorry, I didn't see you." He offered the girl a hand up, which set him several notches above most of the jocks Will had seen at his old school.

The girl clearly disagreed, however. "Stay away from me!" she hissed at him, getting up on her own. "Just go back to your Orcish ways and leave me be!"

"Okay. Sorry." Ben backed up, scooped up the football, and rejoined his friends.

As they walked away, laughing and joking, Will approached the girl.

"Are you all right?"

She had knelt again, this time beside her cello case, and had it open now, inspecting the instrument inside.

"If anything happened to my cello, I'm gonna sue his parents," Will heard her mutter.

"It seems fine," he offered, though he didn't really know much about string instruments beyond guitar. At least he didn't see any cracks.

His comment earned him a scathing look from the girl. "It's impossible to tell until I play it," she announced haughtily, closing the case again and rising to her feet. "I mean, it's not like it's a viola!" Then she stalked off.

"Right." Will watched her go. "Well, I hope that works

**20**

out for you!" He shook his head and walked away as well. School was over for the day, at long last. Time to get out and gone.

"Hey!" Someone shouted as he approached the bus line outside. "Good Samaritan!" Will turned and glanced up as the speaker stepped up beside him—and stared.

Gorgeous. That was the first word that popped into his head. Followed closely by: blond. And: cool. He'd seen girls like her before, at his old school. They ruled the roost, and not just because of their looks. It was their confidence that marked them as being in charge.

And now here was this one, the hottest girl he'd ever seen. The same one, he realized, he'd seen in the cafetorium the other day. And again just now in the hall, he thought. And she was talking to him.

"Do you like kids?" she was saying.

"What?"

"It's a simple question." She laughed, but Will didn't think she was laughing at him. At least, not in a mean way. And he was good at recognizing that, if nothing else. "Do you like kids?" she repeated. "Of course you do. All Good Samaritans like kids. It's in the handbook." She linked her arm through his and swung him back toward the school. "Come on, we don't have a lot of time."

"What?" Will asked again. He was still processing her appearance.

"Do you say anything else besides 'What?'" she asked.

"Yes."

"Yes. Good." She tugged on his arm. "Come. Now."

She began walking back inside, her arm still through his, and Will had no choice but to go with her.

She led him down a short hall and into a classroom Will hadn't seen before. He knew where he was right away, though: the art room. There were easels and paintings everywhere, and pottery wheels off in one corner, and stacks of markers and crayons and chalk and other art implements scattered across the many paint-stained tables.

And there were kids. Lots of kids. Well, ten or twelve, anyway. But these were kid kids, not high school students. He guessed them to be in first grade, maybe second. They were running all over the room, throwing paper and crayons at one another, cutting construction paper, gluing things together, and generally making a mess.

The minute Will and the girl entered, the horde of children stopped dead. But only for a second.

"Quiet, monsters!" the girl shouted, but she didn't actually sound annoyed. She grabbed a canister of something off the teacher's desk, reached into it, and flung several small dark things out at the kids. They grabbed at them frantically, immediately stuffing the catches into their little mouths.

"It's a day care program our fine school set up with Lindsey Elementary around the corner," the girl was saying to Will. "Kids are in at three, out by four thirty. And for that hour and a half, they're mine." She realized Will was staring at the canister, and held it up for his inspection. "Beef jerky. Teriyaki flavor." She shrugged. "They love it."

Will glanced around again, and noticed an adult sitting in the corner, a man with bushy hair and glasses. He was reading a magazine.

"Who's—?" he started to ask.

"Mr. Berry. The art teacher. He supervises." Will could hear the air quotes. "Get it?"

"Got it."

"Good." She favored him with a smile that made his knees go weak. "And that concludes the interview process. I'd say you've got the job."

She tossed him a smock that had definitely seen better days and he found himself putting it on.

"Okay, monsters, listen up," she called out. "I'd like to introduce you to my new 'art'-ner in crime—" she snapped her fingers and pointed at Will. "Name?"

"Will. Will Burton."

"Charlotte Barnes," she said in return, before turning back to the kids. "Ladies and gentlemen, Will Burton is in da house!"

"Yay!" The kids shouted and screamed and cheered. For

a second Will thought he was dreaming. But usually the screaming crowds in his dreams weren't pygmies.

"Gimme your MP3," Charlotte demanded suddenly.

"What?"

"You love 'what!' I've never met a man who loves 'what' more. Your music, man. Fork it over."

Will handed it to her and she grabbed a paint-spattered MP3 dock.

"They're not going to want to listen to this," he warned her as she plugged it in.

"Hey, Rory," Charlotte called out, addressing a little boy spinning in circles nearby. "Do you want to listen to Will's music?"

"Is it like your band?" Rory asked. "Glory Dogs rock!"

"Ex-band," she corrected gently. "As in, ex-pand your horizons, Rory." She hit play—and the Brahms concerto Will had been listening to filled the room.

Everyone was completely silent. The kids stared at him, at Charlotte, and at the MP3 dock.

"I told you they wouldn't want to listen to it," Will muttered, reaching for his player.

"Halt." Charlotte held up a hand to ward him off. Then she pointed.

Will glanced behind him. The kids were now swaying to the music. Most of them were working quietly on one craft or another.

"Way to soothe the savage beast," Charlotte said approvingly. "You are a weirdo, aren't you, Will Burton?" She laughed as she said it, though. "Okay," she told the kids, "clay time is playtime. Anyone who wants to do clay will be with Will over there." This was accompanied by a gesture to the far corner, where Will saw little mounds of clay set out. "Everyone who wants to do pastels, join me over here." She started leading the way to the opposite corner.

Suddenly it sank in that she hadn't been joking. She expected Will to do art with these kids!

"I can't—" he started desperately as she moved away. "I mean, I don't know how—"

"To play with clay better than a seven-year-old?" she interrupted over her shoulder. "If that's true, I pity you, Will Burton."

Will tried to think of a reply but was interrupted by seven little kids suddenly surrounding him. "Clay!" one of them shouted, and the others took up the chant. "Clay! Clay! Clay!"

"Okay, okay!" Will threw his hands up in surrender. "Clay! Let's go!" Swallowing his fear, he led them over to the clay. When he risked a quick glance back, Charlotte was watching him. And smiling.

An hour later, Will was still on clay duty—and loving it. They had made little clay ponies, or at least that's what the kids claimed. Most of the results looked more like footstools with heads. It didn't matter, though, because the kids were having a blast. And so was Will.

When his phone rang, he had to set his pony down carefully, wipe his hands off on a paper towel, and then gingerly extract the phone from his pocket.

"Do I need to call in the National Guard?" Karen demanded as soon as he answered. "It's after four. Why aren't you home?"

"I'm fine, Mom," he told her.

"If you're not going to be home, you have to tell me. That's the law. Everything okay in there, Mrs. Greenwald?" It took a second for Will to realize that last part hadn't been directed at him.

"I'm not going home. Yet," he admitted.

"What? What happened?" He could hear the concern in Karen's voice. "Are you all right?"

"I'm fine," Will assured her. "I sort of got this after-school . . . thing."

"Detention?"

"A job." Will nodded and gave a thumbs-up as Maria came over to show him the yarn mane she'd just added to her pony.

"What kind of job?"

"A helping-out-at-a-day-care-art-class kind of job," Will admitted softly.

There was a pause.

"Can I please speak to Will Burton?" his mother asked finally.

Will laughed. "This is Will."

"The same Will who does nothing and talks to nobody? That Will?"

"That's the one." He took Leo's pony and reattached the front left leg, then handed it back.

"First you go to the mall," Karen said, "which you always warned me would be the first sign of the apocalypse, and now you just walked into this day care place and . . ."

"No," Will corrected. "I didn't walk into anything. Charlotte recruited me."

"Who?"

Just then, Will saw a stream of white out of the corner of his eye. Turning toward it, he realized that Lindsey was pouring a bottle of glue onto Danny's head. And poor Danny was sitting there and letting her do it.

"Oh, Ms. Rice," Lindsey was saying as she set the glue bottle down and began kneading and molding the mass of hair and glue, "your perm is going to be lovely."

"Mom, I gotta go," Will said. Karen sputtered something in reply, but he had already shut his phone, shoved it into his pocket, and lunged forward to prevent Danny from having potentially the worst hair day in his young life.

"Hey, buddy," Charlotte called out as he passed her, "if

you're committing to this every week you gotta cut back on the social life."

Will skidded to a halt. "You want me to do this every week?" he asked.

Charlotte grinned at him. "You catch on fast." Then she glanced pointedly toward the perm-in-progress and Will shelved the discussion until later.

"So she told you to stay and you did?" Karen was asking over spaghetti and meatballs. She absently tossed a meatball to the dog sitting patiently on the floor beside the table.

"What's the big deal? She needed help, so I helped." Will pointed at the dog. "Why is he still here?" The dog panted at him in reply.

"He's getting placed tomorrow," Karen assured him. That was her new job, the one her aunt Nan had offered her here in Lodi. She helped train and place dogs with senior citizens and the disabled. "With a lady with tummy issues. We just want to make sure he's da perfect man for the job, don't we?" she cooed at the dog. "Scout, Maalox."

Scout barked once, wagged his tail, and walked out of the room.

"Since when are you interested in day care?" she asked Will then.

"Since when do you talk like dat to dogs?" Will countered, imitating her baby-talk voice.

"Since when did you get so good at changing the subject?"

Scout returned carrying a bottle in his mouth. It wasn't Maalox, though. It was Ex-lax.

"That's appetizing," Will commented.

"I said Maalox, Scout," Karen corrected. The dog barked again, this time around the bottle, and retreated once more.

"So what's she like, this Charlotte?" Karen asked casually. Too casually.

Will swallowed. "Cool," he answered after a second. "Amazingly cool. The coolest person who's ever spoken to me. The coolest person on the planet." He saw the smirk on his mom's face. "Please, don't make a big deal about it," he pleaded.

"Make a big deal? Me?" Karen protested. "Go ahead and eat."

Will had only managed another mouthful before Karen asked the next question.

"Is she pretty?"

"Mom, stop!" Will demanded, shaking his head to dislodge a sudden image of Charlotte's golden hair and sparkling smile. "I don't want to talk about it, okay?"

He got up and walked out, passing Scout on the way. This time the dog had a bottle of Tylenol in his mouth.

**29**

Behind him, Will heard Karen say, "Thanks, Scout," and the sound of the bottle opening.

"Miles Feltenstein is a puzzle," a student named Harvey was announcing in Human Studies class the next day. "An enigma."

Will and Sa5m sat in back as usual. This was the first of the presentations. Will sincerely hoped they'd get better, because he was afraid to see how they could get worse.

"He has the eyes of a seer," Harvey was insisting, moving a pair of cutout eyes on a canvas he had propped up beside him. Then he added horn-rimmed glasses. "Magnified."

Will bent his head toward Sa5m and rolled his eyes. She did the same. Then they both laughed. They hadn't really talked much since that day at the mall—not that they had conversed extensively then either—but they were at least sharing the humor of the situation. And having lunch together most days.

Sometimes Sa5m even glanced up from her book.

# CHAPTER THREE

"You walk home from school?"

Will started. He'd been so into his music he hadn't noticed the beaten-up old convertible gliding up beside him. Charlotte was studying him from the driver's seat.

He shrugged. "The bus waits for no one. Not even art class."

She smiled and pushed the passenger door open. "I do. Hop in."

The second his butt landed in the seat she hit the gas—and nearly collided with a truck that was passing. The driver honked but Charlotte ignored it. After a few minutes in the car, Will realized that was because she was used to the sound.

"Where do you live?" she asked.

"Holdenn Road."

Charlotte squealed with delight. "*The* Holdenn Road? That's right next to my favorite spot in the whole world." She let loose an evil cackle. "Detour!"

Will clung to the door handle as she swung the wheel over hard and the car leaped across two lanes and down a side road.

"So?" she asked him a little while later. They were sitting on the hood of her car, admiring the view.

"Amazing," Will agreed. And it was. They could see out over the whole valley from here, and had a perfect view of the Manhattan skyline beyond.

"They wanted to put condos here, a parking lot," Charlotte explained. "But each time it somehow got saved." She leaned back against the windshield. "My dad used to bring me here."

Will noticed the past tense. "Is he dead?" he asked softly.

She bolted upright and glared at him. "No! Take it back!"

"I take it back!" Will said quickly, raising both hands to protect himself. "Sorry! It's just the way you were talking about him."

Charlotte took a deep breath and leaned back again. "No, I'm sorry. He was sick last summer, and I don't want to jinx it." The car radio, which had been on in the background, suddenly blared a current Top 40 song. "Ugh. Let's get some decent tunes cranking."

"Can I ask you a question?" Will asked as she hopped into the driver's seat and started sorting through her CDs. "You're a senior—"

"Was that the end of the question?"

"Why are you hanging out with me?" Will finished.

Charlotte shook her head. "I don't do whys." She continued looking. "We need to get you into the modern era," she explained. "Classical music is all well and good, but we are in the twenty-first century now—you should at least be in the twentieth. Aha!" She held up a case— *The Velvet Underground and Nico*. "Might as well start with the best."

"Actually," Will said, "if we're gonna start with the Velvets, I'd rather listen to their self-titled 1969 cut. I mean, it's the first record they produced on their own, so it has a truer sound."

After a second of silence he realized Charlotte was staring at him. "Who are you?" she asked.

Will grinned at her. "Will. Hi."

"Do you know a lot about music?"

He shrugged. "I guess. Yes."

"Why hasn't it come up before?"

"We didn't have a before," he pointed out. "We've only known each other two days."

She considered that. "Okay, good point." She hit PLAY on the CD player.

"My dad's a musician," Will explained.

"No way! Have I heard of him?"

"Nah." Will looked away. "He's just a sideman—plays with anyone who needs him."

"Still, that's pretty cool," Charlotte said.

"So what's with the Battle of the Bands around here?" Will asked, changing the subject.

"Please, it's called BandSlam," she corrected him. She was pacing restlessly now, tossing stray rocks out over the cliff.

"Right, that. Is it some sort of town obsession?"

"Not just our town; it's the whole tristate area." He stared at her to see if she was serious and she nodded. "New York, New Jersey, and Connecticut. The winner gets a bona fide record deal."

"That's amazing."

"It's tough, though," Charlotte added. She was swaying to the music now, and Will felt himself blushing as he watched her. "The entrants all play throughout the day, then the five finalists duke it out that night. It's always some hot but generic New York band that wins. But this year the Dogs have a real shot." She shrugged. "That's big for Van Buren. Huge. We've never won before."

Will was hypnotized. "Any other bands from school enter?" he asked, just to keep her talking and swaying.

She laughed at him, though. "Going up against Glory Dogs would be like burning the flag. Besides, they're great—in that New Jersey Springsteen kind of way." Much to his disappointment, she stopped rocking and slowly returned to the car.

"And you were in the band?" Will asked as he got back in. "Why did you quit?"

"I told you, I don't do why." She hopped in. "But I'm starting another band. Hey, you should come hear us jam on Saturday. Give us the benefit of your vast musical knowledge. There'll be bagels."

"I don't do well in groups," Will admitted.

Charlotte looked him in the eye. "Always do the thing that scares you most," she announced. Then she revved the engine and slammed the car into reverse.

"So I guess we should get together again," Sa5m said as she and Will walked out of class the next day.

"Was that a question or a statement?" Will replied. With her flat tone it was hard to tell.

Sa5m's shrug didn't help much. "Both."

Will shook his head. "Okay, sure. Did you want me to stop by your house?" Will saw her hesitate. "Can you have friends over?"

"Friends." Sa5m rolled the word around in her mouth like it was a foreign phrase. "Don't have those."

"Me neither," Will admitted.

"Maybe," Sa5m suggested softly, "we could not have friends together?"

Will smiled at her. He was pretty sure she was smiling at him, too.

"I actually might have one friend," he said a second later. "Do you know Charlotte Barnes?"

"Since I was ten. She's a senior."

"I thought that was weird, too," Will said. "There's a good chance I'm the punch line of some elaborate joke, but she seems sincere. Are you friends?"

Sa5m shook her head. "She's always been cool. I've always been not. Be careful, Will," she warned.

"Why?"

"Leopards and cheerleaders don't change their spots."

"She's a cheerleader?" Will tried to picture it and couldn't.

"Was," Sa5m corrected. "Last year. Junior prom queen, too."

Will shook his head. That just didn't match the Charlotte he was starting to think he knew.

That Saturday, Will found himself in a garage, listening to Charlotte and two guys play. He certainly wouldn't have called them a band, though. All three of them were very good, but they weren't playing together at all. Each one was in his—or her—own little world.

"Who's this?" the bass player asked after they'd wound down and he'd noticed Will standing off to the side.

Charlotte grinned at Will. "Hey, you came! This would be the coolest kid ever," she told her bandmates. "Knows everything about music. Guys, this is Will. Will, this is guys. So? What do you think?"

"I . . . uh . . ." Will tried to think of how to put it diplomatically. But Charlotte skewered him with her gaze, and shook her head just a little. She wanted the truth. Will sighed. "Okay, look," he said to the bassist, who was dressed skate-punk and had been moshing through the music. "If you're going for a Thin Lizzy harmony, that's very tough to pull off because you can't get the bass to sound fat enough. Especially when your instruments aren't tuned to each other."

The bassist and the lead guitarist, a thin Asian guy with a weak mustache, stared at each other, then at Will. *Well, that's that*, Will thought.

"I bloody well told you," the lead guitarist said after a second. He had an English accent, or at least a bad TV English accent.

"Oh, waah!" the bassist started mocking him. "Waah waah waah!"

"Back off," the lead guitarist warned. "I don't need any of your bloody nonsense."

"And I don't need your bloody English-isms," the bassist snapped back. "You're not English, Omar. You're from Newark."

"Bug. Omar. Can it," Charlotte ordered. Then, to Will, "What else?"

"You need an actual drummer," Will pointed out.

"Hey, I programmed mad beats, yo," Bug complained. "And what about me, then?"

Will rubbed the bridge of his nose. "Yeah, no offense, but you're trying way too hard to be Flea from Red Hot Chili Peppers."

"I am not!"

Will frowned. "What's your name again?"

"Bug."

Will rolled his eyes. "Uh-huh. No resemblance at all."

"Whatever," Bug replied, but it was obvious Will had struck a chord.

"So," Will asked, to change the subject, "what's the name of your band?"

"Glory Dogs," Bug replied proudly.

Will stared at him. "Isn't that the other band's name?"

"No." Bug looked like he was about to spit. "They're 'Ben Wheatly and the Glory Dogs.' Like Bruce Springsteen and the E Street Band. Or Tom Petty and the Heartbreakers. Get it? That way he can fire whomever he wants, whenever he wants to, and it stays his band. But I gave him the name."

"Don't you think he'll object to you taking it back?" Will asked.

Bug laughed. "I don't really care if he objects. Let him try." He glanced at Omar and Charlotte. "Are we through here? Because I'm starving. Jim's?"

"Jim's!" Omar agreed. "Brilliant. Charlotte?"

She glanced at her watch. "Dang. Yeah, come on. You," she told Will. "Food."

"I have to make a call," Will told her as he followed them out the door.

"Your mommy?" Bug asked, laughing.

"Or not," Will amended.

"I notice you didn't say anything about my vocals," Charlotte commented as she drove to Jim's. Bug and Omar had taken Bug's car and were right behind them. "Afraid I'll stop being your friend if you cut me down?"

"No, you were amazing," Will protested.

"Don't get stuck on me, Will," Charlotte warned him gently. "I'm too old for you."

"This has just become my new least favorite memory," Will muttered as they got out of the car and joined Bug and Omar to head into the restaurant. Just then, Will's phone vibrated and he checked it. Karen. He pressed IGNORE.

"Go ahead and sit down, guys—I'll be out in a sec,"

Charlotte said as they stepped inside. She headed off behind the dessert counter and reemerged at their table a few minutes later, decked out in a Jim's apron. Bug, Omar, and Will were already seated and talking about music by then.

"Hey, Charlotte." It was Ben. He intercepted her just as she reached their table. Then he nodded to Omar and Bug. "What's up, guys?"

They pointedly ignored him.

"Oh, come on, guys," Ben pleaded. "Dylan Dyer is an artist. A monster! And he moved two hundred miles just to play with us. What was I supposed to do?"

"What about loyalty?" Bug asked. He and Omar had already explained to Will that they had both been cut loose from Glory Dogs at the start of this year to make room for the new players.

"Look, you guys are good," Ben assured them. "But we need to be great. Sometimes you have to step aside to let others get there."

"Like right now," Charlotte told him sharply. "I have tables."

"Why are you being this way?" Ben asked her. "You quit before any of this even happened!" This surprised Will, but he took a big gulp of water to cover it. Ben softened his voice. "Look, can we talk sometime? How about tomorrow?"

"Busy."

"Monday, then. After last period?"

"I have day care," Charlotte replied. "And then I'm hanging out with Will."

"Who the heck is Will?"

"That the heck is Will," Charlotte answered, pointing at him. "Say hello, the heck is Will."

"Hi," Will managed.

"You've got to be kidding," Ben objected.

Charlotte rounded on him then. "Will happens to be my friend," she announced. "And the manager of our band."

"What?" Will, Omar, and Bug all replied at the exact same time. Ben was only half a second behind.

"And that's not all," Charlotte continued. "This year Van Buren's sending two bands to BandSlam."

"You're going up against Glory Dogs?" Ben looked stunned. "You've changed, Charlotte," he said, shaking his head. "Everybody says so."

Charlotte tossed her hair. "Everybody's right."

"Nice to meet you," Will called out as Ben turned and stalked away.

"Hey, dude," Bug told him. "Welcome to the band!"

"My cell battery died," Will informed Karen as he walked into the house. "Sorry."

"You should have been back hours ago," Karen said after giving him a hug hello. "Where were you?"

"With Charlotte." Will dropped his backpack on the hall table. "I'm managing her band."

"You're what? I thought she wanted you to do day care?"

Will shrugged. "She's very demanding." He saw his mom's look. "Trust me, okay?"

"I do trust you," she assured him. "But five minutes ago you were afraid to get on the school bus. Don't you think you're moving a little fast?"

"I made some friends, Mom," Will replied. "It's new territory for both of us. But it's a good thing, right?"

He headed up to his room before she could reply.

# CHAPTER FOUR

"So what are you listening to?"

After the initial second of surprise, Will smiled. He and Sa5m were sitting together on the school's front lawn after another long, mind-numbing day. They had known each other for a month now. This was the first time she had ever shown any curiosity about his music.

Instead of just answering, he pulled off his headphones and stuck them on her. She listened for a second and then nodded.

"I like it," she decided. "It's like reggae, but they made it their own."

"Exactly!" Will was pleased—most people didn't seem to appreciate the Aggrolites. Sa5m smiled back at him.

"There you are." Charlotte suddenly appeared and plopped down on Will's other side. "Hi," she said to Sa5m. "Don't tell me you're the world-famous Sam-the-five-is-silent. For that alone you're my hero. I'm Charlotte. Nice to meet you."

Sa5m stared at her. "I've known you since fifth grade," she finally managed nervously. It was the first time Will had seen her look a little shaken.

"Really?" Charlotte shrugged. "Huh." Then she stood and turned to Will. "Time for the ankle biters," she reminded him. "They tend to eat their own if we're late."

"Right." Will took the hand she offered and let her haul him up.

"Are we meeting tomorrow after school?" Sa5m asked him quickly, still sounding nervous.

"It's a date," Will answered. Then he remembered that Charlotte was right next to him. "I mean, it's not a 'date' date," he explained quickly. "We're not dating."

"She gets it, Will." Sa5m didn't sound nervous anymore, but she didn't sound amused, either.

"Oh. Okay. See you later." Will followed Charlotte back up the front steps.

"Nice to see you again," Charlotte called over her shoulder. "The five is silent. Genius."

"Excellent," Will declared. "You guys rock." Omar and Bug bowed. They had just finished "I Want You to Want Me."

"Liar," Charlotte accused. "Nobody smiles when they like rock music." It was true, Will did have a smile frozen on

**44**

his face. He had figured it was either that or cry. "What are we doing wrong?"

"Man, I hate this," Will muttered.

"Come on," Charlotte insisted. "Both barrels."

"Both barrels?" Will took a deep breath. "Fine. I can't stress how much you need a real drummer. Why don't you have one?"

"Every decent drummer this side of Philly is taken," Bug answered.

"Well, almost every one," Omar corrected.

Will waited.

"Basher Martin," Bug finally explained. "The best high school drummer in the state."

"Oy, you're our manager," Omar pointed out. "Maybe you can talk him into joining the band."

Will started. "What? Me? No!"

"Sure you can," Charlotte encouraged him. "This is one of those moments where you learn if you have what it takes to step up."

"I already know I don't," Will informed her.

But Charlotte dismissed that with a wave of her hand. "You've got yourself all balled up in this little box marked 'Will,'" she told him. "It's time to make a bigger box."

"Why haven't you tried to get this guy before?" Will asked desperately. He didn't miss the look Bug and Omar exchanged. "What?"

**45**

"He was . . . busy," Bug claimed.

"Doing what?"

Charlotte coughed. "Anger management."

*Bang! Bang! Bang!*

Will heard it the moment he entered the auto shop classroom. Someone was beating on something. A nice, steady, even rhythm. Bug was right—this guy was good.

Will looked around and soon found the source. Basher wasn't really all that big, but he still had that look about him that scared people off—the permanent scowl, the lick of dark hair, the thick arms. He was banging the dents out of an old car fender, and stopped to look up as Will approached. He didn't lower the hammer.

"What are you lookin' at?"

"A legend," Will managed to reply. "I actually saw two kids fight over whether you hit harder than Keith Moon."

Basher grinned. "Whose nickname is Basher?" he pointed out. "That's all I'm saying. Who are you?"

"Will," he answered quickly. "I manage an awesome band and we need a drummer for BandSlam."

Basher stared at him for a moment. "What kind of music?"

"In my dreams?" Will started to breathe again. "We're going for a Led Zeppelin/John Bonham kind of vibe."

"Really? Bonham?" Basher considered, then shook his head. "Nah. Sorry, dude. I need things that keep me calm, not wind me up. Besides, I hate the whole BandSlam thing. Bunch of lemmings chasing a record deal, but they don't give a dang about their art." He went back to banging the fender. Will turned to go, then stopped and forced himself to turn back.

"Look," he said, "I care about art. And if you do, then how can this be enough for you? You're a musician, and you sit here using those skills to repair old cars? Don't you feel like you're wasting your potential? Like no one knows the real you? Like you're walking through life as Clark Kent, aching to bust out as Superman?"

Basher nodded. "I do feel like Clark Kent," he agreed slowly. "Okay, tell you what—make a demo reel and I'll check it out."

But now Will shook his head. "That'd be like licking the pages of a cookbook," he argued. "You have to actually hear them, play with them. Make them great."

Basher frowned. "I don't know . . ."

Just then Will's phone rang. It was Karen.

Basher was close enough to see the picture on the caller ID. "Who's the babe?" he asked.

"My . . . older sister," Will replied slowly. "She hangs out with the band sometimes."

Basher smiled. "Really? I dig older chicks."

Will smiled back and wondered how he was going to explain this one to his mom.

"I can't believe I'm doing this," Karen muttered to Will. They were listening to the band rehearse—with Basher on drums—and she was decked out like a stereotypical rock star groupie. Will had started to ask where she'd gotten the clothes and jewelry from and then had decided he didn't want to know.

"You want to be more a part of my life, right?" he asked her just as softly. "Well, now you are. And besides, you look great." He grinned at her. "We'll run you through a car wash when we get home."

"How old did you tell him I was?"

"Twenty-three."

Karen winced. "Ouch."

The band wound down and Basher finished with an extended drum flourish. He really was amazing.

"Look, it's obviously better," Will told the band afterward. "Much better. But we still need a fuller sound. I'm thinking we bring in some more players, just for BandSlam."

"You mean use sidemen," Charlotte agreed.

"Use what men?" Bug asked.

"Will's dad is a sideman," Charlotte explained. "Plays with lots of bands, fills in as needed. Is that what you meant, Will?"

Will nodded and avoided Karen's questioning look.

Later that night, as he was going to bed, Karen stuck her head in his room. "What's a sideman?" she asked. Will didn't answer.

"Need a hand?" The girl with the cello, Irene Lerman, was lugging it down the hall when Will approached her a few days later. "It looks heavy."

"What are you, Superman?" she asked, peering at him through her glasses.

"No, just trying to help." Will fell in alongside her. After a second he cleared his throat. "I helped you when that moron Ben Wheatly knocked you down. Remember?"

"Vaguely."

"I heard you practice today," Will continued. "You were incredible." She was, too—she and a girl named Kim Lee had been rehearsing a duet in the music room when he'd walked by. Kim played classical piano.

"My legato passages were stiff," Irene claimed, but she

had slowed down a little and Will thought he heard the hint of a smile. "What did you say your name was?"

"Will."

She offered her hand. "Irene." Then she pulled it back quickly, as if he'd squeezed too hard.

"Nice to meet you." Will let a minute pass. "Have you ever considered playing something more . . . contemporary?" he asked.

"Like Offenbach?"

He tried not to roll his eyes. "Even more fun."

"More fun than Offenbach?"

"Crazy, I know. But come play with us after school—you just might like it."

Irene considered, then nodded. "All right. I'm always interested in expanding my musical repertoire."

"Oh, this will expand it," Will assured her. "It'll be so broad it won't fit down the block." He told her the address and watched as she walked away. Then he turned and headed back toward the music room.

Kim Lee was still there. She was so focused on the piece she was playing that she didn't even notice Will enter. He listened for a minute—it was something by Bartók. Then he reached into his backpack and pulled out the sheet music to "Blister in the Sun." Kim was staring so intently at the classical score in front of her that she didn't even notice when Will stuck the new music in front of it. She just continued playing, switching without missing a beat. It took her sixteen bars before she noticed the difference and stopped to stare at him. Will smiled.

"Hi, I'm Will," he told her. "How would you like to be in a band?"

A few days later, he was sitting out on the bleachers, watching the marching band practice. After they'd finished, he hopped down to talk with a few of them.

At the next rehearsal, Will nodded. Now they had Charlotte, Bug, Omar, Basher, Irene, Kim, Phil on trumpet, Lenny on sax, and Dave on trombone. True, the last three were marching around the garage, but he figured they could work on that. The important thing was the sound. It was finally starting to come together. All the pieces were there, anyway. They just needed to synch it all up, smooth it out, get everyone playing together instead of just near one another. And that was starting to happen.

"We've got our first song," Will told them all at Jim's after rehearsal as they listened to their performance playback on his laptop. It was classic Steve Wynn and it actually worked with all those elements thrown in together. "But we need a second one. Something that really says who we are. Ideally something original."

"We only need a second song if we make finals," Bug pointed out.

"When," Charlotte corrected him. "When we make

**51**

finals. What exactly are you looking for?" she asked Will.

"I don't know," he admitted. "But I will when I hear it." He shut the laptop. "We also need to talk about a name."

"We have a name," Bug insisted.

"No, we don't," Will replied. "They're already using the name Glory Dogs. Everyone knows them. And, let's face it, that name sucks. It's generic and lame and sounds like a Springsteen cover band." He was afraid he'd come on too strong but Charlotte and Omar were nodding in agreement.

"What do you want to call us, then?" Bug asked.

Will grinned. He'd given it a lot of thought. "I Can't Go On, I'll Go On," he replied.

Bug laughed. "I what I what I'll do what?"

Will repeated it. "It's memorable," he argued. "It's evocative."

"It's ridiculous," Bug countered.

"It's perfect," Charlotte declared. "It's us, and anyone who might like us." She slugged Will on the arm. "As usual, you're a genius." She raised her glass. "To I Can't Go On, I'll Go On."

Bug raised a fry instead. "How about I Can't Have Sodium, I'll Have Sodium?" he suggested with a grin.

"I Can't Wear Horizontal Stripes, I'll Wear Horizontal Stripes," Charlotte offered.

"I Can't Stand Up, I'll Stand Up," Omar contributed, wedged into the middle seat at the table.

Will laughed and threw a handful of fries at them. "Shut up." He was surprised to realize that this must be what having fun—and having friends—felt like.

# CHAPTER FIVE

"They're really starting not to sound half bad," Will told Sa5m a few days later as they walked down the hall. "Part Arcade Fire, part 'music therapy day at the mental institution.'"

Sa5m didn't laugh. "We still have the stupid Human Studies project to finish," she pointed out, "and we haven't hung out since you've become Joe Cool Rock-and-Roll." Will almost thought he heard a pout in her voice. "You still haven't taken me to your favorite place."

"That's kind of tough," Will explained, "since I've never been there."

Sa5m stopped dead. "You've never been there? How can it be your favorite place, then?"

Will shrugged. "It just is." Then he surprised himself—and her—by reaching out and grabbing her hand. "Come on."

"Where are we going?" Sa5m asked for the hundredth time as he half-dragged and half-led her to the PATH station.

"You'll see," he said yet again. She came to a halt at the top of the stairs and he finally looked back. "What?"

She stared back at him, and finally nodded. Then they started down the stairs.

"Wow." Will looked around as they emerged from the Christopher Street PATH station. He'd seen New York City on plenty of television shows and movies but he'd never been here in person before. It was even cooler than he'd imagined.

And Sa5m seemed to feel the same way. They could have taken the subway, but instead they walked, gawking at everything and everyone they passed. They took videos of each other and strangers on their cell phones, bought pizza from one of the ubiquitous pizza parlors lurking on every street, and admired the varied wares in all the shop windows. They went to the Strand bookstore and Sa5m looked like she'd died and gone to heaven when she saw all the books piled high on every shelf.

"Okay," she asked as Will finally dragged her from the Strand, "where to now?"

Will took her hand again. "Come on."

The building in front of them had seen better times—a lot of them. Its walls and window shutters were covered with graffiti and heavy chains and padlocks barred the scarred old doors. The awning above them had not escaped attention, but out of respect, not a speck of ink or paint had marred the name itself.

"CBGB," Will read reverently. He and Sa5m stood right in front of it. "The nerve center of everything that has mattered in music for the past forty years." He shook his head. "And it closed before I ever got to step inside. Now they're turning CBGB into some cheesy clothing store."

"Maybe it's better that way," Sa5m suggested softly. "Now it will never disappoint you."

Will didn't have an answer for that other than a shrug. But Sa5m wasn't paying attention. She moved away, leaving Will to his grief.

"Over here," she said a minute later, and Will looked around. She was standing off to one side, atop a set of rusty steel doors. Will knew they had been used to make deliveries. He joined her, and she pointed down at the door handles—and the busted lock that held them shut.

Sa5m knelt down and pulled the lock free. "Come on," she urged.

"Are you sure?" Will asked her. "It could be pretty gross down there."

Sa5m pulled the door open, revealing a set of worn concrete stairs. Then she looked up at him. "Do the thing that scares you," she reminded him.

Will nodded and followed her down the stairs and into the dark.

"Look at it," Will said a few minutes later. They had navigated the disgusting, waterlogged, rat-infested basement and found their way up into the club proper. It wasn't much better, its walls still plastered with ancient posters, its floor battered from years of abuse, its ceiling a raw array of metal struts designed to hold stage lights of all sizes. "It's a dive," he added. "A toilet." Then he grinned at Sa5m. "Just like I knew it would be."

They walked around, taking in the history of the place. Will told Sa5m all about the club and who had played there, and the impact they had had on music in general and punk rock in particular. "The Ramones, Patti Smith, Bad Brains," he recited. "Without CB's there's no Sex Pistols or the Clash. So U2 doesn't get inspired to form a band in Ireland. And the Killers don't hear U2 in Vegas and decide to pick up a guitar. The list is endless."

Sa5m laughed. "Okay, Mr. Music Trivia, I believe you."

Will turned—and she was standing right next to him. Up close, all Will could see were her eyes. He'd never noticed before how nice they were. He had an urge to reach out to her, touch her—but he couldn't move.

"Then the rent got jacked," he blurted out, "and the club got shut down. But I knew it would be my favorite place." He finally managed to swallow. "So, what's yours?"

"Now?" Sa5m smiled. "This is."

That night Sa5m came to the band's rehearsal for the first time—she said it was to see just what had been taking all of Will's time. He was surprised at how happy he was to see her there, and how proud he felt when she started swaying along to the music. It was just Omar, Bug, and Charlotte tonight, practicing the Steve Wynn piece on acoustic guitars, but they sounded good. And watching Sa5m listening to them, Will wondered why he'd never realized how pretty she was.

"It's all right, you lived," Charlotte commented as she screeched her car to a halt in front of Will's house after rehearsal.

Will slowly removed his fingers from their death grip on the dash. "I think if you tried signaling, people might honk less," he suggested carefully.

Charlotte shrugged. "They don't need to know my business."

"It's not really a privacy issue."

"Good rehearsal today, don't you think?" Charlotte

said, changing the subject. "It sure got Sa5m going. You like her."

Will looked away. "She's my friend," he replied, but he knew it wasn't the whole truth. Not anymore.

Charlotte knew it, too. "No, you *like her* like her," she insisted. "Have you kissed her yet?" She laughed at his expression. "Have you ever kissed any girl?" She shook her head. "You have to go for it, kiddo. Trust me, that girl is one kiss away from doodling 'Mrs. Will Burton' all over those black sneakers of hers."

Will shook his head. "I wouldn't even know what to do," he admitted quietly.

Charlotte studied him. Then she moved her seat back.

"W-what are you doing?" Will asked with a gulp.

"Don't panic," she replied. "This is strictly educational." She shook her hair out so some of it draped over her face. "Okay, start by slowly, gently moving a strand of hair from her face. That lets you touch her without freaking her out."

With her coaching, Will managed to brush some hair from her forehead, though she had to catch his wrist initially to stop him from poking her in the eye.

"Nice," she said after his small success. "The 'strand of hair' move is key. Now turn that into a caress down her cheek." Will followed her instructions. "Good. Once you've got physical contact, never let it go. Now lower your hand to the back of her neck, lean in—slowly," she corrected when he moved in too fast and almost head-butted her, "part your lips slightly, and . . ." His lips brushed hers and Charlotte shifted forward, bringing them into full contact. Will felt like his heart had stopped, but maybe it was just the whole world. He couldn't feel his hands, his legs, his arms—anything except his lips pressed against hers.

An eternity later, their lips parted. Will blinked once, twice, still unable to believe what had just happened.

Charlotte smiled, a soft sweet smile he'd never seen on her before. Just then a cheesy love song came on the radio, and she glanced at the dash. "How much do you wanna bet you never forget that song for the rest of your life?" Her voice had gone gentle, too. "Good night, Will."

Will found he could breathe again. "Good night, Charlotte." He forced the door open, tripped getting out, pulled himself back up, and closed the door.

Charlotte laughed, though not unkindly. "I am *so* going to heaven," she said. Then she revved the engine and pulled away with a farewell roar.

Will walked up to the front door, opened it, passed through, closed it, and headed to his room, all in a daze. Karen was standing in the living room, staring at him, and some part of his brain realized that she must have seen them. But Will couldn't think about that right now. He couldn't think about anything except a girl—and, amazingly, it wasn't Charlotte.

"Boy, you sure love reading, huh?" It was the next day, after school, and Will and Sa5m were sitting out at the Overlook. It had taken all of his courage that morning to even ask her to go there with him. Now he wasn't sure what to do, and she was buried in a tome as usual.

"Books hold my hand," she replied without looking up.

It's now or never, Will told himself. He reached toward her—and noticed her outfit finally. Really noticed it. Black T-shirt, black jeans, black sneakers, black hat. Black hat!

Now what?

Will tried to think of an alternative, but nothing came to mind. Charlotte had taught him the "strand of hair" trick. He didn't know anything else! He needed that hair! He thought about asking to borrow Sa5m's hat but that would just look stupid. He thought about telling her hats reduced intelligence but that would sound stupid, too. At last he did the only other thing he could think of—he reached out and flicked the hat off her head.

That made her look up from her book, anyway.

"What'd you do that for?" she asked. In the late afternoon light she was beautiful.

"Um . . ." Will cursed Charlotte for not giving him a more thorough training, "You have a . . ." He reached for a strand of Sa5m's hair, now appropriately placed—but she looked down and brought her book up at the same time. He wound up with a strand wrapped firmly around one finger. Too firmly.

"Ow." Sa5m glanced up but didn't actually pull away. Of course, she didn't lower the book again, either.

"Sorry." Will said. He tried to pull his hand free without completely pulling away and only succeeded by laying his left hand on her hair before removing his right. Then he caressed her cheek. She giggled. Giggled! Charlotte hadn't said anything about giggling!

Will knew he had to keep going or he'd regret it forever. He leaned in toward her, lips parting slightly—and Sa5m ducked down, practically planting her nose in her book! He tried again, angling around the book, but she raised that side slightly to block him. Maybe Charlotte had been wrong, he thought. Maybe Sa5m didn't like him after all. Maybe he was just making a fool of himself. Then he remembered the day in New York City, the fun they'd had. And he remembered something else, too:

"Always do what scares you."

He reached down and pulled the book out of her hands—she clung to it fiercely and he almost toppled over when he wrestled it free. Then he set it down behind them, turned back to her, leaned in—and kissed her.

The world stopped.

He was sure of it. He had thought it had last night, but

no—that had just been a preview. This? This was the real thing.

When they parted, they just looked at each other. And Will knew from the look in her eyes, and the slight hint of a smile on her lips, that he'd done the right thing.

"Have you ever seen *Evil Dead 2*?" Sa5m said after a moment.

Will blinked. "Um . . . no." He had no idea where this was going.

"It's my favorite movie ever," she explained. "It's playing at the college Saturday night. They don't card. Would you—would you want to go?"

That didn't require any thought at all. "Sure," he told her honestly. "I'd love to."

"Cool." She glanced down at her hands, but Will still saw her smile. It was the prettiest smile he had ever seen.

# CHAPTER SIX

"Boy, you really tied that shoe to death," Charlotte's voice floated down to him. "Considering it was already tied and everything."

Will rose to his feet. He had been heading for the front doors, the bus, and freedom after another long week when he'd spotted Ben and the rest of the Glory Dogs heading toward him. So Will had ducked down to tie his shoe until they passed. Leave it to Charlotte to show up in time to catch him in the act.

"Can't be too careful," he told her cheerfully. And he was cheerful. In fact, he was on cloud nine, and had been ever since the kiss the day before. He opened his mouth to tell Charlotte all about it—minus a few of the fumbles, perhaps—and to thank her for her expert training, but before he could she handed him a piece of paper.

Will stared at it. It was a single sheet with a date, a time, and an address assembled from cutout letters.

Will is paired with Sa5m for his Human Studies project.

Will meets Charlotte.

Charlotte recruits Will
to help with her
after school art program.

Will and Charlotte bond
over their love of music.

Charlotte's band desperately needs Will's help.

Will and Sa5m visit CBGB—Will's favorite place ever.

Will rallies the band. All they need now is a lead singer . . . like Sa5m!

Charlotte apologizes right before the band takes the stage at BandSlam.

Ben Wheatly and the Glory Dogs perform.

Sa5m leads I Can't Go On, I'll Go On in a rockin' set.

Will and Sa5m at graduation.

I Can't Go On, I'll Go On

"What's this?"

"Underground club," she answered. "Saturday night."

Then she turned it over in his hands. On the back was a stamped logo: a hotel on fire.

"No!"

"Oh yeah." Her smile was huge. "You're getting a sneak peek at the competition, and I'm not talking Glory Dogs."

Will stared at the flyer as if it might change if he looked away. "Burning Hotels? I thought there was no way . . ."

"Hey," Charlotte punched his arm, "where there's a will . . ."

She told him where and when to meet her and the guys tomorrow and Will followed her out, still completely stunned. His first real rock concert! And it was the band Glory Dogs considered the group to beat at BandSlam! He couldn't believe his luck!

Sa5m stood in her room, trying desperately to figure out what to wear. She had initially opted for her usual black but then decided that wouldn't work. No, for this she needed something better.

She scanned her closet. Who put all these black clothes in there? Oh, right, never mind. But a brief flash of something caught her eye. There! Reaching in, she shoved aside black sweaters and black pullovers and pulled out—a black baby-doll dress. It had been a birthday present last year. She had never worn it. Well, there was a first time for everything. She held it up to herself and studied the effect in the mirror, smiling.

Will wouldn't know what hit him.

The concert was unbelievable. Will couldn't stop bouncing, he was so excited. Just getting his hand stamped to enter the club was probably the most exciting thing that had ever happened to him. And then the concert itself! The venue was completely packed, with people jammed up against each other at every turn. It was loud, it was dark, it was smoky. Will loved it all.

Sa5m looked around again. No sign of Will. Where was he? The movie was about to start—they'd be lucky to get seats at this point. She glanced at her cell phone again. Still no answer from him.

She waited a few more minutes, feeling more and more stupid. Finally, as the last person hurried in to see *Evil Dead 2* and the door swung shut behind him, Sa5m gave up. She sank down on the curb and stared out at the street, trying not to cry.

After a little while, she got up and headed home again.

Burning Hotels was, Will had to admit, utterly awesome. They were a classic too-cool-for-school downtown band, very Interpol-into-Joy Division, with their suits and skinny ties and eyeliner and spastic dancing. But they definitely knew how to rock. Will recorded as much as he could on his cell phone, then put it away and lost himself in the screaming, cheering, singing throng. At one point he found himself in the middle of a mosh pit, being tossed around like a rag doll, and after the first minute or two discovered he completely loved the total sense of abandon. He even tried stage-diving, falling backward off the edge of the stage and being caught and carried by the crowd. It was a truly phenomenal experience, one he knew he'd never forget.

By Monday, Will was bursting to tell Sa5m all about it. He'd already tried calling her several times on Sunday but she hadn't answered. Nor could he find her at lunch. When he slid into his chair in Human Studies, he was glad to see her already sitting next to him, but she barely acknowledged his presence.

"Hey," he asked Sa5m after class ended, catching up as she bolted, "where have you been? I tried calling you, like, a billion times!"

She finally did turn toward him, but with a glare. "Movie theater," she snapped. "Waiting for you."

"Waiting for...?" Suddenly Will remembered. Saturday. *Evil Dead 2*. Sa5m's favorite movie ever. Their first date. And he had missed it. "Oh. Oh, man. I'm such a jerk." He appealed to her. "I'm such a jerk. I totally forgot. I'm sorry. There was this thing . . . and it was a flyer . . . and it was Burning Hotels! I had to see the competition." He pleaded. "Come on, don't I get a Burning Hotels pardon?"

Sa5m was still glaring. "Were you with her?" she demanded.

Will knew who she meant. "Yes," he admitted.

"Are you in love with her?"

"What?"

"You are."

Will stared at her, wondering if she was serious. "I'm not," he protested.

But Sa5m had gone completely cold. "You had to think," she pointed out. "I don't care either way," she claimed, "but she's trouble."

"What? Why?"

Sa5m sniffed. "Girls like that always are."

"That's ridiculous," Will replied. "And I'm not in love with her!"

Sa5m pointed at his hand, and Will looked down. The club stamp was still plainly visible.

"You still haven't washed your hand," Sa5m stuttered. "It was that special, being with her." She pushed past him and stormed out, leaving Will staring openmouthed after her. Everything had been going so well just three days ago. How had it all fallen apart now?

"Sa5m should be back any minute now," her mother said as she handed Will a glass of juice. "So what's this project you're doing?"

Will took the glass and thanked her, turning away from the family photos lining the living room wall. Sa5m clearly got her looks from her mother, but the woman lacked Sa5m's reserve and her monochrome wardrobe.

"Each other," he answered. "We're supposed to show the class who the other person really is." Then he looked at Sa5m's mom fully. "Who would you say she is?"

Sa5m's mother smiled. "Let me show you."

She went over to the entertainment center, selected a

DVD, and slid it into the player. The image that appeared on the TV was Sa5m, but Sa5m as Will had never seen her before. She was clearly younger, at least a few years if not more, and wearing a dress, though it was still black. Her hair was pulled back into a single, long braid and she was perched on a stool and strumming an acoustic guitar as she sang. Will recognized the song—it was Bread's "Everything I Own." Her voice was beautiful.

"Middle school talent show," her mother explained softly. "She didn't win. Those judges were idiots."

"Morons," Will agreed automatically. Watching Sa5m on-screen, he couldn't imagine anyone being better.

"What are you doing?" Will looked up as Sa5m stomped into the room and shut off the TV. The picture went dead.

"Nothing," he answered. "We were just . . ."

Sa5m had already marched out of the room and Will jumped to his feet and followed her. "What's wrong?" he asked as she started up the stairs. "That was amazing."

"She had no business showing it to you!" Sa5m stated over her shoulder.

"Why not? What's the big deal?"

Sa5m stopped and turned to look down at him. "Why are you here?" she demanded.

"I came to apologize again." He could see that wasn't going to win him any points, however. "I want to work on our assignment," he offered. "Let's hang out over fall break."

Sa5m started back up the stairs again. "We're going away." She reached the top and paused to glare at him. "You need to go, too. Just go." Then she disappeared down the hall. Will heard a door slam a few seconds later.

"I'm sorry," he called up at her, but he knew she couldn't hear him. "Sorry," he told her mother as he walked to the front door. "Sorry."

"Look at them, everybody." Will and the band were in the garage watching the Burning Hotels concert on his laptop. "They're total posers. But for all that, they have a recognizable sound. Granted, it's the exact same as Interpol, but you get it immediately." He clicked open another file, and now they were watching Glory Dogs, which he had secretly recorded in the school music room. Everyone booed. "Trust me, no one hates these guys more than I do," Will agreed, "but again, ten seconds in and you get it."

He closed the laptop. "That's what we need. We need to find that one song that really says who we are. If we can do that, we're golden."

"Okay," Charlotte said, "so how are we supposed to find it?"

Will scratched his head. "First we need a sound," he

replied. "Basher, get behind your drum kit. Please." Basher did, and Will followed him over. "Now give me a Sly and Robbie kind of groove. Something two-tone."

"I don't do bluebeat," Basher protested. "I do Bonham. Dave Grohl."

Will sighed. "Look, everyone knows you can beat that kit senseless," he argued. "Real power is in holding back. In control. Go on." When Basher started banging, he stopped him. "Less. Still less." The banging changed, simplified, and became something smooth and loping. "Sweet! No wonder you're a legend. Bug!"

Bug stepped up, bass guitar in hand.

"Listen to what he's doing and play against it," Will instructed. "But leave some air. Don't fill up every second." Bug nodded, listened for a few seconds, and then joined in. It was the most controlled Will had ever heard him. "Perfect!" Will enthused. "That's what I'm talking about! Now stay on the F. Everybody else, just make up a part. Don't worry about being perfect, just fit with what you're hearing."

Everyone else picked up their instruments and started jamming, and for the first time they really fit together. It was brilliant.

"What song should we actually play, Will?" Omar asked, but softly, as if afraid to disturb the group vibe.

"Yeah," Charlotte chimed in. "I can't just sing 'F, F, F . . .'"

"It doesn't matter," Will replied. "Anything with simple changes. Just make it heartfelt. It should . . ." He stopped. "Wait." Moving back to his laptop, he flipped it open again, powered it up, and pulled up "Everything I Own," Sa5m's song.

"Here," he said, carrying it over to show Charlotte and then everyone else. "Let's try this . . ."

It wound up being the best rehearsal they had ever had. Everyone congratulated one another, and especially Will. They really felt like a band, and like they actually had a shot at BandSlam. And Will was excited, and proud. It was almost enough to make him forget the ache inside.

# CHAPTER SEVEN

"Hey, check it out!" Will pointed over Charlotte's shoulder to a spot on the computer screen. "We got our first post!" They were in the school's computer room, looking at the web page he'd designed for the band. "'Lower your mortgage rate now,'" he read. "Hm, does spam count?"

Charlotte laughed. Then a message window popped up. "Love you," it said. It was from a Phil239. Will noticed it was tagged as a reply, meaning Charlotte had sent him a message first. He quietly straightened up and moved over to the next cubicle, sinking down so Charlotte could have some privacy.

"Were you reading my message?" she asked him a second later.

"You mean the one from Phil that said 'Love you'?" Will asked. "No."

"Good."

"You're entitled to have men pop out of cyberspace and say they love you," Will commented.

"He's my father."

Oh. "You call him Phil?"

"That is his name." Well, that made sense.

"I saw a few things I want to clean up on the site," Will told her. "Only take a minute." *More than enough time to message your dad again*, he thought.

"Cool." They worked in silence for a bit, save for the sound of keys clattering and mice clicking.

"I've been looking for you." Will started and glanced around. He hadn't heard anyone else come in, but he recognized the voice. It was Ben Wheatly.

"Well, you found me." Charlotte didn't sound very welcoming.

"How was your break?"

"All right." Will noticed she didn't bother to ask Ben about his.

"Hey, guess what?" Ben offered. "I went back to Hunter Mountain. Got stuck on that lift again."

"Get out!" Charlotte replied. Will frowned. That had sounded a lot friendlier.

"I swear. Turns out it's not so magical when you're by yourself." Ah. Ben was invoking a shared happy memory. And it sounded like it was working.

"What'd you do?" Charlotte sounded genuinely interested.

"Same thing as last time," Ben admitted. "I cried like a little girl."

She laughed at that. Laughed!

"It was pathetic," Ben continued. "A five-year-old on the opposite lift sang an Elmo song to cheer me up." Charlotte laughed again. "Listen, Charlotte," he said, his tone softer and more serious, "it's a new year. I think it's time to give me a second chance, don't you?"

Will noticed she didn't instantly spurn the idea. He wasn't sure why he cared so much. He and Charlotte were pals, nothing more. But he just didn't like Ben.

Then he heard the sound of objects moving about—and, a second later, music. Piano and acoustic guitar, both clearly prerecorded, but accompanied by a live guitar as well. Damn, this guy was smooth!

"What's this?" Charlotte sounded both surprised and intrigued. Half of Will wished he could see what was going on. Half of him wished he were anywhere else.

"This is me risking all-out humiliation," Ben replied. "Now hush—if I miss the entrance I have to wait for it to come around again."

And he started to sing.

He really did have a good voice, Will had to admit. And it was a pretty song. A love song, but barely cheesy at all. Charlotte wasn't saying anything, but Will thought he heard her foot tapping along after the first few verses.

Then the door to the hall opened, and suddenly the music got louder. Will risked glancing around his cube, and was amazed to see two of the other Glory Dogs—that new guy Dylan and the drummer whose name he didn't know—playing alongside Ben. Will quickly ducked back into his cube. This was a private concert, and he hadn't been invited.

Finally the song ended.

"So?" Ben asked. There was a muted clatter that was probably him setting his guitar down, and then footsteps as he moved closer. "What do you say?" Will looked up to see Ben staring at him—he had approached at just the right angle to see both Charlotte and the cubicle next to her. Busted!

"Will and I were just updating our band's web page," Charlotte explained. She actually sounded a little embarrassed, or maybe a little disappointed.

"Hey," Will offered. He couldn't think of what else to say.

"Hey." Ben stared at him a bit more, then turned on his heel. Grabbing his guitar, he exited the room, with Dylan and the drummer right behind. Will saw the glare Ben directed his way as they left, and cringed. Great. Like he needed more enemies.

"Don't sweat it," Charlotte reassured him, reading his mind. "He's just jealous. Come on, you'll be late for class." Ben and his two cronies were still in the hall when they left but didn't glance around. Ben seemed to be giving instructions to the other two, and Will shuddered to think what they might be.

"I almost got into a fight with Ben Wheatly today," Will told Sa5m as they boarded the school bus after the last class. "Because he was jealous. Of me. Whose life am I living?" But Sa5m had her face buried in a book, as usual. "Come on, how long are you going to be mad at me?" Will pleaded. "Our project is due next week. Can't we at least call a truce to work on it?"

"Mine's done," Sa5m replied. Then she climbed onto the bus and took a seat next to someone else. She hadn't even bothered to look at him.

That night, Will lay in bed and stared at his ceiling, wishing he knew how to fix things. He'd screwed up with Sa5m, he knew that, but he had to get her to give him a second chance. He had to! For a second he imagined borrowing Ben's trick and serenading her, but immediately saw several problems with that, not the least of which was his own complete and utter lack of musical ability. So it had to be something else. Something that would show Sa5m he really cared about her.

Their class project.

It was perfect—it was supposed to be about her, about who she really was. If he could knock Sa5m's socks off with it, she'd know how he really felt. So would the rest of the class, but Will didn't care about that. What was a little humiliation in the service of true love?

But what to do for the project? Especially since Sa5m wouldn't even look at him? He missed her looking at him, that shy smile, those eyes. He missed seeing her face.

Will sat bolt upright. That was it!

He spent the rest of the week working on it. It required several side trips with his camcorder, and several visits to an art supply store and a photocopy shop, plus long hours putting everything together on his computer afterward, but Will didn't care. This had to be perfect.

"Okay, guys," Ms. Wittenberg said. "Best for last. Sa5m, Will, tell us who you are."

Sa5m got up first, and that was fine by Will. He wanted to go last, to really wow her. And he was curious what she was going to do for her half. She had a shopping bag with her, and Will saw now that it held a large mirror.

"My project is Will Burton," she announced once she was in front of the class. Then she pointed toward him. "I'm pointing," she explained, "because it's hard to tell who he is. How many people here know him? Raise your hands."

No one did.

"Or have spoken to him?" she asked.

Again no one moved. Will felt a chill creep down his spine. This didn't bode well.

"Well, I have." Sa5m shook her head. "I was going to use photographs for this presentation. But I realized the real Will Burton can't be captured on film. Instead, you need this." She pulled out the mirror, held it up, and began walking up and down the aisles, pausing in front of each student and holding it up for them to see their own reflections.

"Will is a reflective surface," Sa5m explained. "He mirrors back at you whatever you want to see. He reflects you back at yourself, so you think he's someone like you. Someone you can talk to. Someone you can trust. And it's nice for a while. Until you realize he's doing that with everyone."

She had reached the back of the room now, and faced Will himself. He looked up at her, but she held the mirror so all he could see was his own reflection.

"The only one he can't do that for is himself," Sa5m announced. "Because he doesn't have a clue who he is. Because he's not really there. He's just a reflection."

She sat down, keeping the mirror between them. Will stared at her, wishing he knew what to say, how to respond, how to tell her how wrong she was about him. But he knew she wouldn't listen.

"Okay," Ms. Wittenberg said after a minute. "Well, that was very creative, Sa5m. And really mean." She sighed. "Will, are you ready?"

Will took a deep breath and nodded. *Now or never*, he thought. She'd have to listen. They all would. He got up and approached the projector, his disc in hand. He dropped it in and set it to play, then scooted over toward the door to hit the lights.

The movie came on the screen, but Will didn't need to watch it. He already knew it by heart. He'd used Peter Bjorn and John's "Young Folks" for the sound track, figuring it was just the right level of sweet without being obnoxious. The title page read "Sa5m You Am." After that was the montage, showing shots of him and Sa5m in a variety of settings. Only he'd used a life-size foam cutout with photos of her face on it, swapping out the photos to change her expression. There was the one of them sitting in the park with her drinking Coke through a Twizzler. Her frowning by the fountain at the mall. Her grinning in the library, surrounded by books. All of them had captions: "Her favorite straw," "Her least favorite place," "She looooves to read." There was a shot of her double signing out a library book, the camcorder closing in on the signature: Sa5m. The caption explained, "The 5 is silent."

Will heard the class laughing in a few places, but he didn't watch them. He only had eyes for Sa5m. She stared at the screen, eyes wide. Even from here Will was pretty sure he saw the glint of tears. The last image was of him and "Sa5m" dancing in the park, and for a moment he turned the camera toward himself so she could see how happy he was to be with her. When the movie ended he flipped the lights back on and Sa5m looked at him. And smiled.

"Nicely done, Will," Ms. Wittenberg congratulated him. "Very, very nicely done."

Looking at Sa5m, Will knew she was right.

"English, Irene. English," Will begged. "There's no such thing as conversational Elvish."

They were walking down the hall together. It was the middle of the day, only an hour before Human Studies—Will and Sa5m had spent lunch together just like they used to, and Sa5m had set the book aside to talk to him and joke with him and share Twizzlers and Coke with him. He was still flying from it.

"Scre-e-e-ech!" Ben Wheatly came careening down the hall, making car sounds, miming a vain attempt to steer. He came to a screaming halt right in their faces, slamming into Will.

"Oh man, sorry, Dewey," Ben said casually.

Will stared at him, then forced himself to keep moving.

"That's what they call you, right?" Ben asked, following them.

"No." Will refused to turn around.

"It was at your last school," Ben insisted. "Or do you prefer Junior?" He directed his next question to Irene. "Did you know your buddy here is actually named Will Burton Jr.?"

"Did you know I don't care?" Irene shot back.

"His dad is kind of famous," Ben continued, ignoring her indifference. "Or infamous, really. Right, Dewey? You still close to your old man? I guess you don't get to see him much, do you? Just visiting hours?"

"I don't know what you're talking about," Will insisted through gritted teeth.

"Oh, I think you do. Later, Dewey." Ben made a few more car sounds but didn't follow them farther.

"Okay, that was surreal," Irene commented as they walked away. "You okay?"

"What?" Will started. "Yeah, fine. Listen, I need to . . ." he wandered away, not even finishing his sentence. Irene called something after him in Elvish but he didn't have any idea what is was, and right now he didn't care.

# CHAPTER EIGHT

Will was lying on his bed, staring up at the ceiling but not really seeing it. Yet again his life was headed for the toilet, and fast. No, not just heading. Already there and ready to flush. And he'd just gotten things mended again here.

He rolled over onto his side—and jerked upright, flailing as he lost his balance and almost fell off the bed. There was someone outside his window! Will gasped loudly for air and finally managed to get his heart to stop racing and the room to stop spinning. Then he looked again, hoping it had just been one of those "half-glimpsed objects looking like something else" mind-tricks. But no, there really was someone outside his window.

It was Charlotte. And she was peering in at him. When he stared at her, she waved at him, then gestured for him to open the window. Will didn't move. Finally Charlotte grabbed the bottom lip of the window, gave it a good hard yank—

—and nearly fell over backward herself when the window shot up.

It was a good thing Karen had only rented a one-story house.

"Don't you know enough to lock your windows?" Charlotte asked as she climbed into Will's room. "This is New Jersey, you know. Someone could sneak in through one of those things."

"You just did," Will pointed out.

"See? I told you." She leaned against the windowsill and looked around. "Nice," she commented. "Very 'I'm a teenage boy with raging hormones and an obsession with music who won't let his mom even think about cleaning in here.'"

"What are you doing here?" Will asked her.

She shrugged. "You didn't answer my texts and you left me alone with the monsters. Why weren't you in school?"

Will considered telling her the truth but just couldn't. "Sorry," he said after a second. "I was sick."

Charlotte put her hands to her head and waggled them around. "My Spidey-sense tells me you're lying," she declared. "So, what gives?"

Will looked away. "I'm thinking of changing schools."

"What? No way, my little friend." In two quick steps she was next to his bed, hands on her hips. "I'm not facing the Neanderthals without you. Besides, if you change schools you can't be our band manager. And you have to be our manager to gain access to—this!" With a triumphant flourish she pulled a beaten-up old notebook from her bag and raised it high like it was the Olympic torch. Despite himself, Will was intrigued.

"What's that?" he asked.

"Something private," Charlotte answered, lowering it. "Something I would only show the manager of my band . . . or my best friend." Will stared at her, wondering if she was teasing him, but she seemed serious. "Scootch," Charlotte insisted, and when he shifted over she sank down onto the bed beside him. "You said we needed one song that says who we are," she explained. "Well, these say who I am."

She handed Will the notebook. It was covered in graffiti and stickers, he noticed, some of them years old. The pages were filled with Charlotte's quirky but clear handwriting, both words and notes. Song lyrics and rhythms. He scanned a few of the songs and nodded, already hearing them in his head. They were good.

Charlotte reached over him and turned the notebook to a page that was more dog-eared than the rest. At the top it read "Phil's Song." Below that was the real song title, "Someone to Fall Back On."

"For your dad?" Will asked.

"No," she answered, surprising him. Then she corrected herself. "I mean, not for him, exactly. Or not just him, anyway. Just something he said when I was mad about something once. That inspired this. It's not really about my dad, not anymore—that would be too weird. It's about . . . everything."

Will was only half-listening now. He was reading the song instead, and nodding along as he hummed it under his breath. Charlotte's talking petered out as she watched him read.

"There's other stuff in here, too," she told him once he finished it. "I'm not saying any of it's any good, I just thought—"

Will looked up at her. "Thanks." He meant it, too. Knowing that Charlotte was on his side made a big difference. Somehow things seemed bearable again.

Then Charlotte snatched the notebook away from him. "By accepting this," she warned, holding it just out of his reach, "it means no more talk of changing schools. Agreed?"

Will grinned and reached for the notebook, and Charlotte smiled back at him.

"Man, I'm good," she congratulated herself. Will laughed at her and swatted her with the pillow, which made her topple over. "Hey!" She retaliated by leaping onto him and smothering him with the same pillow, drowning out his laughter. "Oops." She shifted off him and sat back down on the edge of the bed, and Will shoved the pillow aside, ready to counterattack—and saw Karen standing in the doorway staring at them both.

"Hey, Mom," he said weakly.

"Does somebody want to explain what's going on here?" Karen demanded. "Will?"

The way she was glaring at Charlotte, and at him—Will wanted to die. He did the next best thing, crawling back under his covers and pulling them up over his head. Maybe this is all just a bad dream, he told himself.

"Get off his bed," he heard Karen tell Charlotte. "Now."

The bed shifted as Charlotte hopped to her feet. "Hey, whatever," she said. Then he heard her snort. "Wait, you don't think . . . ewwww!" Now Will was very glad they couldn't see him. He just wished he couldn't hear them, either. Then he wouldn't have had to hear what they said next.

"I saw you kiss him in your car," Karen accused. "Don't you think he's a little young for you?"

"That was for educational purposes only," Charlotte explained. "I mean . . . ewwww!"

"I want to die," Will moaned.

"Did you hear that?" Charlotte said. "He wants to die. He needs help, Karen."

"Then I'll help him," Karen replied. "I'm his mom."

"But I am wise in the ways of Will," Charlotte countered.

Will couldn't take it anymore. He threw off the covers and sat up again, glaring at them both. "I am actually here, you know," he told them both. "These covers don't literally make me disappear. So stop talking like I'm not here!"

Both of them ignored his outburst. "I don't trust you," Karen declared, walking up to Charlotte and looking down at her. "I don't know why you're messing my son around, but I want it to stop."

"Mom, stop meddling," Will pleaded.

"Sorry, I'm the mother," she replied. "It's my job."

"No, actually it's not," Will told her. "You're supposed to give me some space and let me have a life. Not just say that's what you want and not do it."

"He's got a point," Charlotte agreed.

"And you!" Will turned toward Charlotte. "Let's face it, I'm not a manager. I can't just take on the biggest band in school, and I'm not sure you can, either, but you want to. I don't. I just want to be the kid everyone ignores again."

"Too late," Charlotte said. "You're our fearless leader, Will. We need you." She paused a second. "I need you," she admitted quietly.

"You can't have him," Karen warned her.

Will looked at them both, glaring at each other and silently appealing to him, trying to make him pick a side. It wasn't fair. But then, what was? "Just leave me alone," he begged them both. "Please!" He pulled the blanket back over his head so he wouldn't have to look at them.

After a few seconds he heard the sound of footsteps moving out of the room.

"Which one of you left?" he asked after a minute.

"Guess." It was his mom who answered. Then Will heard the front door open and close. It didn't slam, which at least was a good sign. He didn't need still more enemies.

He pulled the covers back off his head and looked at his mom. "Someone called me Dewey today," he told her softly.

"What?" Karen sank onto the bed beside him, Charlotte completely forgotten. "How?"

Will shook his head. "This guy, Ben, doesn't like me much. I should have guessed he'd try to dig up dirt on me." He sighed. "I'm sure everyone knows about Dad by now."

"I hate them all," Karen said fiercely.

"Me too."

"You, however," she slugged him on the arm, "you I love."

"Yeah, but you loved Dad," Will reminded her. "We can't trust your taste."

"I was nineteen," Karen protested. "He was a drummer. And it made my mother take me seriously overnight, which was really all I wanted."

"Mom, you're doing that thing where you talk to me like I'm Oprah," Will warned.

**90**

Karen laughed. "I'll tell you this, though." She turned to face him fully. "I'd marry him all over again to get you." She grabbed Will and hugged him tight. "I promise," she whispered into his hair, "you're going to get everything you deserve out of life. Plus a little bit of the next guy's."

Will hugged her back. "Thanks." After a minute he pulled away. "I should probably get some sleep."

"Yeah." Karen let him go, and tousled his hair. "No more late-night visitors though, okay? Or at least make them use the front door."

"Deal." Will curled up in bed again, and Karen kissed him on the forehead and then turned out the light and left, closing the door behind her. After she left, Will thought about his life. School was eh, but it was school. But he had three amazing women in his life: his mom, Charlotte, and Sa5m. And all of them were pulling for him. That had to be enough, right? It had to be.

The next day Charlotte and Will commandeered one of the music rooms. Charlotte sat down at the piano, her notebook open to Phil's song, and began to play it. Will sat next to her. Neither of them said a word about the previous night, which was probably for the best.

"That's it," Will agreed after she'd finished the first verse and the chorus. "That's the song we need."

They brought it to the band and got everyone in on it. Every single one of them loved the song the minute they heard it, and they all took immediately to their respective parts. Will helped them focus their attention, helped each of them find the perfect rhythm and groove for themselves, helped coordinate them all back together. Then he sat back and listened.

It was beautiful. It was intense. It was haunting. It was about love, and relationships, and the bonds that form between people, and how those can be a lifeline through difficult times. The music conveyed all of that, the words built upon it, driving the message home. Will was impressed beyond words. This was brilliant stuff.

Sa5m knew it, too. She was coming to their rehearsals again, which thrilled Will. And he saw her nodding along to the song, swaying to it slightly. But for the most part his eyes were on Charlotte. He had seen her sing in rehearsals before and he'd known she was good, but this song was hers and she owned it completely. For her every word came straight from the heart. Will had never seen her pour herself into the music like this. It was breathtaking. He hoped Sa5m didn't get jealous, but a quick glance at her showed him she felt it, too. So did the rest of the band. Charlotte's intensity forced all of them to a new level, and it did more than that. It bonded them all together, forging the same lifelines the song talked about. Now they really were a band. And they had undeniably found their song.

Will was still humming the song when he walked into the art classroom after school a few days later. But he stopped humming as he glanced around. Where was everyone? The room was completely empty. No, not completely, he realized. Someone was sitting in the corner reading a magazine. It was Mr. Berry, the art teacher. Their supervisor.

"What's going on?" Will asked him. "Where is everyone?"

Mr. Berry glanced up. Will was pretty sure it was the first time the guy had ever actually seen him. "Art class is canceled today," he explained.

"What? Why? What happened?"

Mr. Berry stared at him. "Charlotte's father passed away," he answered slowly. "I assumed you knew." But Will was already running for the door.

# CHAPTER NINE

"This was a mistake." Will sat in the car beside Karen. They were parked across the street from Charlotte's house. It was a nice house, bigger than theirs and better looked after, with cheerful flowers lining the front walk and underneath the first-floor windows. Toys littered the well-tended lawn. Cars filled the driveway and the curb near the house. Will recognized Charlotte's right up against the garage.

"She's your friend," Karen replied. "She needs you."

"I thought you didn't like her," Will reminded her.

"I don't," his mom agreed. "But that doesn't mean I want her to suffer through this, and especially not alone."

Will glared out through the windshield. "I'd hardly call that alone." Charlotte had just stepped out of the house. Ben was with her. They walked over to a car, talking softly. Will noticed they were standing very close the whole way. When they reached the car, Ben gave her a long hug. She didn't pull away.

"We shouldn't be here," Will insisted. "She didn't return any of my calls."

"She's going through a lot," Karen pointed out. "Go."

Will stayed motionless a moment longer, watching a few other people exit the house and hug Charlotte good-bye before leaving. Then he slowly climbed out of the car. As he crossed the street, he saw two more adults, this time with a pair of five-year-olds between them, and paused as the quartet approached Charlotte. The adults said something to her, and she squatted to tousle one kid's hair and hug the other quickly before standing again and letting them traipse past her. They disappeared around the house, presumably toward the backyard.

After they'd left, Will approached her. "Charlotte?" She glanced his way but her face was blank. He might have been anyone. "I'm sorry." That got a brief nod. "I called. I don't know if you got my messages."

"I got them." Charlotte nodded again. "Thanks." Her voice was as flat as Sa5m's at its worst. After a moment, she bent and began picking up the scattered toys, piling them up to one side of the front steps. Will automatically began helping her.

"I wish you'd called me," he said after a while.

"Why?"

"Why?" Will paused. "So I could . . . I don't know," he admitted. "I was just . . . when I heard . . . I mean, I wish I'd known."

She shrugged. "You heard. So?"

Will frowned. "Did you tell Ben?"

"Yeah. What of it?"

Will couldn't figure out why she was acting so distant toward him. Grief, yes, but there was something else going on. "Is anything wrong?" He cursed himself the minute he'd said it, but it was too late to take the words back.

"My dad died," Charlotte reminded him, her voice cold.

"No, I know," he said quickly. "I'm sorry. I wish I could have met him." Will struggled for something else to say. "I'm sure he was a great guy."

For just a second, Charlotte smiled. "He was." Then it was gone and she turned back toward the front door. Will could see through the window that there were still more people inside. "Listen, I've got to do this."

"I'll come with you," Will offered.

He followed her as far as the front door before she stopped and studied him. "What do you want, Will?" she asked.

He shrugged. "I just want you to know I'm here for you."

"Thanks." She eyed him a second, then turned away. "Listen, I'm sorry, okay? But it's a lot to deal with right now. I sort of want to be alone."

"Yeah, I get it. No problem."

"And look," Charlotte added as he backed away, "about the band . . ."

"Don't worry," Will assured her. "We'll work around you. We're locked on the Steve Wynn song for the qualifying round, anyway, and if—I mean when—we make finals we'll use Phil's song—or not," he corrected as she stiffened. "I mean, we don't have to use it . . ."

"Go ahead," Charlotte told him. "Knock yourself out."

"It's a beautiful song," Will said. "Your dad would be proud. It'll be like he's there with us, and—"

"Stop," Charlotte cut him off. "Just stop. There is no us, Will. I'm not going to be in the band anymore."

"What?" Will stared at her, unable to believe what he was hearing. "No. No, no. We'll find another song—we have time, we can—"

"It's not about the song," she told him, turning away. "I just . . . I quit. That's all. I quit."

"Why?" She didn't answer. "Charlotte, why?" he asked again. "I at least deserve an answer."

"You want to know why?" She turned to face him again. "You really want to know? Fine. When my dad got sick last year, I promised God, the universe, anyone who'd listen that if he got better I'd be different. Better. Nicer. I'd drop my old habits, my old friends. Dad hated the way I acted with them—the way I acted when I was with Ben. Hanging out at all hours, worrying him and my mom half to death. Looking down on anyone who wasn't popular." She wiped angrily at her eyes. "So I changed. Started volunteering

**97**

with the monsters. Left my friends, left cheerleading, left the band, tossed out everything that set me apart from people like . . ."

". . . me," Will finished for her. He felt numb.

"I made a deal, Will." She was almost begging him to understand. "And I kept my end of it. I did!"

"So we were just this . . . bargain," Will demanded, anger replacing the shock, "this experiment to see if it would make your dad okay?"

"I know how crazy this must sound . . ." Charlotte started, but this time Will cut her off.

"You know what was crazy?" he told her, his voice rising. "What was crazy, what never made any sense, was you being my friend in the first place. Leopards and cheerleaders. I guess deep inside I knew it was a lie."

"I didn't lie, Will," Charlotte insisted. "The universe did. I kept my end of the bargain."

She took a step after him as he turned back toward where Karen still waited in the car. "And who are you to judge me about lying anyway, Dewey?" That stopped him in his tracks. "Yeah, I know," she continued, circling around him until she was in his face. "Dewey—D.U.I., right?" She crossed her arms over her chest and shook her head, her expression half disgust and half pity. "I don't know which is worse," she declared. "Losing a father you loved so much you changed your whole life for him, or having a father you're so ashamed of you make up a whole fake life for him."

Will didn't have anything left to say, anything left to fight with. He pushed past her without another word and hurried back toward Karen. He hoped he'd left too quickly for Charlotte to see his tears.

"Experiment?" Omar said again. "We were just her experiment?" He and Bug and Basher were leaning against the fence behind the school with Will and Sa5m. Will had just told them about Charlotte quitting the band, and why.

"Damn, I feel used," Bug commented. "Not to mention cheated, cheap, and horribly depressed."

"I keep thinking," Sa5m said suddenly, to no one in particular.

"What?" Will asked when she didn't elaborate.

"Never mind."

"No, what?"

"Well," Sa5m flicked her hair back out of her face, "if you were. Just part of her experiment this whole time, I mean. If that's true, then what is reality, really?"

They all stared at her. Omar put their group thought into words. "Huh?"

"What if Charlotte and her experiment were just part of someone else's larger experiment?" Sa5m asked them all. "I mean, what if we're all just being manipulated by some greater intelligence. Call it God, call it the Divine Impulse, call it aliens, whatever you like. If something is controlling us, is there really such a thing as free will?" She held up her right hand and began waving it back and forth. "Am I moving my hand," she asked, "or was it predetermined by some force I'm not even aware of? Are we all being used every second of every day? Like Charlotte but times a trillion?"

The others continued to stare. Then they all began waving their hands around at once.

"You see," Bug said after a second, "this is why you don't have friends."

"Someone change the subject," Basher begged. "Anything, I don't care. Bunny rabbits. Ice cream cones. My poor little head can't take all this highbrow stuff."

They all laughed, and Will smiled at Sa5m. He had no idea where that had come from, but it had certainly snapped them out of their funk. For the first time since seeing Charlotte, he wasn't depressed. He was just angry.

"This is ridiculous," he announced, climbing to his feet. "She doesn't get to make our whole lives a lie. So what if it was just an experiment for her? It was real for me. Was it real for you?" The others all nodded. "I say we refuse to let Charlotte screw this up for us. We've worked too hard to stop now." He faced them. "I say we're doing BandSlam."

"You're crazy," Bug replied, but he was grinning as he let Will pull him to his feet.

"Yeah? Why?" Will challenged him.

"How long have you got?" Omar answered. But he was grinning, too.

"It won't work," Basher argued. "What song are we gonna do, for one?"

"Phil's song," Will replied. "She said we could."

"Yeah?" Basher pushed Will's hand away and stood on his own. "Who's going to sing it?"

Will thought about that. Then he remembered a performance he'd seen recently. He turned toward Sa5m, who was still sitting and watching them. And he smiled.

Rehearsal the next day did not start well. Without Charlotte, everyone floundered, unsure where to look or how to act. Until Sa5m let loose with a whistle that almost burst their eardrums.

"Geez!" Basher clapped his hands to his ears, slapping his head with his sticks as he did. Everyone shut up instantly and focused on Sa5m, who was standing in front, a Rickenbacker guitar slung low in front of her.

"One week from now," she announced, "we're going on stage in front of a thousand people." Her hair was pulled back and there was a fire in her eyes Will had never seen there before. It was mesmerizing. "And you daffodils," she accused, "are not going to embarrass me! Now get your heads in the game and let's melt some faces!"

"Yeah!" Bug replied, strumming his guitar and starting the lead-in. Omar followed suit. Basher was still staring at Sa5m, however.

"Marry me," he begged her. Sa5m snorted and Basher laughed and began the drumbeat. Then Sa5m turned and winked at Will before clutching the microphone and starting to sing.

# CHAPTER TEN

Will gaped shamelessly. He'd only been to one concert in his entire life—the underground club where Burning Hotels had played—and that had been mind-blowing enough. But this! BandSlam was held in a major sports arena, just as if it were a world-class rock concert. And the arena was jam-packed with students, parents, and other music lovers. It was unbelievable.

He wasn't the only one in shock. Sa5m had taken one look at the crowd massed around the stage and had turned right around. Only Will's quick reflexes, grabbing her wrist as she darted past, had kept their lead singer from running back to the prep area and hiding behind the equipment. Basher looked a bit overwhelmed as well. Omar and Bug were taking it in stride—they had been here last year, after all. But, surprisingly, it was Irene and Kim and the marching band trio who were the least fazed by the waiting crowd. They had all performed in front of big audiences before, and often with far closer scrutiny. Playing in a rock band with people yelling and screaming everywhere was a lot less pressure.

"You'll be fine," Karen assured all of them. "Just go out there and wow each and every one of them."

"Not helping," Will hissed at his mom. She ruffled his hair in reply.

"I'll go save our seats," she told Will. "Good luck, guys. You'll be awesome. Trust me." Then she threaded her way past other waiting bands and toward the doors that led back out into the general audience section.

"Okay," Will said after she'd left. "You guys can totally do this." The band members didn't look all that convinced. "Come on," he urged. "Look at everything we went through just to get here! And now we're here—you're not going to walk away without giving it everything you've got, are you?"

"No." Sa5m took his hand and smiled. "No, we're not." The others nodded slowly. Will thrust his and Sa5m's linked hands out in front of him, and one by the one the others added their hands as well.

"All right!" Will shouted when they were all in. "Who are we?"

"I Can't Go On, I'll Go On!" the others shouted back.

"And what are we going to do?" Will demanded.

"We're going to rock!"

"That's right!" He shoved all their hands up into the air. "Now get out there and rock this place!"

Sa5m leaned in and gave him a quick but sweet kiss. Then she turned to her bandmates. "You heard the man!" she shouted. "Let's do this thing! Let's get out there and make some noise!" And, whooping like a crazed savage on the warpath, she charged out onto the stage. The others only stared at her for half a second before they followed, screaming as well.

"Go get 'em," Will whispered after them. Then he rushed to find Karen and their seats.

"You okay?" she asked as he sank down next to her. Onstage, the band was warming up and getting ready to play.

"I don't know," he admitted. "What are the early warning signs of a heart attack?"

"You'll be fine," Karen told him, putting her arm around his shoulder. "We all will." She watched the band, and eyed all the other bands waiting in the wings for their turn to perform, and sighed. "But it's going to be a long day."

It *was* a long day. Will and Karen were exhausted, and they weren't even the ones performing. But the band did a great job, hitting each beat perfectly. They'd sailed through the semifinals, and now they and everyone else waited anxiously to hear the results.

Gordy Kaye, a well-known local radio jockey who was emceeing the event, stepped out onto the stage. The crowd went nuts, most of them already hoarse from screaming throughout the day, and he waited patiently for them to settle down.

"We've heard a lot of music today," he said finally, when it was quiet enough for everyone to hear him, "and a lot of it was awesome! But only five can go on, and so the judges have whittled it down. So here are the finalists for this year's BandSlam!"

Will, standing with the band just offstage, gripped Sa5m's hand tight.

"Band number one," Gordy announced, "is from Erasmus High in Brooklyn, New York—Straightfork! From Greenwich High School in Greenwich, Connecticut—The Daze! From Robert Moses High School in Manhattan—Burning Hotels!" As each band's name was called, the band hurried out onto the stage behind Gordy. "From Martin Van Buren High School in Lodi, New Jersey," he continued, and Will's heart almost stopped, "Ben Wheatly and the Glory Dogs!" Ben and his bandmates high-fived and chest-bumped as they walked out, sneering as they passed Will and the others.

"And for the first time ever," Gordy went on, "two bands have made the finals from the same school. From Martin Van Buren High, in Lodi, New Jersey, I Can't Go On, I'll Go On!"

Will exploded. He screamed louder than he'd screamed in his entire life, and all but shoved Sa5m and Basher and the others out onto the stage. They were stunned but recovered quickly, shouting and laughing and hollering right along with him. From where he stood, Will could see Karen shouting her head off, too, and throwing attitude at the Van Buren cheerleaders near her, who had of course come out to support Glory Dogs.

Ben, he noticed smugly, did not look happy.

But Will ignored him. He was focused on the crowd, on the announcer, and on his band.

"Congratulations to all five outstanding bands!" Gordy declared, clapping and encouraging the audience to do the same—not that they needed the urging. "The finals will begin at nine o'clock sharp." He shook hands with the members of each band and then shooed them gently offstage, to eat something and get some fluids back in them and give their voices a rest and mentally psych themselves up for their final performances. As soon as the band returned, Will found himself in the middle of a group hug, and he happily returned the affection. Then, acting like a good manager, he ushered them all back to the prep area to relax as best they could before their turn to perform. Karen texted him to say she'd be out in the lobby—they had printed up band T-shirts and she was hoping to sell a few of them to audience members. Will wasn't sure anyone would actually want to buy anything from their band, but he admired his mom's optimism.

Out in the lobby, Karen quickly found that Will's silent fear was right. She had set up a makeshift booth and was displaying the T-shirts, which said "I Can't Go On" on the front and "I'll Go On" on the back. A few people stopped to check them out, but no one was buying. Other people had set up booths as well, selling shirts and CDs from some of the other bands. A few of them, particularly Burning Hotels and Glory Dogs, were actually raking in the cash. Karen tried not to glare at them too much.

"Anybody buying?" Karen looked up, and the salesman smile she'd put on froze when she saw who it was. Charlotte.

"Yeah, you just missed a whole busload of 'em," Karen replied.

Charlotte politely pretended to believe that. "Cool. How are the guys holding up? Have you been backstage?"

"They're fine," Karen replied. "Actually, they're great. They're all great."

Charlotte nodded. "Cool," she said again. "I think I'll just go and wish them luck." She turned to walk away, heading toward the backstage entrance, and Karen came around the booth to block her path.

"Dennis Ardmore," she said, forcing the name out.

"What?"

"Dennis Ardmore," Karen repeated. "He would have been your age now. Except Will's father got drunk in the middle of the afternoon, like he did every afternoon, and ran Dennis over while he was walking home from school."

Charlotte had the good grace to look embarrassed. "I heard," she admitted. "I'm sorry."

But Karen wasn't about to stop. "Did you hear that Will insisted I bring him to the funeral?" she demanded. "Twelve years old and he walked right up to Dennis Ardmore's parents"—she was fighting to speak through the tears—"and asked their forgiveness. That's the kind of kid he is. People hated his dad. Who wouldn't, right? After he was sentenced, though, they turned it on his kid. What could I do except get him out of there?"

Charlotte didn't look away. "I'm glad you did," she said.

Karen wiped at her eyes. "Music became Will's only friend—until he met you." She took a deep breath. "So give him a break, okay? Not many people have. Just, please, don't make up with him. Don't be his friend."

Charlotte stared at her. "Why not?"

"Because," Karen told her bluntly, "I don't think he'll recover if you leave him twice."

Charlotte looked like she was fighting back tears herself. "I've never met anyone like Will," she said softly. "He's smart, he's funny, he can talk about Beethoven and the Kinks and OutKast all in one breath. He's amazing. And I want you to let me apologize to him because I want to keep knowing him." She sighed. "All this time, I thought I was just doing things to make my dad happy. I didn't notice it was making me happy. I like who I am when I'm with Will." She raised her chin and met Karen's gaze, though there were tears in her eyes. "And I will do anything in the world to be that person again. So please don't ask me not to."

They stared at each other for a moment, each one measuring the other. Then Karen made her decision and, hoping and praying it was the right one, she stepped aside.

"Thank you," Charlotte told her. Karen watched her as she disappeared backstage.

"We're toast," Bug said. They had stepped out into the alleyway behind the stadium to get some air. Burning Hotels was performing their final piece, and it was amazing.

"I don't know," someone replied, "they're okay but I hear the band to watch is I Can't Drive Stick, I'll Drive Stick, or something like that." They all recognized the voice instantly.

"Charlotte." Will turned around. She was standing in the doorway.

"Let me just speak," she asked, stepping toward them. "The whole experiment thing? Not my finest hour. I was angry and stupid and really, really confused. I'm sorry."

Nobody else moved.

"Are you kidding me?" Charlotte burst out after a second of silence. "Quick recap: Charlotte dumps Ben, turns you guys into a band, finds the genius that is Will, writes the song you're using for finals, then does one stupid thing *because her father has died*, realizes, and comes to apologize. And you're not going to accept it? What are you, cheerleaders?" She paused. "I also really, really missed you," she admitted.

"Is that real?" Will asked her carefully.

"One hundred percent," she assured him. "All that matters is seeing you guys kick serious butt tonight. You guys rock!" She turned to Sa5m. "And you're singing Phil's song."

Will nodded. "Absolutely," he agreed.

Charlotte grinned. "And I'll be the girl in front, screaming my head off while you do."

Charlotte held out her arms to Will, but he still wasn't sure he could trust her again. So she grabbed him and hugged him instead. After a few seconds he awkwardly returned the gesture.

**111**

"This is not the hug of someone forgiving someone," Charlotte pointed out. She locked her arms around Will, lifted him off the ground, and shook him like a rag doll. "*This* is the hug of someone forgiving someone." Will couldn't help but laugh at that. The old Charlotte, the real Charlotte—his friend Charlotte—was back. The others sensed it as well, and slapped her on the back or gave her hugs. But then they heard the crowd applauding. Burning Hotels had finished their number. Time to go back out there.

"Go get 'em, guys," Charlotte told them all as they headed back in. "I'll be rooting for you."

Karen looked up as Charlotte sank into the seat next to her.

"So," she asked, "how many pieces is he in?"

"One," Charlotte replied. "I, however . . ."

Karen surprised herself by putting an arm around the girl. She was even more surprised when Charlotte leaned against her and she felt the girl's tears on her shoulder. It seemed she'd made the right choice after all.

# CHAPTER ELEVEN

Will and Sa5m and the others slowed to a stop halfway to the stage, relieved. They'd been afraid they were up next, but there was still one band before them. Glory Dogs.

"Hey," one of the Dogs called out as they brushed past I Can't Go On, I'll Go On. "I didn't know BandSlam was being sponsored by Mountain Dewey." The other Glory Dogs laughed and Will gritted his teeth. Of course Ben had told them. He'd probably told the entire school. He glared at Ben, who returned his look with a calm "Yeah? What're you gonna do about it?" sneer.

"Come on, let's go!" Ben told the rest of the Dogs after a second. "Let's show these losers how to rock and roll!"

He led his band out onto the stage, and the audience erupted into cheers and shouts. Great.

"Thank you, thank you!" Ben shouted back as he stepped up to the mic. "I want to dedicate this song to someone very special. She taught me a lot, and she wrote this song. Charlotte, this is for you."

Will felt a chill run down his spine. Something horrible was about to happen. He just knew it.

And then the Glory Dogs started playing—"Someone to Fall Back On."

"No way!" Omar whispered. Bug and Basher had more colorful replies, and if he hadn't been in shock Will suspected he might have blushed at some of the language they used. As it was, he crept forward to the very front edge of the wings and peered out into the audience. There was Karen, and he was surprised to see Charlotte right next to her. Charlotte looked pale. She saw Will looking, and began frantically signaling to him, shaking her head emphatically. *Okay*, Will thought. *I get it. You didn't know.*

The question was, what should they do now?

He rejoined his band, all of whom were panicking.

"What are we going to do?" Bug demanded from him. "We can't sing the same song!"

"We have to," Sa5m whispered. "I don't know anything else." Her eyes pleaded with Will not to blame her for that lack, and he reached out and took her hand to reassure her. The smile she gave him reminded her of something else, something he'd seen not too long ago—a younger Sa5m, singing to someone else. And he smiled.

"Yes, you do," he reminded her. "You all do." Then he gestured toward the side door. "Alley. Now!"

They rushed outside. Will filled them in on the way.

"You're crazy," Basher stated as the door shut behind them. "We can't play that."

"We have to," Will replied. "It's that or nothing. And we've come way too far to just do nothing."

"But we've never—" Omar started.

"I haven't—" Bug added.

"It's been years since—" Sa5m gasped.

"I don't care," Will told them. "Look, you can do this. We can do this! I know we hadn't planned on it, I know we haven't practiced it with Sa5m, I know we've never performed it together. But here we are, and we're in the finals at BandSlam! BandSlam! And right now Glory Dogs is finishing up awing the judges and the crowd with *our* song! Are we just going to take that lying down?"

"No way!" Basher replied, slamming one fist into the other.

"Not a chance!" Bug agreed.

The others all shouted their agreement as well. Will had them riled up. Good.

"Okay, we need to talk through the changes, the intros, the rhythms," he told them. "We all know the song, it's just a matter of bringing it together. But we can totally do this."

Just then the door opened and Ben stepped through. He was pouring a water bottle over his head. Clearly the Glory Dogs had finished, and judging by the huge smile on his face the reaction had been everything they'd hoped for. Will left the others talking to approach Ben.

"She didn't know you were going to sing that, did she?" Will asked.

Ben eyed him for a second. Then his grin widened. "Nope," he admitted. "It was a surprise. Blew her away, too."

*Yeah, she wasn't the only one*, Will thought.

Ben tossed the now-empty water bottle into the dumpster.

"Good luck out there, man," he called over his shoulder as he headed back inside. Will didn't for a second think it was sincere.

Once Ben opened the door, Will could hear the noise from the arena again. And, far worse, he could hear the announcer.

"Our last band is also from Martin Van Buren High," Gordy was saying. "I don't know what they put in the water over there, but give it up for I Can't Go On, I'll Go On!"

The cheers and applause were certainly gratifying, but after a minute they petered out. And Will and the band were still here in the alleyway.

"That's us," Will told the others. "Come on!"

"We need another minute," Sa5m replied without looking up.

"We don't have another minute," Will pointed out. "He just introduced us!"

This time Sa5m did look at him, and her glare was laser-sharp. "We. Need. Another. Minute!" she snapped.

A stage manager came to the door. "What's going on?" he asked.

"Maybe they can't go on?" Will heard Gordy saying.

"Get onstage," Basher whispered to Will.

Will stared at him. "What?"

"Onstage."

"Why?" Will felt the blood draining from his face. "No. What am I going to do?"

"Stall," Bug suggested.

"They hate me!" Will whined.

"Go!" Sa5m ordered. Will could feel himself sweating like he was trapped in a car wash. He hated being in front of people! There was a reason he was the manager! But the band was desperate, and they needed him. And this was what good managers did—they took care of their bands.

And their friends.

Will brushed past the stage manager and headed indoors. He marched past the prep area, through the wings, and out onto the stage. Gordy handed him the microphone, and Will took it, staring out into the crowd—

—and froze.

What the hell should he do now?

His mind was a complete blank. His hands and feet felt

numb. He was light-headed. His mouth was bone-dry even though the rest of him was drenched. And he didn't have a clue what to say.

The crowd was completely silent, wondering who this guy was and what he was doing onstage.

But apparently a few people recognized him. A girl—it had to be one of the Van Buren cheerleaders—shouted, "Dewey!"

A few other kids picked up the chant. "Dewey! Dewey! Dewey!" they shouted. Will was sure they didn't have a clue what it meant.

But someone did. He saw Karen and Charlotte clutching each other, faces white, eyes urging him to take charge, to shout back, to do something. Anything.

And it was the support he saw there—and the anger he felt at having all the old baggage dragged back up again—that finally freed him.

"Dewey!" he shouted back. "Dewey!" He began pacing the stage, waving his arms, exhorting everyone to join in. And they did. "Dewey! Dewey! Dewey!"

Then he turned that hated name on its ear.

"Do we?" He shouted. "Do we want to rock?"

A few people cheered or shouted "yes."

"Wake up, New Jersey!" Will demanded. "I said, 'Do we want to rock?!'"

This time more people joined in.

"Let's try it one more time," Will encouraged them. "DO WE WANT TO ROCK?"

"YES!!!" came the thunderous reply.

A movement in the wings caught his eye, and Will glanced over. It was Sa5m, with the rest of the band right behind her. She gave Will a thumbs-up and he nodded back.

"You'd better," he shouted at the crowd, "because I have seen the future of rock and roll! And its name is I Can't Go On, I'll Go On!" He raised his arms high and the band swept out behind him. And the crowd leaped to its feet and cheered like it was raining money.

Will bowed to the crowd, handed the mic to Sa5m, winked at her, and then scurried offstage. He stopped just inside the wings, turned around, and leaned on the wall there. That had been the hardest thing he'd ever done in his entire life. Even harder than talking to Dennis Ardmore's parents. But it had been worth it.

Because I Can't Go On, I'll Go On warmed up quickly, and then broke into song.

Bread's "Everything I Own."

And it was brilliant.

Everything they had done in rehearsal, everything they'd learned—about music, about performing, and about each other—came together. It was part pop, part reggae, part rock—and all amazing. Sa5m was beautiful and edgy and vulnerable. Omar and Bug were perfectly controlled.

Basher was a marvel. Irene, Kim, and the trio were indie-nerd cool. And it all worked.

Glancing out over the audience, Will could see they got it, too. Some of them more than others. Some were just grooving to the music, but others were totally getting where it came from. Karen was crying. And Charlotte? Charlotte was serene, a soft smile on her face—she had her eyes closed and her head back, letting the music simply wash over her.

The band ended the song and the crowd roared. Those who had sat during the performance surged to their feet again. It was unbelievable. Will knew he was crying, too, and as soon as the band came offstage he grabbed Sa5m in a fierce hug, reaching out to include the others as well. This was what music was all about. Taking these people, these great, odd, misunderstood people, and all of them coming together to produce something truly breathtaking, something that moved anyone who heard it.

Will felt honored to be a part of that. And he was most definitely a part of it. He belonged.

Which was the best feeling of all.

# CHAPTER TWELVE

Minutes later, Will was still in a daze when he saw a blur approaching. Then he was lifted off his feet as someone tackled him in an enormous hug.

"You were amazing!" Karen crowed, squeezing him tight before setting him down again. "They were amazing! Who are you?"

Will smiled but ducked his head as Karen started to squeeze him again. "Mom," he whispered, "kids are staring! I have to face them in school tomorrow!"

She laughed at him and started deliberately planting huge, noisy kisses all over his face. Sa5m cracked up. The others laughed as well.

"Mom," Will pleaded. "Cute lead singer I hope to make my girlfriend is laughing at me!" Sa5m heard him and her eyes got huge. Then she smiled at him, a smile that made the whole room glow.

"Yeah, I don't think she cares," Charlotte pointed out, slugging him on the shoulder. "Nice try though, champ."

"Shh!" Omar motioned. "Look!"

One of the judges stood up and turned to where Gordy Kaye stood waiting, then handed him a sealed envelope. Gordy took it and walked out to the center of the stage, motioning for all five bands to line up behind him. Will stayed in the wings again. Karen and Charlotte had returned to their seats, and he could see them clutching each other's hands right in front.

"And the winner of this year's BandSlam," Gordy announced, "is—" He tore open the envelope and read it. "The Daze!"

The crowd cheered and The Daze jumped and cheered. Will felt like crying. He watched The Daze's lead singer step forward to shake hands with Gordy and receive an enormous trophy from a tall, leggy, blond woman.

I Can't Go On, I'll Go On shuffled offstage, as did the other three bands. They all looked as crushed as Will felt. Behind them, photographers were rushing to take pictures of The Daze, and a record company exec was approaching them, carrying a thick contract and a huge cardboard check. Will turned away, unable to watch any longer.

"Come on," he told the others. He led them out the stage door and back into the audience area. The place was emptying rapidly.

"I can't believe we didn't win," Omar muttered. The others nodded.

"We should have won!" Basher insisted.

"Yes, you should have," Charlotte agreed as she and Karen rejoined them. "You rocked. You guys were amazing."

"So why didn't we win?" Bug asked her. He gestured toward the stage, where The Daze was still taking photographs and talking to the record company guy. "Why did they win and not us?"

Charlotte shrugged. "Who knows? Maybe they're more 'now.' Maybe they're easier to label, easier to market. Maybe they have blackmail photos of the judges playing mini-golf in clown costumes. Does it matter? The important thing is, you guys killed. And no one can take that away from you."

Just then two kids walked past, heading for the exit. They looked to be freshman, and Will didn't recognize them— they were probably from one of the other participating schools. One was holding up his cell phone, and Will could just hear "Everything I Own" playing on it.

"Forget The Daze," the kid was saying to his friends. "These guys were better than anyone!"

"I know," his friend agreed. "Cool name, too. You should totally post that online."

The other kid nodded. "Totally!"

Charlotte watched them go. "There, see?" she said after the kids had gone. "Your adoring public."

"We really did rock," Sa5m agreed.

**123**

"Hell yes, we did!" Basher chimed in, and everybody laughed.

"Aw, who wants a big record deal, anyway?" Bug claimed. "Indie is the only way to go."

Talking and laughing, they collected their gear and headed for the door. Will took one last look up at the stage, and Sa5m followed his gaze.

"Idiots," she said, taking his hand.

"Morons," he agreed. They walked out together.

# CHAPTER THIRTEEN

"Congratulations, Class of 2009!"

Everyone cheered as the principal nodded and the graduating seniors switched their tassels from the right side of their caps to the left. Another school year done, another crop of students ready for the world beyond.

After the ceremony, Will and Sa5m sought out Charlotte, Bug, Omar, and Basher.

"You guys did it!" Will exclaimed, hugging each of them in turn.

"What, you doubted?" Charlotte demanded with a smile. Then she whacked him on the arm. "Jim's?"

"Jim's!" everyone agreed.

"You look great," a new voice intruded. It was Ben. He was looking at Charlotte, of course.

"It's my new makeup," Charlotte replied. "I Can't Wear Blush, I'll Wear Blush." They headed for her car, and Ben fell in alongside them.

"Room for one more?" he asked as they reached it and

Charlotte slid into the driver's seat. Will and Sa5m hopped in back. Omar and Basher headed for Basher's van, saying they'd meet the others there.

Charlotte glanced at the others, lingering on Will. He considered it for half a second. But losing BandSlam had taken the wind out of Ben's sails a bit. He didn't seem as cocky now. And he had asked, rather than demanded. Charlotte must have read Will's mind yet again, because she nodded.

"Shotgun," Ben called out, but Bug laughed and angled past him, dropping into the front passenger seat.

"No way, dude," Bug told him. "I called shotgun like an hour ago."

Ben glanced at Charlotte for support, and Bug rolled his eyes. So did Will. But they should have known better.

"No, Bug called it," she told Ben. "Shotgun must be earned."

Surprisingly, Ben smiled. "Fair enough." He climbed into the back with Will and Sa5m, forcing them to cuddle together. Will didn't mind one bit.

"Hold on," he murmured to Sa5m, who obliged by clinging to him. Charlotte flung her graduation cap into the air, gunned the engine, and peeled out. Then they were off.

And Will smiled. He couldn't wait to tell the others about how he'd checked their band website just before graduation. Kids all across the country were playing the "Everything I Own" video and flooding their site with messages. He'd even heard from a few record producers—nothing definite yet, but there was real interest out there. They'd even seen changes at school, with kids wearing homemade I Can't Go On, I'll Go On shirts, singing their songs, and even adding silent letters to their names. They were practically celebrities at Van Buren.

It seemed strange that, less than a year ago, he and Karen had been driving out here. Now he had good friends, an amazing girlfriend, a red-hot band—

Now he belonged.

It really couldn't get much better.

Yet he had a feeling it would.

# PREFACE

## INTRODUCTION

The *Auto Upkeep Workbook* contains Internet-based and hands-on activities that are extensions of the text. The *Auto Upkeep* text and activities provide the fundamental knowledge and experience in owning and maintaining an automobile.

## FEATURES OF THE WORKBOOK

Each chapter in the workbook corresponds to a chapter in the text.
Features include:
- Think Safety
- Web Exploring
- Study Questions
- Activity Journal

## ON THE INTERNET

*Auto Upkeep* can also be experienced online at www.AutoUpkeep.com. This website provides answers to commonly asked questions, links to industries, educational institutions, and individuals teaching basic automotive programs. It serves as an additional resource for you to communicate to people within the automotive field or purchase automotive supplies. The website is continually updated with new links, so keep checking it for additional automotive resources and new publications.

## WEB EXPLORING

Due to the nature of the Internet, Internet search words listed throughout the book may direct students to unanticipated content. If this text is used in an educational institution it is recommended that the instructor review websites before sending students to them.

## QR CODES

A QR (quick response) Code is provided at the beginning of each chapter. With a smartphone and a scanning app you can use the QR codes to easily access additional resources online.

## NATEF CONNECTIONS

Many of the activities presented in the *Auto Upkeep Workbook* have connections to the 2012 National Automotive Technicians Education Foundation (NATEF) Maintenance and Light Repair Task List. Where applicable, the connections are listed at the beginning of each activity. *Auto Upkeep* correlates to over 50% of these standards. A correlation matrix can be accessed at www.3rd.AutoUpkeep.com/standards. However, *Auto Upkeep* is designed to promote basic car care and repair. It is not designed to prepare students for comprehensive ASE certification. Comprehensive texts and workbooks are available from other publishers that cover Automobile Service Technology and Master Automobile Service Technology in depth. To learn more about NATEF, go to www.NATEF.org.

## LIMITED PHOTOCOPY PERMISSION

With the purchase of this workbook, permission is granted by Rolling Hills Publishing to make copies from the following list of appendix pages for unlimited use in the classroom:
- Safety Rules
- Activity Completion Record
- Competency Profile/Task List
- Daily Reflection Log
- Article or Website Review
- Career Exploration
- Repair Invoice/Work Order
- Vehicle Reference Information
- Order Information

All other pages of this workbook may not be reproduced, stored in a retrieval system, or transmitted in any form or by any means (electronic, mechanical, photocopying, recording, or otherwise) without prior written permission from the publisher, except by a reviewer, who may quote brief passages in a review or as permitted by the United States Copyright Act.

# TABLE of CONTENTS

# Auto Upkeep
## Basic Car Care, Maintenance, and Repair
## Workbook

EDITION

3RD

RESOURCES

QR

## Michael E. Gray
## and
## Linda E. Gray

Rolling Hills Publishing
www.rollinghillspublishing.com
Ozark, Missouri

www.rollinghillspublishing.com

## Auto Upkeep: Basic Car Care, Maintenance, and Repair
### Workbook
3rd Edition
Michael E. Gray and Linda E. Gray

Printed in the United States of America
20  19  18  17  16  15  14  13          10  9  8  7  6  5  4  3  2

ISBN-13: 978-1-62702-002-2
ISBN-10: 1-62702-002-0

For more information contact: Rolling Hills Publishing, Ozark, Missouri
Phone:        1-800-918-READ (1-800-918-7323)        Fax:        1-888-FAX-2RHP (1-888-329-2747)
Email:        info@autoupkeep.com        Website:        www.autoupkeep.com

NOTICE TO THE READER
The publisher, authors, www.rollinghillspublishing.com, www.autoupkeep.com, reviewers, and those associated with the text do not warrant or guarantee any procedure, process, products, or websites presented in the text. Extensive effort has been made to ensure accuracy in the text and illustrations throughout the book. However, due to the vast number of automotive manufacturers and related products, the reader should follow all procedures provided with the vehicle or by the product manufacturer. The book is sold with the understanding that the publisher, authors, www.rollinghillspublishing.com, www.autoupkeep.com, reviewers, and those associated with the text are not engaged in rendering any specific mechanical, safety, diagnostic, legal, accounting, or any other professional advice. The reader assumes all risks while following activity procedures, is warned to follow all safety guidelines, and should avoid all potentially hazardous situations. The publisher, authors, www.rollinghillspublishing.com, www.autoupkeep.com, reviewers, and associates shall not be liable for damages to vehicles, their components, or injuries to individuals using or relying on this material.

PRODUCT DISCLAIMER
The publisher, authors, www.rollinghillspublishing.com, www.autoupkeep.com, reviewers, and associates do not endorse any company, product, service, or website mentioned or pictured in the book. The company names, products, services, and websites were noted and pictured because they are readily available, easily recognizable, and may help the reader understand the content. It is acknowledged that other company names, products, services, and websites could work as substitutes for those given throughout the text.

# 1

# INTRODUCTION AND HOW CARS WORK

## Think Safety

Moving and/or hot engine components can be dangerous. Shut off the engine and remove the key before opening the hood.

## Objectives

After reading the *Auto Upkeep* text and completing the following activities, you will be able to:

- Identify people that have impacted the development of the automobile.
- Differentiate between vehicle manufacturers, makes, models, and types.
- Describe how cars work.

## Summary

In a little over one hundred years, automobiles have become extremely popular. The automobile has made personal land transportation easy, allowing people to work great distances from where they live. Cugnot, Benz, Ford, and Porsche, among others, changed the development of the automobile forever. With an ever-growing number of vehicles on the road and demand for oil increasing, fossil fuel prices will certainly rise. Today, manufacturers are mass-producing hybrid and 100% electric vehicles to increase efficiency, minimize pollution, and reduce our reliance on fossil fuels.

## Web Exploring

### Key Terms/Internet Search Words

Visit **www.google.com** to investigate any of the following terms or phrases. Summarize your findings in a research paper.

- Automotive Manufacturers
- Automotive Milestones
- Carl (Karl) Benz
- Cugnot Steam Traction Engine
- Diesel Engines
- Ferdinand Porsche
- Four-Stroke Engine
- Gasoline Engines
- Henry Ford
- How Cars Work
- Internal Combustion Engine
- Leonardo da Vinci Automobile
- Model T
- Nicholas Cugnot
- Nikolaus Otto
- Ransom Olds First Assembly Line
- Vehicle Identification Number
- Volkswagen Beetle
- What is MPGe

## 📖 Study Questions - Introduction and How Cars Work

1. What was the earliest self-powered road vehicle?

   _____

   _____

2. Who was credited with the world's first motorcar?

   _____

   _____

3. How do cars work?

   _____

   _____

4. How are vehicles classified?

   _____

   _____

5. What is the difference between a manufacturer and make?

   _____

   _____

6. What does the acronym VIN represent?

   _____

   _____

7. What two units of measurement are used to classify engine sizes?

   _____

   _____

8. What is an engine configuration? List several examples.

   _____

   _____

9. What is the difference between a gasoline and diesel engine? What are the strokes in a four-stroke internal combustion engine?

   _____

   _____

10. Why is it a good idea to know the size of your vehicle's engine?

    _____

    _____

| Name | Class | Date / / | Score |
|------|-------|----------|-------|

# Car Identification Activity

## Objective

Upon completion of this activity, you will be able to correctly identify an automobile by manufacturer, make, model, year, and type.

## NATEF Connections

**Preparing Vehicle for Service**
- Vehicle identifying information.

## Tools

None

## Supplies

None

## Cautions

Follow all procedures and safety guidelines specified by your instructor.

## Directions

Check off the boxes ❑ when completed. When you see a hand ✍ next to the task, write the information in the activity journal. If you have any questions during the duration of this activity, stop and ask the instructor for assistance.

## Procedure

❑ Open the driver's door and look for the vehicle certification label.

Vehicle Certification Label

✍ Identify the date of manufacture.
✍ Identify the vehicle manufacturer.
✍ Look in the front windshield and find the VIN. Write down the VIN.

VIN

❑ Look on the outside of the vehicle. The make and model are usually identified on the rear, front, or side of the vehicle.
✍ Note the make and model.
✍ Identify the vehicle type (e.g., Microcar, Subcompact Car, Compact Car, Mid-size Car, Full-size Car, Sports Car, Compact SUV, Mid-size SUV, Crossover SUV, Full-size SUV, SUT, Compact Pickup, Full-size Pickup, Minivan, or Van).
❑ Open the hood. If unsure how to open the hood, refer to the owner's manual. A release latch should be under or near the steering column.
❑ Once the hood is popped, there is a safety latch on the outside.

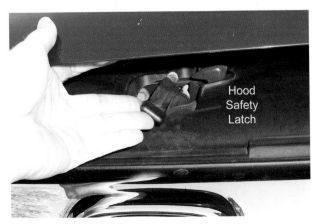

Hood Safety Latch

❑ Locate the vehicle emission control information (VECI) sticker under the hood.

✍ Look on the VECI sticker to determine the model year.

✍ Look on the VECI sticker to determine the size (e.g., 2.4 L) and type (e.g., gasoline or diesel) of engine in your vehicle.

Model Year (MY)

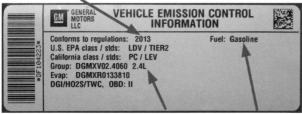

Size of Engine    Type of Engine

✍ Look at the engine design to determine the configuration (e.g., inline, opposed, slant, or V).

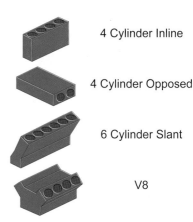

4 Cylinder Inline

4 Cylinder Opposed

6 Cylinder Slant

V8

✍ Look at the engine to try to determine the number of cylinders. Identifying the number of spark plugs may help you. ***Note: Most engines have one spark plug per cylinder, but some have two.***

❑ Close the hood.

## ✍ Activity Journal

1. What is the date of manufacture for the vehicle?

_____

2. What company manufactured the vehicle?

_____

3. What is the VIN for the vehicle?

_____

4. What is the make and model of vehicle?

_____

5. What is the vehicle's type?

_____

6. What is the model year according to VECI sticker?

_____

7. What is the engine size and type?

_____

8. What is the engine configuration?

_____

9. How many cylinders does the engine have?

_____

# 2

# BUYING AN AUTOMOBILE

## Think Safety

All automobiles are not designed and manufactured equally safe. When buying an automobile always research unbiased test safety ratings and consider new safety features.

## Objectives

After reading the *Auto Upkeep* text and completing the following activities, you will be able to:
- Determine your automobile budget.
- Differentiate between needs and wants in relation to good transportation.
- Identify the steps in buying an automobile.
- Identify the places to buy an automobile.

## Summary

Automobiles are expensive to own. Identifying your budget, wants, needs, ways to finance the deal, and the abundant places to purchase a vehicle will give you a step up. Remember that this is a large financial purchase – take your time, complete research, and be educated about the car buying process.

## Web Exploring

**Key Terms/Internet Search Words**
Visit www.google.com to investigate any of the following terms or phrases. Summarize your findings in a research paper.
- Auto Trader
- Automobile Loans
- Automobile Safety Features
- Buying a Car
- Buying a Used Vehicle
- Car Buying Guide
- Car Buying Steps
- CARFAX
- CarMax
- Co-signing a Loan
- Dealer Cost
- Dealer Invoice
- Edmunds
- Insurance Institute for Highway Safety
- Kelley Blue Book
- MSRP
- NADA
- Online Car Dealerships

Name _____ Class _____ Date __ / __ / __ Score _____

## 📖 Study Questions - Buying an Automobile

1. Why do you need an automobile?

   _____

   _____

2. If you worked 16 hours a week earning minimum wage, how much money would you gross per week?

   _____

   _____

3. If you buy an automobile and have to make payments, why is it best to shop around for interest rates?

   _____

   _____

4. What is the difference between MSRP, Dealer Cost, and Dealer Invoice?

   _____

   _____

5. What is a reasonable offer to make on a new automobile in relation to Dealer Cost?

   _____

   _____

6. What does it mean if someone has to co-sign a loan with you?

   _____

   _____

7. What is the difference between buying and leasing an automobile?

   _____

   _____

8. What are some expenses (other than the monthly payment) you will encounter in owning an automobile?

   _____

   _____

9. What safety features are available on automobiles?

   _____

   _____

10. What is a comparable when selling an automobile?

   _____

   _____

| Name | Class | Date / / | Score |
|------|-------|----------|-------|

# Buying a New Automobile Activity

## Objective

Upon completion of this activity, you will be able to differentiate between MSRP, dealer invoice, and dealer cost.

## NATEF Connections

None

## Tools

Computer with Internet access, calculator (or use the calculator on the computer)

## Supplies

None

## Cautions

Follow all procedures and safety guidelines specified by your instructor.

## Directions

Check off the boxes ❑ when completed. When you see a hand ✍ next to the task, write the information in the activity journal. If you have any questions during the duration of this activity, stop and ask the instructor for assistance.

## Note

Internet addresses were accurate at the time of printing. If the webmasters of these domains change links or home pages, please look for similar navigational items to complete this activity.

## Procedure

❑ Log on to your computer and open up an Internet browser.

❑ Type in the following Internet address - www.kbb.com.

❑ Click on *New Car Pricing*.

❑ Follow the instructions on the website to price out a vehicle of your choice.

✍ Note the manufacturer, make, model, and year.

✍ Identify the dealer invoice.

✍ Identify the MSRP (Manufacturer's Suggested Retail Price).

❑ Click on *Incentives*.

✍ Calculate the adjusted invoice cost by subtracting any customer rebates or incentives.

**Example**

$$\$21{,}000 \ - \ \$1{,}000 \ = \ \$20{,}000$$

| Dealer Invoice | (Rebates + Incentives) | Adjusted Invoice Cost |
|----------------|------------------------|-----------------------|

✍ Calculate dealer cost by also subtracting a 3% factory holdback to represent the incentive a dealership may receive from the manufacturer to sell the vehicle.

**Example**

$$\$20{,}000 \ - \ \$600 \ = \ \$19{,}400$$

| Adjusted Invoice Cost | (3% Factory Holdback) | Dealer Cost |
|-----------------------|-----------------------|-------------|

✍ Calculate a reasonable offer for the vehicle.

**Example**

$$\$19{,}400 \ \times \ 1.04 \ = \ \$20{,}176$$

| Dealer Cost | 4% Over Dealer Cost | Reasonable Offer |
|-------------|---------------------|------------------|

✍ Calculate your cost for the vehicle by including the sales tax.

**Example**

$$\$20{,}176 \ \times \ 1.05 \ = \ \$21{,}185$$

| Reasonable Offer | 5% Sales Tax | Cost with Sales Tax |
|------------------|--------------|---------------------|

✍ Calculate your 20% down payment.

**Example**

$$\$21{,}185 \ \times \ .20 \ = \ \$4{,}237$$

| Your Cost with Sales Tax | 20% Down Payment | Down Payment |
|--------------------------|------------------|--------------|

❑ Use a search engine (e.g., www.google.com) to find an online loan calculator (keyword: *loan calculator*).

✍ Calculate your monthly payment on the remaining balance if you financed the loan for 48 months at the current average interest rate.

❑ Log off your computer.

## ✍ Activity Journal

1. What is the manufacturer, make, model, and year of the vehicle you are researching?

_____

2. What factors caused you to choose the specific type of vehicle that you researched?

_____

3. What is the dealer invoice for the selected vehicle?

_____

4. What is the MSRP for the selected vehicle?

_____

5. If there is an incentive or rebate subtract if from the dealer invoice. Show calculation below.

_____

6. Calculate estimated dealer cost by subtracting another 3% (holdback). Show calculation below.

_____

7. Calculate a reasonable offer (Reasonable Offer = Dealer Cost x 1.04). Show calculation below.

_____

8. Calculate your cost for the vehicle by including the sales tax. Show calculation below.

_____

9. Calculate your 20% down payment (Down Payment = Your Cost x 0.20). Show calculation below.

_____

10. What is the current bank interest rate for new automobiles?

_____

11. Does the manufacturer offer low interest rate incentives? If yes, what is the rate?

_____

12. Use an online loan calculator to determine your monthly payment on the remaining balance if you financed the loan for 48 months at the current average interest rate. What is the monthly payment?

_____

13. How does a monthly payment change by increasing the loan duration?

_____

14. How does a monthly payment change by increasing the interest rate?

_____

15. How can automotive retailers sell vehicles under dealer invoice?

_____

# Buying a Used Automobile Activity

## Objective
Upon completion of this activity, you will be able to research prices, reliability ratings, recalls, technical service bulletins, and safety ratings on used automobiles.

## NATEF Connections
None

## Tools
Computer with Internet access

## Supplies
None

## Cautions
Follow all procedures and safety guidelines specified by your instructor.

## Directions
Check off the boxes ❑ when completed. When you see a hand ✍ next to the task, write the information in the activity journal. If you have any questions during the duration of this activity, stop and ask the instructor for assistance.

## Note
Internet addresses were accurate at the time of printing. If the webmasters of these domains change links or home pages, please look for similar navigational items to complete this activity.

## Procedure
- ❑ Log on to your computer and open up an Internet browser.
- ❑ Type in the following Internet address – **www.consumer.ftc.gov**.
- ❑ Click on *Money & Credit*.
- ❑ Click on *Buying & Owning a Car*.
- ❑ Read the article titled *Buying a Used Car*.

- ❑ Research one vehicle of your choice.
- ✍ Note the manufacturer, make, model, model year, and trim level that you chose. The trim level is the vehicle's level of luxury or accessories.
- ✍ Identify and note the estimated miles per gallon (MPG) that the vehicle should achieve. Use **www.fueleconomy.gov** to assist you.
- ❑ Research three potential used vehicles that match your chosen vehicle type. Use three Internet sites from the following list or ones provided to you by your instructor for your research. *Note: Make sure you are researching the same vehicle. All three vehicles should be the same year and have the same trim level. For example, if you chose a 2010 Honda Civic with a trim level of an EX, don't compare it to a 2010 Honda Civic with a trim level of DX. That is not an accurate comparison.*
  Car Buying Sites
  www.autobytel.com
  www.autotrader.com
  www.carmax.com
  www.cars.com
  www.craigslist.org
  www.motors.ebay.com
- ✍ Note the website, mileage, and listed price for the three vehicles that you researched. For example: **www.autotrader.com**, 56,242 miles, $8,995.
- ❑ Visit **www.edmunds.com**, **www.kbb.com**, and **www.nada.com** and research your chosen used vehicle's suggested dealer retail price.
- ✍ Note the suggested dealer retail price.
- ❑ Research the reliability ratings of your chosen vehicle. Use the three Internet sites from the following list or ones provided to you by your instructor for your research.
  Reliability Ratings Sites
  autos.jdpower.com/ratings/index.htm
  www.autos.msn.com
  www.carfax.com/safety/index.cfx
- ✍ Note the reliability ratings.

❑ Research recalls and technical service bulletins (TSBs) on your vehicle. Use the three Internet sites from the following list or ones provided to you by your instructor for your research.

**Recall and Technical Service Bulletin Sites**
www.alldatadiy.com/recalls
www-odi.nhtsa.dot.gov/tsbs
www-odi.nhtsa.dot.gov/recalls

✍ Note any recalls and technical service bulletins (TSBs) on your vehicle.

❑ Research safety ratings on your vehicle. Use three of the Internet sites from the following list or ones provided to you by your instructor for your research.

**Safety Ratings Sites**
www.automobilemag.com/used_car_safety
www.carfax.com/safety/index.cfx
www.euroncap.com
www.iihs.org
www.safercar.gov

✍ Note the safety ratings of your vehicle.

❑ Log off your computer.

## ✍ Activity Journal

1. What do you need to consider when purchasing a used vehicle?

_____

2. What vehicle did you choose to research?

| Manufacturer | Make | Model | Model Year | Trim Level |
|---|---|---|---|---|
|  |  |  |  |  |

3. What MPG should the vehicle achieve?

| City MPG | | Highway MPG | | Combined MPG | |
|---|---|---|---|---|---|
|  |  |  |  |  |  |

4. What prices did you find on your chosen vehicle?

| | Website | Mileage | Listed Price | Suggested Dealer Retail Price | | |
|---|---|---|---|---|---|---|
| | | | | Edmunds | KBB | NADA |
| Vehicle 1 |  |  |  |  |  |  |
| Vehicle 2 |  |  |  |  |  |  |
| Vehicle 3 |  |  |  |  |  |  |

5. What factors other than differences in mileage do you believe influenced price variations between the vehicles?

_____

6. What did the reliability ratings search reveal about your vehicle?

_____

7. What recalls or TSBs where posted about your vehicle?

_____

8. What did the safety rating search reveal about your vehicle?

_____

9. After completing research, do you still believe your chosen vehicle was a good one? Why or why not?

_____

# 3

# AUTOMOTIVE EXPENSES

## Think Safety

Budgeting for routine maintenance is important to your safety. Potentially hazardous situations can be avoided by doing maintenance on your vehicle as recommended or required.

## Objectives

After reading the *Auto Upkeep* text and completing the following activities, you will be able to:

- Identify automotive expenses.
- Identify ways to save money.
- Describe insurance coverage levels.
- Calculate specific automotive expenses.

## Summary

Automobiles are expensive to own. The financial obligations to own and operate a vehicle range from monthly car payments to insurance premiums to unexpected repairs. Knowing your budget and planning for routine maintenance and unexpected expenses will prepare you for the financial responsibility of vehicle ownership.

## Web Exploring

### Key Terms/Internet Search Words

Visit **www.google.com** to investigate any of the following terms or phrases. Summarize your findings in a research paper.

- Allstate Insurance Company
- American Automobile Association (AAA)
- American Family Insurance
- Automobile Collision Insurance
- Automobile Comprehensive Insurance
- Automobile Liability Insurance
- Buying a Car
- Cheap Gasoline Prices
- Country Companies Insurance
- Department of Motor Vehicles
- Farmers Insurance Group
- Gasoline Prices
- Geico Direct
- Hybrid Electric Vehicles
- Insurance Companies
- Progressive Insurance
- State Farm Insurance
- Towing Insurance

Name _____  Class _____  Date ___/___/___  Score _____

## 📖 Study Questions - Automotive Expenses

1. What are common automotive expenses?

   _____

   _____

2. What are three things that your monthly car payment is dependent on?

   _____

   _____

3. What is the minimum insurance policy that your state/province requires?

   _____

   _____

4. What do the numbers 50/100/20 represent in an insurance policy?

   _____

   _____

5. What does collision insurance cover?

   _____

   _____

6. What does comprehensive insurance cover?

   _____

   _____

7. How much would you spend on gasoline each year if you drove 10,000 miles over the year and your vehicle achieves 15 miles per gallon with gasoline priced at $4.00 a gallon?

   _____

   _____

8. Using the same scenario as question seven, substitute your vehicle for a hybrid-electric automobile that achieves 60 miles per gallon. Calculate the yearly cost for fuel with this vehicle.

   _____

   _____

9. How often do license plates need to be renewed in the state/province that you reside?

   _____

   _____

10. Why is it important to keep up with routine maintenance?

   _____

   _____

| Name _____ | Class _____ | Date __/__/__ | Score _____ |
|---|---|---|---|

# Automotive Expenses Activity

## Objective

Upon completion of this activity, you will be able to calculate automotive expenses.

## NATEF Connections

None

## Tools

Computer with Internet access, telephone, calculator (or use the calculator on the computer or a spreadsheet program such as Microsoft Excel)

## Supplies

None

## Cautions

Follow all procedures and safety guidelines specified by your instructor.

## Directions

Check off the boxes ❏ when completed. When you see a hand ✍ next to the task, write the information in the activity journal. If you have any questions during the duration of this activity, stop and ask the instructor for assistance.

## Note

Internet addresses were accurate at the time of printing. If the webmasters of these domains change links or home pages, please look for similar navigational items to complete this activity.

## Scenario 1

You have been saving for years for your first vehicle and have accumulated $2,500. Recently you passed your driver's test and received your license. Your parents have agreed to match the amount of money that you have saved for your vehicle, so your budget is now $5,000. However this sum of money needs to last you six months until you get a summer job. You must calculate a six-month budget that will cover the vehicle's purchase, insurance, fuel, registration,

license, routine maintenance, and $100 worth of unexpected repairs. Your parents have decided that they don't want you to take out any loans. Use the table in the activity journal or a computer spreadsheet to organize the data that you collect.

## Procedure 1 - Saved for Purchase

❏ Log on to your computer and open up an Internet browser.

❏ Type in the following Internet address - www.autotrader.com.

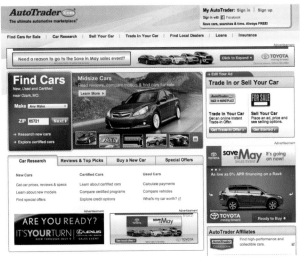

*Screen Capture from* www.AutoTrader.com

❏ Use this site to search for possible vehicles. Remember that you only have $5,000 to spend on the vehicle and expenses.

✍ Note the manufacturer, make, model, year, and engine size.

✍ Note the cost of the vehicle.

✍ Call your local Department of Motor Vehicles (DMV) or check online for the cost of license plates, registration, and title transfer fees for the specific vehicle you are researching.

✍ Calculate the sales tax (if applicable) on the vehicle. This tax is often collected by your local DMV if you bought a vehicle from a private party.

## Example

| **$4,000.00** | x | **.05** | = | **$200.00** |
|---|---|---|---|---|
| Vehicle Cost | | 5% Sales Tax | | Sales Tax |

✍ Complete research to identify the vehicle's fuel efficiency in miles per gallon or L/100 km.

✍ Visit or call gas stations (or search online) to determine the cost of fuel per gallon.

✍ Calculate a six-month expenditure on fuel costs if you travel 1,000 miles (1,609 km) a month or use an online calculator (e.g., www.fueleconomy.gov) to assist you.

## Example MPG

| **200** | x | **$4.00** | = | **$800.00** |
|---|---|---|---|---|
| 6,000 Miles ÷ Fuel Efficiency of 30 MPG | | Price of Fuel per Gallon | | 6 Month Fuel Costs |

## Example L/100 km

| **757** | x | **$1.00** | = | **$757.00** |
|---|---|---|---|---|
| (9654 km ÷ 100) x Fuel Efficiency of 7.84 L/100 km | | Price of Fuel per Liter | | 6 Month Fuel Costs |

Screen Capture from www.fueleconomy.gov

✍ Call a local insurance agent or check online for the cost of a six-month liability policy. Your parents want you to have 100/300/50 coverage. Gather at least three quotes from different insurance companies. Choose a policy from a company that best meets your needs.

✍ Budget for two oil and filter changes in the six-month period. Include labor costs if you do not intend to complete the service. Call repair facilities for estimates.

✍ Budget for one major tune-up in the six-month period. You will need to calculate the cost for spark plugs, spark plug wires (if applicable), distributor cap (if applicable), distributor rotor (if applicable), air filter, and fuel filter. *Note: A distributorless ignition system does not have a cap or rotor. Coil-on-plug (COP) ignition systems will not have spark plug wires.* Include labor costs if you do not intend to complete the service. Call repair facilities for estimates.

✍ Calculate your total vehicle expenditures. To do this, add the following.
- Vehicle Cost
- License Plates, Registration, and Title Transfer Fees
- Sales Tax on Vehicle
- Fuel Costs for Six Months
- Insurance for Six Months
- Two Oil Changes
- Tune-Up
- Unexpected Repairs (Estimate $100)

✍ Compare your total vehicle expenditures with the amount of money ($5,000) that is available.

❑ Log off your computer.

| Name | | Class | Date  /  / | Score |
|------|--|-------|------------|-------|

## Scenario 2

You have not saved much money for your first vehicle, but you have recently started working a part time job clearing $8.00 an hour. Your parents have offered to give you $1,000 towards your first vehicle and will co-sign a loan with you for another $4,000. Now you have $5,000 to spend towards a vehicle. Your job should cover the loan payment and the costs for the monthly expenses. You purchased a vehicle for $5,000 including the sales tax. You are curious to calculate how many hours a month you need to work to keep your vehicle operational. Your goal is to calculate the average monthly cost of owning this vehicle. Use the table in the activity journal or a computer spreadsheet program to organize the data that you collect.

## Procedure 2 - Loan for Purchase

🖎 Use an online loan payment calculator (keyword: *loan calculator*) to determine the monthly payments on a $4,000 loan for 48 months at the current interest rate.

Auto calculator — Amortization schedule Calculator

Auto loan amount: $ 10000.00

Auto loan term: 5.000  years or  60  months

Interest rate: 7.5  % per year

Auto loan start date: May ÷ 16 ÷ 2012 ÷

Monthly auto loan payments: $ 200.38

[Calculate]

*Screen Capture from* www.bankrate.com

🖎 Call a local insurance agent or check online for the cost of a six-month liability policy. Your parents want you to have 100/300/50 coverage. Since you have a loan on the vehicle, the lending institution will also require collision and comprehensive coverage. Gather at least three quotes from different insurance companies. Choose a policy from a company that best meets your needs.

🖎 Calculate the cost of the insurance policy on a monthly basis.

## Example

$600.00 ÷ 6 = $100.00

Insurance for 6 Months    Months    Insurance Cost per Month

🖎 Complete research to determine the fuel mileage per gallon (MPG) or L/100 km of the chosen vehicle.

🖎 Visit or call gas stations (or search online) to determine the cost of fuel per gallon.

🖎 Calculate your monthly expenditure on fuel if you travel 1,000 miles (1609 km) a month.

### Example MPG

33.33 x $4.00 = $133.32

1,000 Miles ÷ Fuel Efficiency of 30 MPG    Price of Fuel per Gallon    Approximate Fuel Cost per Month

### Example L/100 km

126.15 x $1.00 = $126.15

(1609 km ÷ 100) x Fuel Efficiency of 7.84 L/100 km    Price of Fuel per Liter    Approximate Fuel Cost per Month

🖎 Pro-rate (per month) the cost for licensing and registering. Call your local Department of Motor Vehicles (DMV), Motor Vehicle Administration (MVA), or check online for the cost of license plates, registration, and title transfer fees for the specific vehicle you are researching.

## Example

$120.00 ÷ 12 = $10.00

Annual License & Registration    Months    License & Registration Cost per Month

🖎 Traveling 1,000 miles (1609 km) a month will determine that your vehicle will need an oil change every 3 months. Pro-rate (per month) the cost of an oil change.

## Example

$30.00 ÷ 3 = $10.00

Oil Change Price    Months    Oil Change Cost per Month

✎ Pro-rate (per month) the cost of a tune up. You will need to calculate the cost for spark plugs, spark plug wires (if applicable), distributor cap (if applicable), distributor rotor (if applicable), air filter, and fuel filter. ***Note: A distributorless ignition system does not have a cap or rotor. Coil-on-plug (COP) ignition systems will not have spark plug wires.*** Include labor costs if you do not intend to complete the service. Call repair facilities for estimates. Estimate that your vehicle will need a major tune-up every two years.

**Example**

$$\$240.00 \div 24 = \$10.00$$

| Tune-Up Cost | Months | Tune-Up Cost per Month |

✎ Pro-rate (per month) the cost for one set of tires. With your driving habits, you will need to buy a new set of tires every four years. Check online or with a local tire distributor for the cost to replace the tires for your vehicle. You want to buy 50,000 mile (80,470 km) tires with the following minimum UTQG ratings: Traction A, Temperature B, Treadwear 400. You also want new valve stems installed, the tires mounted and balanced, and the old tires properly disposed.

**Example**

$$\$480.00 \div 48 = \$10.00$$

Set of 4 Tires Cost — Months — Tire Cost per Month

✎ Pro-rate (per month) the cost for one battery. You live in a harsh climate and will probably need a new battery in the next four years. Check online or with a local battery distributor for the cost to replace the battery in your vehicle.

**Example**

$$\$72.00 \div 48 = \$1.50$$

Battery Cost — Months — Battery Cost per Month

✎ Pro-rate (per month) the cost for new windshield wiper blades. You will probably need to replace your wiper blades every year. Check online or with a local parts distributor for the cost to replace the wipers on your vehicle.

**Example**

$$\$24.00 \div 12 = \$2.00$$

Set of 2 Wiper Blades — Months — Wiper Blades Cost per Month

✎ Pro-rate (per month) the cost for two new headlamp bulbs in the next four years. Check online or with a local parts distributor for the cost for two new headlamp bulbs.

**Example**

$$\$32.00 \div 48 = \$0.66$$

Set of 2 Headlamps — Months — Headlamp Cost per Month

✎ Pro-rate (per month) the cost for one complete brake job in the next four years. Check online or with a local service facility for the cost to replace the brake pads/shoes and resurface the rotors/drums.

**Example**

$$\$240.00 \div 48 = \$5.00$$

Cost for Brake Job — Months — Brake Expense Cost per Month

Rotor    Brake Pad

✎ Calculate your total monthly expenses by adding the following:
- Monthly Car Payment
- Monthly Insurance Cost
- Monthly Fuel Cost
- License Plates, Registration, and Title Transfer Fees Cost Pro-Rated Monthly
- Oil Change Cost Pro-Rated Monthly
- Tune-Up Cost Pro-Rated Monthly
- Tire Cost Pro-Rated Monthly
- Battery Cost Pro-Rated Monthly
- Wiper Cost Pro-Rated Monthly
- Headlamp Cost Pro-Rated Monthly
- Brake Job Cost Pro-Rated Monthly
- Miscellaneous Monthly Car Expenses

❏ Calculate the minimum number of hours you need to work each month to keep your vehicle on the road.

## Example

| **$320.00** ÷ | **$8.00** = | **40** |
|---|---|---|
| Total Monthly Expense | Hourly Income After Withholdings | Hours Needed to Work |

❏ Log off your computer.

## ✎ Activity Journal

1. Complete the Procedure 1 table below or organize your data in a computer spreadsheet program.

| Vehicle Information | |
|---|---|
| Manufacturer | |
| Make and Model | |
| Model Year | |
| Engine Size | |
| Fuel Efficiency (MPG or L/100 km) | |

| Six Month Budget | | Cost |
|---|---|---|
| Vehicle Cost | | |
| Six Month Cost of License Plates, Registration, and Title Transfer Fees | | |
| Sales Tax = Vehicle Cost x Sales Tax Percent in decimal form | | |
| Price of Fuel per Unit Measure (Gallon or Liter) | | |
| Six Month Fuel Expenditure if you travel 1,000 miles (1,609 km) a month Fuel Costs = (6,000 miles/Fuel Efficiency in MPG) x Price of Fuel per Gallon or Fuel Costs = ((9,654 km/100) x Fuel Efficiency in L/100 km) x Price of Fuel per Liter | | |
| Cost of Six Month Liability Insurance Policy | Quote 1 Quote 2 Quote 3 | Quote Chosen |
| Cost of Two Oil and Filter Changes (Include Labor Costs if Applicable) | | |
| Cost of One Major Tune-up (Include Labor Costs if Applicable) | | |
| Unexpected Repairs | | $100.00 |
| Estimated Total Vehicle Expenditures | | |
| $5,000 Budget - Total Vehicle Expenditures = Amount Under or Over Budget | | |

2.  Complete the Procedure 2 table below or organize your data in a computer spreadsheet program.

| Vehicle Information | |
|---|---|
| Manufacturer | |
| Make and Model | |
| Model Year | |
| Engine Size | |
| Fuel Efficiency (MPG or L/100 km) | |

| One Month Budget | Cost |
|---|---|
| Current Interest Rate | |
| Monthly Payment on $4,000 loan for 48 Months at Current Interest Rate | |
| Cost of Monthly Insurance Policy       Quote 1<br>Monthly Policy = Six Month Policy/6     Quote 2<br>Quote 3 | Quote Chosen |
| Price of Fuel per Unit Measure (Gallon or Liter) | |
| One Month Fuel Expenditure if you travel 1,000 miles (1,609 km)<br>Fuel Costs = (1,000 miles/Fuel Efficiency in MPG) x Price of Fuel per Gallon or<br>Fuel Costs = ((1,609 km/100) x Fuel Efficiency in L/100 km) x Price of Fuel per Liter | |
| Cost of License Plates, Registration, and Title Transfer Fees Pro-Rated Monthly | |
| Oil Change Cost Pro-Rated Monthly | |
| Tune-Up Cost Pro-Rated Monthly | |
| Tire Cost Pro-Rated Monthly | |
| Battery Cost Pro-Rated Monthly | |
| Wiper Cost Pro-Rated Monthly | |
| Headlamp Cost Pro-Rated Monthly | |
| Brake Job Cost Pro-Rated Monthly | |
| Miscellaneous Monthly Vehicle Expenses | $16.00 |
| Estimated Total Monthly Vehicle Expense | |
| Hours Needed to Work per Month = Total Monthly Expenses/$8.00 | |

3.  Why should you obtain several insurance quotes?

_____

4.  What is the second most costly pro-rated monthly expense?

_____

5.  Why is it important to budget for expenses?

_____

6.  How could you reduce your monthly expenses?

_____

# REPAIR FACILITIES

## Think Safety

When choosing a technician for your vehicle it is important to look for one that has had updated training or is ASE certified in the specific area of repair needed.

## Objectives

After reading the *Auto Upkeep* text and completing the following activities, you will be able to:
- Identify a quality repair facility.
- Communicate effectively with a technician or service writer.
- Interpret a repair invoice.
- Locate a car care education program.

## Summary

Whether your vehicle needs an oil change or transmission overhaul, there is a wide choice of repair centers. When choosing a facility, check its quality, service, price, reputation, and warranties. Have a clear understanding of what service work is being completed and how you are being charged for that service with a written estimate. Maintain an open communication with the technician and service writer. Keep good records of all work completed on your vehicle.

## Web Exploring

### Key Terms/Internet Search Words
Visit www.google.com to investigate any of the following terms or phrases. Summarize your findings in a research paper.
- American Automobile Association (AAA)
- Auto Repair Law
- Automotive Service Excellence (ASE)
- Be Car Care Aware
- Better Business Bureau
- Blue Seal of Excellence
- Bumper-to-Bumper Warranty
- Certified Auto Repair
- Certified Repair Facilities
- Certified Used Cars
- Choosing a Repair Facility
- Consumer Rights Auto Repair
- Corrosion Perforation Warranty
- Federal Emission Warranty
- Motorist Assurance Program
- National Institute for Automotive Service Excellence
- Writing an Automotive Repair Order

**Name** _____    **Class** _____    **Date** ___ / ___ / ___    **Score** _____

## 📖 Study Questions - Repair Facilities

1. What does it mean when a technician is ASE certified?

   _____

   _____

2. What are AAA Approved Auto Repair facility characteristics?

   _____

   _____

3. What are examples of an ASE technician's Code of Ethics?

   _____

   _____

4. What is the purpose of the Better Business Bureau?

   _____

   _____

5. What are different types of service facilities?

   _____

   _____

6. What is the difference between an estimate and a repair invoice?

   _____

   _____

7. What types of warranties are available on new vehicles?

   _____

   _____

8. Why might a chain warranty be better than an independent repair facility warranty?

   _____

   _____

9. What does it mean when a warranty is pro-rated?

   _____

   _____

10. Why do some repair facilities offer community education programs?

   _____

   _____

Name _____ Class _____ Date __/__/__ Score _____

# Repair Facilities Activity

## Objective

Upon completion of this activity, you will be able to choose a quality repair facility and interpret a repair invoice.

## NATEF Connections

**Preparing Vehicle for Service**
- Identify information needed and the service requested on a repair order.
- Demonstrate the use of the three C's (concern, cause, correction).
- Review vehicle service history.
- Complete work order to include customer information, vehicle identifying information, customer concern, related service history, cause, and correction.

## Tools

Computer with Internet access

## Supplies

None

## Cautions

Follow all procedures and safety guidelines specified by your instructor.

## Directions

Check off the boxes ❏ when completed. When you see a hand ✍ next to the task, write the information in the activity journal. If you have any questions during the duration of this activity, stop and ask the instructor for assistance.

## Note

Internet addresses were accurate at the time of printing. If the webmasters of these domains change links or home pages, please look for similar navigational items to complete this activity.

## Procedure 1 - Choosing a Repair Facility

✍ Interview at least three adults that have been driving for at least ten years each. Ask questions related to choosing repair facilities (e.g., Where do you bring your vehicle for service? Why do you bring your vehicle there? What do you look for when choosing a repair facility?).

❏ Log on to your computer and open up an Internet browser.

❏ Go to ASE's YouTube Channel online at **www.youtube.com/asetests**.

❏ Click on *Videos*.

❏ Click on and view the video titled *Why Car Owners Should Look For ASE Certified Technicians*.

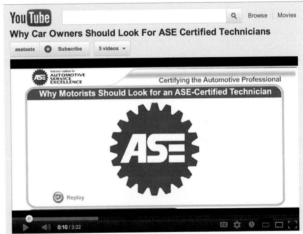

*Screen Capture from* www.youtube.com/asetests

❏ Type in the following Internet Address - **www.ase.com**.

❏ Using the ASE website, review the characteristics of a *Blue Seal Shop*.

❏ Click on the tab *Car Owners* and then *Find an ASE Blue Seal Facility Near You*.

*Screen Capture from* www.ase.com

❑ Use the Blue Seal Shop Locator to see if any repair facilities in your geographical area meet the quality standards.

❑ Use www.google.com to search for *AAA Approved Auto Repair Facilities*.

❑ Click on www.aaa.com link in the search results to access the AAA Facility Search Tool to locate facilities in your geographical area.

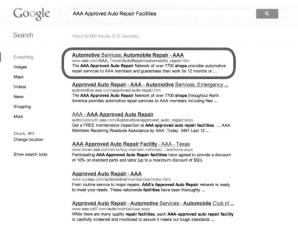

*Screen Capture from* www.google.com

❑ Type in the following Internet address - www.motorist.org.

❑ Click on and view the video *How to Select An Automotive Repair Facility with Confidence.*

*Screen Capture from* www.motorist.org

❑ Use the Service Center Search tool to locate local repair shops that participate in the Motorist Assurance Program (MAP) and adhere to the MAP Pledge of Assurance to Customers and the Standards of Service.

❑ Review any old repair invoices that you may be able to obtain.

❑ Identify if the invoice has a written *Customer Rights* list that is clearly stated.

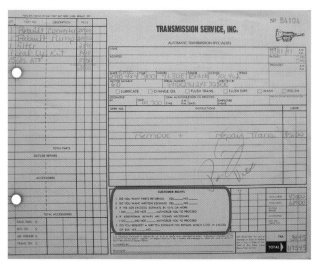

❑ Compare responses from the interviews, ASE Blue Seal Shop search, AAA Approved Auto Repair Facilities search, and Motorist Assurance Program search. See if any of the facilities meet all four criteria:
   1. Recommended by someone you interviewed
   2. ASE Blue Seal Shop
   3. AAA Approved Auto Repair Facility
   4. Motorist Assurance Program Accredited Automotive Shop

❑ Log off your computer.

## Procedure 2 - Interpreting a Repair Invoice

✍ Interview at least three adults that have been driving for at least ten years each. Ask questions related to repair invoices and estimates (e.g., What do you expect to see on a repair invoice? Do you have any old repair invoices I could review? Did you ever have a dispute with an auto repair shop regarding a repair? If so, what did you do?).

❑ Log on to your computer and open up an Internet browser.

❑ Complete an Internet search using *Auto Repair Law* as the search phrase.

Screen Capture from www.google.com

❑ Some states have comprehensive auto repair laws, others do not. Michigan Department of State has a well designed brochure titled *A Guide to the Auto Repair Law – For Mechanics and Repair Facilities*. Complete an Internet search to find this brochure that is available online. Read the brochure.

❑ Repair invoices should have the vehicle's VIN, year, make, model, odometer reading, and date of repair. It should also list parts and labor costs, the name of the parts installed, guarantee (if applicable), and whether the parts were rebuilt, new, or used.

### REPAIR INVOICE/WORK ORDER

Repair and Service Facility
123 Any Town, USA
(555) 555-0100

Work Order Number: _____
Date & Time Received: __/__/__ __:__ A.M. P.M.
Promised: __/__/__ __:__ A.M. P.M.
Order Written By: _____

| Customer Contact Information |
| --- |
| Name: |
| Address: |
| City:    State:    Zip: |
| Phone Home: ( ) |
| Work: ( )    Cell: ( ) |

| Vehicle Information | | |
| --- | --- | --- |
| Make and Model | | |
| Year/Color | | |
| License Number | | |
| Odometer Reading | IN | OUT |
| Engine Size | | |
| VIN | | |

| Description of Customer Concern |
| --- |
| |
| |
| |

| Customer Rights | |
| --- | --- |
| Do you want your parts returned? | Yes ❑ No ❑ |
| If the job exceeds the estimate by 10% or more, do you authorize us in proceeding? | Yes ❑ No ❑ |
| If additional repairs are found necessary, do you authorize us in proceeding? | Yes ❑ No ❑ |
| Do you request a written estimate for repairs with cost in excess of $50.00? | Yes ❑ No ❑ |

| Service History |
| --- |
| |
| |

I hereby authorize the above repair work to be done with the necessary material, and hereby grant you and/or your employees permission to operate the vehicle herein described on streets, highways, or elsewhere for the purpose of testing and/or inspection. An express mechanic's lien is hereby acknowledged on above vehicle to secure the amount of repairs thereof.
X _____

| Estimate of Repair | |
| --- | --- |
| Parts | $ |
| Labor Rate $ ___ Per Hr. x ___ Hrs. | $ |
| Other/Supplies | $ |
| Preliminary Estimate Total | $ |

| ❑ Lubricate Chassis | ❑ Change Oil | ❑ Check All Fluids | ❑ Rotate Tires | ❑ Wash |
| --- | --- | --- | --- | --- |

| Parts Required | | | |
| --- | --- | --- | --- |
| Qty. | Item No. | Description | Price |
| | | | |
| | | | |
| | | | |
| | | | |
| | | Total Parts | |

| Labor Required | | |
| --- | --- | --- |
| Service Description | Hours | Charge |
| | | |
| | | |
| | | |
| | | |
| | Total Labor | |

| Other/Supplies Required | | | |
| --- | --- | --- | --- |
| Qty. | Item No. | Description | Price |
| Towing | | | |
| Environmental Fees | | | |
| Supplies | | | |
| | | Total Other/Supplies | |

| Repair Total | |
| --- | --- |
| Total Parts | $ |
| Total Labor | $ |
| Total Other/Supplies | $ |
| Subtotal | $ |
| Tax | $ |
| Total Amount Due ▶ | $ |

❑ Obtain a blank Repair Invoice/Work Order. Use the one in Appendix G or one that your instructor provides to you.

❑ Work with a partner. Take turns role playing. One person acts as a customer the other acts as a service writer. It is the job of the service writer to complete the Repair Invoice/Work Order to include customer information, vehicle identifying information, customer concerns, related service history, possible causes, and proposed corrections. It is the job of customer to clearly convey to the service writer the vehicle's problems. After you play one role, switch and play the other.

❑ Log off your computer.

## ✍ Activity Journal

1. What type of facility did the drivers with ten or more years of experience that you interviewed choose most often for major service - a dealership, independent, or specialized repair facility?

   _____

2. Why did they choose to bring their vehicle to a specific repair facility?

   _____

3. Did someone recommend the repair facility to them? If yes, who recommended it?

   _____

4. What are characteristics of a quality auto repair facility?

   _____

5. Why should you look for a facility that has ASE certified technicians?

   _____

6. What did the drivers that you interviewed expect to see on a repair invoice?

   _____

7. Did they have any old repair invoices? If yes, was the cost of labor identified separate from the cost of parts and/or supplies?

   _____

8. What are auto repair facilities required to provide on estimates and repair invoices in your geographical location?

   _____

9. Did the drivers that you interviewed ever have a dispute about service? If so, what did they do?

   _____

10. What should you do if you have a dispute with the service facility over the quality or price of an auto repair?

   _____

11. Why is it important to clearly communicate vehicle issues?

   _____

# 5

# SAFETY AROUND THE AUTOMOBILE

## Think Safety

Always wear eye protection. Eyes are very fragile and foreign materials can easily damage them when you least expect it.

## Objectives

After reading the *Auto Upkeep* text and completing the following activities, you will be able to:

- Safely work on and around a vehicle.
- Safely jack and support a vehicle.
- Identify basic types of vehicle lifts.
- Safely raise and lower a vehicle on an automotive lift.
- Identify types of fire extinguishers.

## Summary

Safety in an automotive lab or shop is essential. Fires are classified by the type of material burning. The best type of fire extinguisher to have when working on an automobile is a combination A-B-C. Proper jack procedures enable you to lift a vehicle safely and without damage. Two types of lifts are common in automotive shops: inground and surface-mounted lifts. Surface-mounted lifts come in two-post and four-post designs. The four-post is easier to use than the two-post, but it is not as versatile without special adapters. The four-post lift is generally used for oil changes and undercarriage inspections, while the two-post is commonly used for tire, brake, or suspension work. Be extremely careful when working around airbag system components. They can be dangerous if accidentally deployed.

## Web Exploring

### Key Terms/Internet Search Words

Visit www.google.com to investigate any of the following terms or phrases. Summarize your findings in a research paper.

- Airbag Safety
- Ammco Lifts
- Automotive Lift Institute
- Decibel Ratings
- Ear Muffs
- Ear Plugs
- Fire Extinguisher Ratings
- Fire Extinguishers
- Hydraulic Jacks
- Jack Stands
- Rotary Lifts
- Safety Glasses
- Using Hydraulic Jacks
- Using Hydraulic Lifts
- Using Jack Stands
- Uvex Safety Products

Name _____   Class _____   Date __ / __ / __   Score _____

## 📚 Study Questions - Safety Around the Automobile

1. Why is it important to "think safety" while working on an automobile?

   _____

   _____

2. What things should you be able to locate in a garage, shop, or laboratory facility?

   _____

   _____

3. What safety equipment is required when working on vehicles?

   _____

   _____

4. Why do you need to be extremely cautious around electric fans?

   _____

   _____

5. What is the procedure for jacking up a vehicle?

   _____

   _____

6. What are two types of automotive lifts? How are they different?

   _____

   _____

7. How are fire extinguishers classified? What type of fire extinguisher should you have in an automotive shop?

   _____

   _____

8. What is the procedure to lift a vehicle on a two-post lift?

   _____

   _____

9. What is the procedure to lift a vehicle on a four-post lift?

   _____

   _____

10. What should you do if a vehicle starts to fall off an automotive lift?

    _____

    _____

| Name | Class | Date / / | Score |
| --- | --- | --- | --- |

# Automotive Safety Activity

## Objective

Upon completion of this activity, you will be able to identify the location of emergency and safety equipment.

## NATEF Connections

**Shop and Personal Safety**

- Identify general shop safety rules and procedures.
- Identify and use proper placement of floor jacks and jack stands.
- Identify and use proper procedures for safe lift operation.
- Utilize proper ventilation procedures for working within the lab/shop area.
- Identify marked safety areas.
- Identify the location and the types of fire extinguishers and other fire safety equipment; demonstrate knowledge of the procedures for using fire extinguishers and other fire safety equipment.
- Identify the location and use of eye wash stations.
- Identify the location of the posted evacuation routes.
- Comply with the required use of safety glasses, ear protection, gloves, and shoes during lab/shop activities.
- Identify and wear appropriate clothing for lab/shop activities.
- Secure hair and jewelry for lab/shop activities.
- Demonstrate awareness of the safety aspects of supplemental restraint systems (SRS).
- Locate and demonstrate knowledge of material safety data sheets (MSDS).

## Tools

None

## Supplies

None

## Cautions

Do not use an automotive lift unless properly supervised. Follow all procedures and safety guidelines specified by your instructor.

## Directions

Check off the boxes ❏ when completed. When you see a hand ✍ next to the task, write the information in the activity journal. If you have any questions during the duration of this activity, stop and ask the instructor for assistance.

## Procedure

❏ Re-read the laboratory safety precautions in the textbook.

❏ Locate the shop's exhaust evacuation system and watch a demonstration from the instructor on how to use it.

✍ Identify any marked safety areas in the shop.

✍ Identify any posted evacuation routes in the shop.

❏ Locate SRS safety labels on a vehicle in the shop.

✍ Locate the Material Safety Data Sheets (MSDS) in the shop.

✍ Locate fire extinguishers in the shop. Read all labels so you understand the proper procedures for using each fire extinguisher. Note the type(s) of fire extinguisher accessible in the shop.

A-Type  B-Type  C-Type  D-Type

✍ If you are in a school laboratory or shop setting, locate the load capacity ratings on the automotive lift(s). Note the ratings.

❏ If there are automotive lifts available, locate the lift safety and caution labels. Read them.

❏ Identify where the closest telephone is for emergencies.

❑ Locate the rag waste can for combustible materials.

❑ If there is an eyewash station, read the instructions on how to use it.

*Courtesy of Guardian Equipment Company*

✍ If you are in a school laboratory or shop setting draw an overhead (bird's eye) view of the garage layout in the activity journal. Note the location of fire extinguishers, eyewash stations, exits, evacuation routes, safety areas, MSDS sheets, exhaust evacuation controls, trash cans, rag waste can, extension lights, electrical outlets, automotive lifts, supply cabinets, tools, workbenches, and safety glasses. List as many items as possible to make yourself familiar with the shop.

❑ After reading the procedure in the textbook on "Jacking a Vehicle", work with a partner to safely lift a vehicle with a jack and jack stands.

❑ After the instructor demonstrates the use of an automotive lift, work with a partner to safely lift a vehicle on the automotive lift.

## ✍ Activity Journal

1.  What types of fire extinguishers are located in the shop?

    _____

2.  What are the load capacities of the automotive lifts?

    _____

3.  What are some safety rules when using an automotive lift?

    _____

4.  What do you have to be cautious about when using an automotive lift?

    _____

5.  How do you use an eyewash station?

    _____

6.  Why is it important to use a shop exhaust evacuation system?

    _____

7.  Why is it important to be cautious around SRS systems when working on a vehicle?

    _____

8.  Why is it important to use jack stands to support a vehicle that is lifted by a jack?

    _____

9.  What is an MSDS sheet? Where are they located? Why are they important?

    _____

10. Sketch an overhead view of garage layout on a blank sheet of paper.

CHAPTER

# 6

RESOURCES

QR

# BASIC TOOLS

## Think Safety

Improper use of a tool may cause it to slip or break when force is applied. Be sure to choose tools that fit snuggly and are designed for the task.

## Objectives

After reading the *Auto Upkeep* text and completing the following activity, you will be able to:
- Recognize basic hand tools.
- Identify the correct tool for the job.
- Use tools properly.
- Identify types of service manuals.

## Summary

Quality tools can be expensive, but having the right tool can make a difficult job easier. Start off with a basic tool set and then periodically add more specialized tools as you see a need and as your budget permits. Remember that caring for and cleaning your tools will help them last longer. Having the proper tools makes working on a vehicle easier, faster, and ultimately more enjoyable.

## Web Exploring

### Key Terms/Internet Search Words

Visit **www.google.com** to investigate any of the following terms or phrases. Summarize your findings in a research paper.
- ALLDATA
- Chilton Repair Manuals
- Coolant Testers
- Converting Measurements
- Dial and Vernier Calipers
- English Customary System
- Floor Jacks
- Haynes Repair Manuals
- Jack Stands
- Micrometers
- Mitchell Repair Manuals
- Multimeters
- Pliers
- Safety Glasses
- SI Metric System
- Socket and Ratchet Sets
- Tire Pressure Gauges
- Torque Wrenches
- Wrench Sets

**Name** _____    **Class** _____    **Date** ___ / ___ / ___    **Score** _____

## 📖 Study Questions - Basic Tools

1.  Sketch a drawing to illustrate the difference between an open-end and a box-end wrench.

    ┌─────────────────────────────────────────────────┐
    │                                                 │
    │                                                 │
    │                                                 │
    │                                                 │
    └─────────────────────────────────────────────────┘

2.  If a 6-point wrench is less likely to strip a fastener, when would you need a 12-point wrench?

    _____

    _____

3.  What is the most common ratchet size?

    _____

    _____

4.  What specialty tool can be used to test voltage, resistance, and amperage in a circuit?

    _____

    _____

5.  What tool could be used to cut an exhaust pipe?

    _____

    _____

6.  What are the two types of measurement systems commonly used?

    _____

    _____

7.  What is the function of an air gauge?

    _____

    _____

8.  What are two common types of screwdrivers? How do you know what type of screwdriver tip to use?

    _____

    _____

9.  If you only had one wrench in your toolbox, what type would it be?

    _____

    _____

10. Why is it important to use the correct tool?

    _____

    _____

| Name | Class | Date / / | Score |
|---|---|---|---|

# Basic Tools Activity

## Objective

Upon completion of this activity, you will be able to correctly identify basic tools that are used in automotive shops.

## NATEF Connections

**Shop and Personal Safety**
- Utilize safe procedures for handling of tools and equipment.

**Tools and Equipment**
- Identify tools and their usage in automotive applications.
- Identify standard and metric designation.
- Demonstrate safe handling and use of appropriate tools.
- Demonstrate proper cleaning, storage, and maintenance of tools and equipment.
- Demonstrate proper use of precision measuring tools.

**Preparing Vehicle for Service**
- Identify purpose and demonstrate proper use of fender covers, mats.

## Tools

All tools needed for identification

## Supplies

None

## Cautions

Follow all procedures and safety guidelines specified by your instructor.

## Directions

Check off the boxes ❑ when completed. When you see a hand ✍ next to the task, write the information in the activity journal. If you have any questions during the duration of this activity, stop and ask the instructor for assistance.

## Procedure

❑ Listen to your instructor's description and demonstration on how to handle and use various automotive hand tools.
❑ Listen to your instructor's description regarding the specific cleaning, storing, and maintenance of the shop tools.
❑ Listen to your instructor's demonstration on how to use the shop's precision measuring tools.
❑ Listen to your instructor's demonstration on how to properly use fender covers and mats to protect a customer's vehicle.
❑ Your instructor will have tools displayed for you to identify. Each tool will be labeled with a number (e.g., 1, 2, 3).

## Example

Identify Tool

❑ Each student will be at a different tool. You will have one minute to inspect and identify the tool.
✍ Once you have identified the tool, write its correct name and function in your activity journal next to the corresponding number.

## Example

Name Tool

❑ Rotate every minute to identify the next tool until you have identified all the tools that your instructor displayed.
❑ At the end of the rotation, your instructor will assign you a tool. When called on you will be required to identify the assigned tool and describe/demonstrate how it is used.

## Example

Describe Tool Use

❑ Clean up and put away all tools.

## ✍ Activity Journal

1. How are pliers different than wrenches?

   _____

2. What is the difference between a socket and a ratchet?

   _____

3. In what way is a spark plug socket different from a regular deep well socket?

   _____

4. Why is it important to be able to identify, safely handle, properly store, clean, and know the specific function of automotive tools?

   _____

5. Write the name and function of each tool next to the corresponding number.

| | |
|---|---|
| 1. _____ | 21. _____ |
| 2. _____ | 22. _____ |
| 3. _____ | 23. _____ |
| 4. _____ | 24. _____ |
| 5. _____ | 25. _____ |
| 6. _____ | 26. _____ |
| 7. _____ | 27. _____ |
| 8. _____ | 28. _____ |
| 9. _____ | 29. _____ |
| 10. _____ | 30. _____ |
| 11. _____ | 31. _____ |
| 12. _____ | 32. _____ |
| 13. _____ | 33. _____ |
| 14. _____ | 34. _____ |
| 15. _____ | 35. _____ |
| 16. _____ | 36. _____ |
| 17. _____ | 37. _____ |
| 18. _____ | 38. _____ |
| 19. _____ | 39. _____ |
| 20. _____ | 40. _____ |

# 7

# AUTO CARE AND CLEANING

## Think Safety

Windows that are dirty are a potential hazard while driving, especially at night when oncoming headlights create glare. Keep your windows clean to maximize visibility.

## Objectives

After reading the *Auto Upkeep* text and completing the following activities, you will be able to:
- Identify different automotive finishes.
- Explain the importance of washing, drying, and waxing a vehicle.
- Explain the importance of cleaning the inside of a vehicle.
- Correctly clean a vehicle inside and out.

## Summary

Keeping a vehicle clean is not difficult; it just takes a little time. Washing, waxing, and vacuuming will make your vehicle worth more and make it more appealing to drive and own. Finishes on vehicles have changed over time from basecoats to basecoat/clearcoats. Clearcoats add a deeper shine and a more durable finish. By spending a little extra time on paint repair and forgotten part lubrication you can keep your vehicle looking good and functioning properly. Most importantly control the environmental impact by selecting biodegradable cleaners and learning local laws regarding washing vehicles at home.

## Web Exploring

### Key Terms/Internet Search Words

Visit **www.google.com** to investigate any of the following terms or phrases. Summarize your findings in a research paper.
- Armor All
- Automotive Detailing
- Biodegradable Car Wash Soap
- Car Cleaning
- Car Wash Soaps
- Carnauba
- Chamois
- Dupont Corporation
- Eco-friendly Car Washing
- How to Wash a Car
- How to Wax a Car
- Microfiber Towels
- Mothers Polishes
- Nu Finish
- Paintless Dent Repair
- Simoniz Wax
- STP Cleaners
- Synthetic Automobile Waxes
- Turtle Wax

## 📚 Study Questions - Auto Care and Cleaning

1.  What are two types of automotive paint finishes? What is the difference?

    _____

    _____

2.  What types of weather, climatic, or road conditions affect vehicle finishes?

    _____

    _____

3.  What is a chamois?

    _____

    _____

4.  Why shouldn't you use dish detergent when washing your vehicle?

    _____

    _____

5.  What is carnauba?

    _____

    _____

6.  What is the purpose of waxing a vehicle?

    _____

    _____

7.  Why is it important to vacuum the inside of a vehicle?

    _____

    _____

8.  Why should you wash a vehicle before waxing it?

    _____

    _____

9.  Why should you dry a vehicle after washing?

    _____

    _____

10. How often should you wax a vehicle?

    _____

    _____

**Name** _____     **Class** _____     **Date** / /     **Score** _____

# Interior Cleaning Activity

## Objective

Upon completion of this activity, you will be able to clean the inside of a vehicle.

## NATEF Connections

**Preparing Vehicle for Customer**
- Ensure vehicle is prepared to return to customer per school/company policy (floor mats, steering wheel cover, etc.).

## Tools

Vacuum, bucket

## Supplies

Detail towels, shop rags, car wash soap (environmentally safe), cotton swabs, auto glass cleaner, vinyl cleaner, fabric cleaner, lint-free cloths, multipurpose cleaner, water

## Cautions

Read all product labels. Follow all procedures and safety guidelines specified by your instructor.

## Directions

Check off the boxes ❑ when completed. When you see a hand ✍ next to the task, write the information in the activity journal. If you have any questions during the duration of this activity, stop and ask the instructor for assistance.

## Procedure 1 - Interior Cleaning

❑ Pull out all floor mats. Shake out, wipe clean, or vacuum as necessary.

❑ Clean all garbage out of the vehicle and put in the trash can. Recycle aluminum cans, plastic, and paper. Remember to clean out the door pockets and storage areas.

❑ Thoroughly vacuum the headliner, seats, back window area, door panels, floor mats, trunk, sun visors, and carpet.

❑ Dampen a towel with soap and water and wipe down the doorjambs and the seal around the trunk area.

❑ Spray a vinyl cleaner on a detail towel to clean and protect vinyl and rubber components (e.g., the dash, door panels, and weather-stripping around the doors and trunk). Do not use cleaner on the gas pedal, brake pedal, clutch pedal, or steering wheel. Using cleaners on these components may cause a hazardous driving condition for the operator of the vehicle.

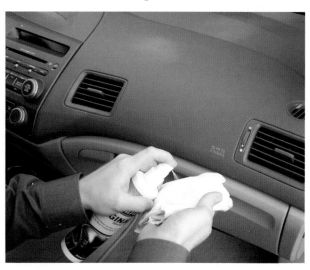

❏ Use cotton swabs to clean tight areas like the heater vents and radio controls.

❏ Use the appropriate fabric cleaner to get stains out of the seats, carpet, and trunk. Always read the directions on the product label. Use detail towels to scrub and dry the fabric. Test in an inconspicuous area.

❏ Spray glass cleaner on windows and wipe off with lint free cloths. Clean all mirrors and both sides of the windows.

❏ Put the clean floor mats back in the vehicle.
❏ Open the hood. Wet a shop rag with a multi-purpose cleaner and wipe grime, dirt, and dust from the engine compartment. Close the hood.

## Clean Up

❏ Dump the debris out of the shop vacuum into a trash can.
❏ Clean and put away all tools and supplies.
❏ Wash your hands thoroughly.

## Procedure 2 - Customer Care

❏ Listen to your instructor's demonstration on the expectations of maintaining a clean customer vehicle when completing repairs or servicing. Locate shop supplies (floor mats, steering wheel cover, etc.) to ensure customer vehicles are returned according to the shop's policy.

## ✍ Activity Journal

1. What are some tools and supplies needed to properly clean the inside of a vehicle?

_____

2. Why is it important to read and understand all product labels?

_____

3. Why do you think it is important to test cleaners in inconspicuous areas?

_____

4. What product can be used to clean and condition weather-stripping?

_____

5. How did cotton swabs help you in cleaning your vehicle?

_____

**Name** _____    **Class** _____    **Date** __/__/__    **Score** _____

# Exterior Cleaning Activity

## Objective

Upon completion of this activity, you will be able to clean the outside of a vehicle.

## NATEF Connections

None

## Tools

Hose with spray nozzle, bucket, chamois or microfiber towel, wash mitt, tire scrub brush

## Supplies

Car wash soap (environmentally safe), whitewall/ blackwall cleaner, shop rags, water

## Cautions

Read all product labels. Follow all procedures and safety guidelines specified by your instructor.

## Directions

Check off the boxes ❑ when completed. When you see a hand ✍ next to the task, write the information in the activity journal. If you have any questions during the duration of this activity, stop and ask the instructor for assistance.

## Procedure

❑ If the vehicle has been in the sun, let it cool. Never wash a hot vehicle.

❑ Rinse out the wash bucket. Put about 1/4 cup of car wash soap into the bucket and fill with warm water. Read the product label for the recommended water to soap ratio.

❑ Rinse off the wash mitt to avoid scratching the finish.

❑ Rinse the vehicle thoroughly from top to bottom with a hose. Spray off the wheels and wheel wells. Get off as much loose dirt as possible before scrubbing.

❑ Wash the vehicle one section at a time, scrubbing with a wash mitt. Work your way from the top down.

❑ Periodically rinse off the section that you just washed. The key is to make sure the car wash soap doesn't begin to dry while you are still washing.

❑ Spray whitewall/blackwall cleaner on the tires and scrub with the tire brush. Use a shop rag to scrub the wheels/rims with soapy water. Always read the labels on the products that you use.

❑ Rinse the tires, wheels, and wheel wells thoroughly.

❑ Rinse the wash mitt, tire scrub brush, and shop rag thoroughly.

❑ Give the whole vehicle a final rinse to avoid water spots.

❑ Use a chamois or detail (e.g., microfiber) towel to dry the vehicle. When using a chamois, wet it first to make it soft. Make sure the chamois is clean to prevent scratches.

❑ When using a chamois, drag it across the finish to pull water off. Then squeeze the excess water out until the chamois is just damp.

❑ Use a damp shop rag to clean the inside of the doorjambs.

❑ Pop open the hood and trunk and dry the surrounding lip with a shop rag.

## Clean Up

❑ Clean and put away all tools and supplies.

❑ Wash your hands thoroughly.

## ✎ Activity Journal

1. Why do you think you should rinse the vehicle thoroughly before scrubbing?

_____

2. What water to soap ratio was recommended?

_____

3. Why should you wash one section of the vehicle at a time?

_____

4. Why should you wet the chamois before using it?

_____

Name _____ Class _____ Date ___/___/___ Score _____

# Waxing Activity

## Objective

Upon completion of this activity, you will be able to wax the finish on a vehicle.

## NATEF Connections

None

## Tools

None

## Supplies

Detail towels, wax applicator or cloth, automotive wax, bug and tar remover, auto glass cleaner, lint-free cloths

## Cautions

Read all product labels. Do not wax a vehicle's finish when hot, in the direct sun, or dirty. Follow all procedures and safety guidelines specified by your instructor.

## Directions

Check off the boxes ❑ when completed. When you see a hand ✍ next to the task, write the information in the activity journal. If you have any questions during the duration of this activity, stop and ask the instructor for assistance.

## Procedure

❑ Wash and dry the vehicle according to the *Exterior Cleaning Activity*.

❑ Use bug and tar remover to clean any stubborn spots. Read the product's label before use.

❑ Wipe off any remaining bug and tar remover from the area with a soft and clean detail towel, then wash, rinse, and dry the area.

❑ Read the back of the wax bottle/can. Follow directions supplied by the product manufacturer.

❑ Do not wax a hot vehicle or one that is in direct sunlight.

❑ Dampen the wax applicator or cloth. This will help in applying a thin consistent layer. Apply the wax to the applicator or cloth and then to the finish. Some products suggest using linear motions while others suggest large circular motions. Read and follow the directions on the wax container.

❑ Wax one area at a time. Do not get wax on trim, molding, logo badges, or black plastic parts. It can be extremely difficult to remove wax from these pieces.

❑ The wax will dry to a haze. The drying time depends on the temperature and humidity in the air.

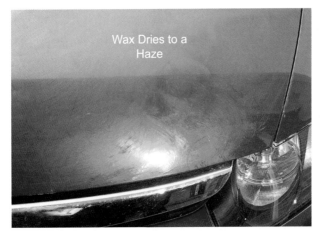
Wax Dries to a Haze

❑ Wipe off the dry section with a clean detail towel. You should let one section dry at a time, while applying wax to the next section.

❑ Continue waxing and drying until the vehicle is complete.

❑ Wipe down the whole vehicle to ensure that you have not left any wax haze on the finish.

❑ Spray auto glass cleaner on windows and wipe off with lint-free cloths. Clean all mirrors and both sides of the windows. If your vehicle has a rear window defroster, use linear motions in the direction of the heating wires.

## Clean Up
❑ Clean and put away all tools and supplies.
❑ Wash your hands thoroughly.

## ✎ Activity Journal

1.  Why should you use bug and tar remover before you wax?

_____

2.  Why should you dampen the wax applicator or cloth before use?

_____

3.  Why did you wax one area at a time?

_____

4.  Why should you wipe down the whole vehicle in the end?

_____

5.  What type of motion (linear or circular) did the product label indicate to use?

_____

# FLUID LEVEL CHECK

## Think Safety

Do not leave antifreeze in an open container or spilled on the floor where it might be accessible to children or animals. Antifreeze is toxic and can be fatal if ingested.

## Objectives

After reading the *Auto Upkeep* text and completing the following activities, you will be able to:
- Identify different types of fluids used in the automobile.
- Analyze fluid conditions.
- Perform basic fluid level checks.

## Summary

Fluids in the automobile have critical functions. Fluids that are neglected and run low for long periods of time add stress to components and can cause premature damage. Practice preventative maintenance by checking fluid levels frequently. Always refer to the owner's manual to identify the correct type of fluid for your specific vehicle. Using incorrect fluids can harm vital systems and could cause a hazardous situation while driving. Most of the fluids used in automobiles are toxic. Antifreeze has a sweet taste to animals and can be fatal if ingested. Dispose of all fluids properly. Always wash your hands thoroughly after checking and adding fluids.

## Web Exploring

### Key Terms/Internet Search Words

Visit **www.google.com** to investigate any of the following terms or phrases. Summarize your findings in a research paper.
- American Petroleum Institute
- Automatic Transmission Fluid
- Battery Electrolyte
- Coolant Color
- Coolant Confusion
- Dex-Cool
- Ethylene Glycol
- Extended Life Coolants
- Exxon-Mobil
- How to Check Motor Oil
- No Oil Dipstick
- No Transmission Dipstick
- Phillips Petroleum
- Power Steering Fluid
- Prestone
- Propylene Glycol
- Society of Automotive Engineers
- STP
- Synthetic Oil

Name _____    Class _____    Date __/__/__    Score _____

## 📖 Study Questions - Fluid Level Check

1.  What functions do various fluids provide to vehicle components?

    _____

    _____

2.  What is the process to check engine oil?

    _____

    _____

3.  What is the color of clean oil? What is the color of dirty oil?

    _____

    _____

4.  What is the process to check automatic transmission fluid?

    _____

    _____

5.  What is the color of clean automatic transmission fluid?

    _____

    _____

6.  What is the process to check antifreeze (coolant) level?

    _____

    _____

7.  What are the two common types of antifreeze? What is the difference between them?

    _____

    _____

8.  What is a common color for windshield washer fluid?

    _____

    _____

9.  What are some safety precautions when handling brake fluid?

    _____

    _____

10. What is the process to check power steering fluid?

    _____

    _____

# Fluid Level Check Activity

## Objective

Upon completion of this activity, you will be able to safely check the fluid level in various vehicle components.

## NATEF Connections

**Engine Repair – General**

- Research applicable vehicle and service information, vehicle service history, service precautions, and technical service bulletins.
- Inspect engine assembly for fuel, oil, coolant, and other leaks; determine necessary action.

**Engine Repair – Lubrication and Cooling Systems**

- Check coolant condition and level.

**Electrical/Electronic Systems – Battery Service**

- Fill battery cells.

**Automatic Transmission and Transaxle – General**

- Research applicable vehicle and service information, fluid type, vehicle service history, service precautions, and technical service bulletins.
- Check fluid level in a transmission or a transaxle equipped with a dipstick.
- Check fluid level in a transmission or a transaxle not equipped with a dipstick.
- Check transmission fluid condition; check for leaks.

**Automatic Transmission and Transaxle – In-Vehicle Transmission/Transaxle**

- Inspect for leakage at external seals, gaskets, and bushings.

**Manual Drivetrain and Axles – General**

- Research applicable vehicle and service information, fluid type, vehicle service history, service precautions, and technical service bulletins.
- Check fluid condition; check for leaks.

**Manual Drivetrain and Axles – Clutch**

- Check and adjust clutch master cylinder fluid level.
- Check for system leaks.

**Manual Drivetrain and Axles – Differential Case Assembly**

- Check and adjust differential housing fluid level.

**Suspension and Steering – Related Suspension and Steering Service**

- Determine proper power steering fluid type; inspect fluid level and condition.
- Inspect for power steering fluid leakage; determine necessary action.

**Brakes – Hydraulic System**

- Select, handle, store, and fill brake fluids to proper level.

## Tools

Safety goggles, chemical resistant gloves, basic hand tools, fender cover

## Supplies

Shop rags, correct type and amount of fluids needed

## Cautions

Read the owner's manual to identify the correct type of fluids to be used. Never remove a hot radiator cap. Follow all procedures and safety guidelines specified by your instructor.

## Directions

Check off the boxes ❑ when completed. When you see a hand ✍ next to the task, write the information in the activity journal. If you have any questions during the duration of this activity, stop and ask the instructor for assistance. Reread the procedures in the text to correctly check and add fluids. Since variations can occur from one vehicle manufacturer to another and from one model to another, reread the owner's manual for specific procedures and type of fluids. The following are general procedures.

## Pre-Service

- ❏ Use the vehicle's maintenance records, the owner's manual, a service manual, and the Internet to research applicable vehicle and service information, fluid type, vehicle service history, service precautions, and technical service bulletins.
- ❏ Apply the parking brake.
- ❏ Remove the key from the ignition. *Warning: On a push button keyless ignition refer to the owner's manual for specific safety procedures to prevent an unintended engine startup.*
- ❏ Put on your safety glasses.
- ❏ Pop open the hood.
- ❏ Use a fender cover to protect the vehicle's finish.
- ❏ Inspect the engine compartment and underneath the vehicle for fluid leaks.

## Procedure 1 - Engine Oil

- ❏ Locate the engine oil dipstick and oil filler cap.

- ❏ Pull out the dipstick, inspect the oil condition, and wipe it off with a paper towel.

- ❏ Reinsert the dipstick completely, remove it again, and note the reading.

- ❏ Clean around the oil filler cap.
- ❏ If low, remove the oil filler cap and use a clean funnel to add the correct type of oil. Do not overfill. Allow the oil time to flow to the pan.
- ❏ Recheck the level and correct if needed.

## Procedure 2 - Transmission Fluid

- ❏ Locate the transmission dipstick (if automatic transmission). *Note: Some automatic transmissions do not have a dipstick and must be checked with a special tool and/or procedure.*

- ❏ With the engine idling (most vehicles), pull out the dipstick, inspect the fluid condition, and wipe it off with a paper towel.
- ❏ Reinsert the dipstick completely, remove it again, and note the reading. Shut off the engine.

Keep ATF In This Range — Full Hot
Full Cold (Add 1 Pint if Transmission is Hot)

- ❏ If low use a clean funnel to add the correct fluid directly into the dipstick tube or hole. Do not overfill.
- ❏ Recheck the level and correct if needed.

## Procedure 3 - Power Steering Fluid

- ❏ Locate the power steering fluid cap and dipstick unit. Some power steering reservoirs are translucent with "MIN" and "MAX" lines.

- ❏ Clean around the power steering fluid cap.
- ❏ Remove the dipstick, inspect the fluid condition, and wipe it off with a paper towel.
- ❏ Reinstall the dipstick, remove it again, and note the reading.

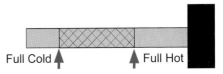

Full Cold    Full Hot

- ❏ If low, add the correct type of power steering fluid to the reservoir. Do not overfill.

## Procedure 4 - Brake Fluid

- ❑ Locate the brake fluid reservoir.
- ❑ Clean around the cap and reservoir.
- ❑ Check the brake fluid level through the translucent reservoir with "MIN" and "MAX" lines.

- ❑ If low, remove the cap and add the correct type of fluid. Do not overfill.
- ❑ When reinstalling the cap, make sure that the rubber gasket seats properly.

## Procedure 5 - Clutch Fluid

- ❑ Locate the clutch fluid reservoir (manual transmissions only). It is usually next to the brake master cylinder.
- ❑ Clean around the cap and reservoir.

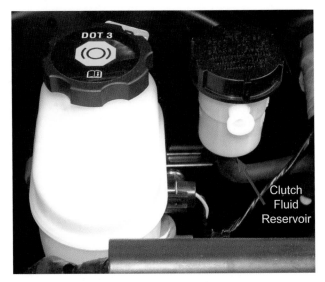

- ❑ Check the clutch fluid level. It should be at or near the top.
- ❑ If low, remove the cap and add the correct type of fluid. Do not overfill.

## Procedure 6 - Differential Fluid

- ❑ Locate the differential fluid check plug on the rear and/or front axle housings (where applicable on RWD and 4WD vehicles).
- ❑ Clean around and then remove the check plug.

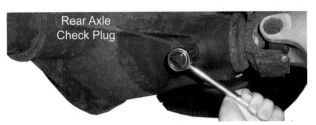

- ❑ If low, add the correct type of fluid. On most vehicles the level should be at the bottom of the plug hole, but check the owner's manual.

## Procedure 7 - Coolant

- ❑ Locate the overflow reservoir and radiator.

- ❑ Clean around the overflow reservoir and caps.
- ❑ When the engine is cool, check the coolant level in the reservoir.
- ❑ If low, remove the reservoir cap and add the correct type and mixture of coolant. Do not overfill.
- ❑ Remove the radiator cap and check the coolant level. *Warning: Never remove a hot radiator cap - severe burns could result.*

- ❑ If low, add the correct type and mixture of coolant.

## Procedure 8 - Battery Electrolyte

❑ Refer to the owner's manual or read the top of the battery to determine if it is a sealed battery. Some battery caps are not removable.

❑ Take off your rings and watch.

❑ Put on chemical resistant gloves and safety goggles.

❑ Wipe off the top of the battery with a shop rag.

❑ Check the battery electrolyte level if applicable.

❑ Remove the battery caps.

❑ Shine a flashlight into the cells and inspect the level in each cell. Commonly a split ring indicator in each cell identifies the correct electrolyte level.

❑ If any cells are low, add only distilled water to make all cells the proper level. Be sure the electrolyte covers the plates. Do not overfill.

❑ Replace the caps.

❑ *Warning: Batteries contain sulfuric acid. Wash your hands thoroughly to remove any battery acid after removing gloves.*

## Procedure 9 - Windshield Washer Fluid

❑ Check the windshield washer fluid level.

❑ To add windshield washer fluid, remove the cap and fill until the fluid almost reaches the top.

## Clean Up

❑ Clean and put away all tools and supplies.

❑ Wash your hands thoroughly.

## ✍ Activity Journal

1. What type and viscosity of oil does the owner's manual recommend to use?

_____

2. What type of transmission fluid is recommended to use in your vehicle?

_____

3. What type of power steering fluid does the owner's manual recommend to use?

_____

4. What type of brake fluid is recommended for your vehicle?

_____

5. What type and mixture of coolant is recommended for your vehicle?

_____

# ELECTRICAL SYSTEM

## Think Safety

It is dangerous to recharge or jump-start a battery that has a low electrolyte level or is frozen, damaged, or cracked.

## Objectives

After reading the *Auto Upkeep* text and completing the following activities, you will be able to:

- Define electricity in terms of voltage, current, and resistance.
- Identify and describe the components in the starting and charging system.
- Explain battery performance ratings.
- Identify the importance of fuses in the electrical system.
- Test the starter and alternator.
- Clean and test a battery safely.

## Summary

The electrical system may seem quite complex to the do-it-yourselfer, but there are simple ways to maintain it and save money. Start by keeping your 12-volt DC battery maintained. The starting system converts chemical energy to electrical energy to mechanical energy in order to start the engine. The charging system converts mechanical energy to electrical energy to chemical energy to recharge the battery. Fuses are overcurrent protection devices. Lights are used in many places on the automobile and periodically need replacing. In addition to a 12-volt DC battery

system that powers the computer systems and accessories, electric and hybrid vehicles have a high voltage electrical system that runs electric motors for propulsion. The electrical system activities will assist you in testing and replacing automotive electrical system components. Keep in mind that integrated computer technology can help you keep your vehicle running smoothly and help diagnose problems with trouble codes.

## Web Exploring

### Key Terms/Internet Search Words
Visit **www.google.com** to investigate any of the following terms or phrases. Summarize your findings in a research paper.

- Cold-Cranking and Cranking Amps
- Composite Light Bulbs
- How to Test a Car Battery
- How to Test a Starter
- How to Test an Alternator
- Jump-Starting a Vehicle
- Replacing a Headlamp
- Replacing Automotive Fuses
- Serpentine Belts and V-Belts

Name _____ Class _____ Date ___ / ___ / ___ Score _____

## 📚 Study Questions - Electrical System

1. What is electricity?

   _____

   _____

2. What is electrical voltage?

   _____

   _____

3. What is electrical current and how is it different from voltage?

   _____

   _____

4. What is the purpose of the battery?

   _____

   _____

5. What does a starter do?

   _____

   _____

6. How does an automotive battery get recharged?

   _____

   _____

7. What is an ohm? What is the relationship between voltage, current, and resistance?

   _____

   _____

8. How is the cold-cranking rating different from a cranking-rating?

   _____

   _____

9. Why should you not bypass a fuse?

   _____

   _____

10. What could cause a fuse to blow?

   _____

   _____

# Battery Activity

## Objective

Upon completion of this activity, you will be able to safely clean and test the battery.

## NATEF Connections

**Electrical/Electronic Systems – General**

- Research applicable vehicle and service information, vehicle service history, service precautions, and technical service bulletins.
- Demonstrate proper use of a digital multimeter (DMM) when measuring source voltage, voltage drop (including grounds), current flow, and resistance.

**Electrical/Electronic Systems – Battery Service**

- Perform battery state-of-charge test; determine necessary action.
- Confirm proper battery capacity for vehicle application; perform battery capacity test; determine necessary action.
- Maintain or restore electronic memory functions.
- Inspect and clean battery; fill battery cells; check battery cables, connectors, clamps, and holddowns.
- Identify high-voltage circuits of electric or hybrid electric vehicle and related safety precautions.
- Identify electronic modules, security systems, radios, and other accessories that require reinitialization or code entry after reconnecting vehicle battery.

**Shop and Personal Safety**

- Demonstrate awareness of the safety aspects of high voltage circuits.

## Tools

Safety goggles, chemical resistant gloves, basic hand tools, VOM (volt-ohm meter/multimeter), battery load tester, battery hydrometer, wire brush, battery terminal cleaner, battery post spreader (top mount batteries only), battery terminal puller (top mount batteries only), parts cleaning brush, mixing cup, fender cover

## Supplies

Shop rags, baking soda, distilled water, anti-corrosion spray

## Cautions

Wear safety goggles and chemical resistant gloves while performing this activity. Know where the eyewash station is and how to use it. Battery electrolyte will eat through clothing. Do not touch the battery against your shirt or pants. Electrolyte will irritate your skin. If you do get electrolyte on your skin, clean promptly with soap and water. Do not allow flames or sparks near battery gases. Battery gases can explode. Follow all procedures and safety guidelines specified by your instructor.

## Directions

Check off the boxes ❑ when completed. When you see a hand ✍ next to the task, write the information in the activity journal. If you have any questions during the duration of this activity, stop and ask the instructor for assistance.

## Pre-Service

❑ Use the vehicle's maintenance records, the owner's manual, a service manual, and the Internet to research applicable vehicle and service information, vehicle service history, service precautions, and technical service bulletins.

❑ Apply the parking brake.

❑ Remove the ignition key. *Warning: Push button keyless ignitions may have specific safety procedures to follow before working on electrical components. Check the owner's manual.*

- ❑ Remove rings and watch.
- ❑ Put on chemical resistant gloves.
- ❑ Put on your safety goggles.
- ❑ Pop open the hood.
- ❑ Use a fender cover to protect the vehicle's finish.

## Procedure

- ❑ Identify if the vehicle being serviced has a high voltage system, such as those on hybrid and electric vehicles. *Warning: Be extra careful around high voltage systems. High voltage lines are orange. Check for any warning labels.*
- ❑ Locate the battery rating label and compare the cold cranking amps and cranking amps with the minimum requirements listed in the owner's or service manual. *Note: Make sure the battery meets these minimum requirements.*
- ❑ Complete a visual inspection of the battery. Check for loose battery cables, corroded terminals, deposits on connections, cracks or leaks in the case, and frayed or broken cables.
- ❑ Remove the negative (-) battery cable. Use a puller, if needed, on top mount connections.

- ❑ Remove the positive (+) battery cable. Be careful not to touch the wrench against the body of the vehicle or engine components. A spark could occur causing the battery to explode. Use a puller, if needed, on top mount connections.

- ❑ Remove the battery hold-down bracket. Use penetrating oil if rusted.

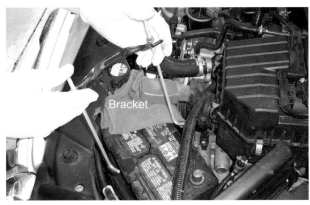

- ❑ Remove the battery from the vehicle and set in a utility sink. Do not turn the battery upside-down or on its side.
- ❑ Use a battery post cleaner tool to remove corrosion from the posts.

- ❑ Make a water/baking soda solution - 1/8 cup of baking soda to 1 cup of warm water.

- ❑ Dip the part's brush in the solution and scrub the battery. Do not allow the solution to enter the battery.
- ❑ Rinse the battery thoroughly with clean water.
- ❑ Dry with a shop rag.

✎ Set a VOM to Volts DC. Connect the VOM. Positive (+) first, then the Negative (-). Note the voltage reading.

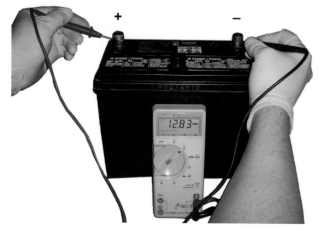

❏ Remove VOM. Negative (-) first, then Positive (+).

❏ Connect a battery load tester to evaluate the battery's capacity. Positive (+) first, then Negative (-).

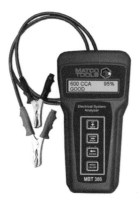

✎ Follow the instructions on the battery tester to complete the capacity test. Note the reading.

❏ Remove the battery tester. Negative (-) first, then Positive (+).

❏ If the battery has removable vent caps, remove them at this time. Ask the instructor or refer to the owner's manual if unsure.

❏ To test the specific gravity in each cell, you will use a battery hydrometer. Squeeze and release the bulb so the electrolyte (water and acid mixture) enters the battery hydrometer. Complete this procedure for each cell (there should be six cells).

✎ Note the readings of each cell. A fully charged battery will have a specific gravity rating between 1.254-1.280.

❏ Check the electrolyte level. The fluid in each cell should be even with the bottom of the filler ring. If the fluid is low, add only distilled water.

❏ Replace the vent caps.

❏ Clean the battery cable ends with a wire brush or battery terminal cleaner tool.

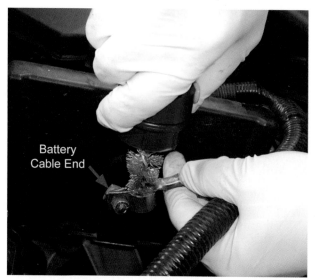

Battery Cable End

❏ Before putting the battery back in the vehicle, clean the battery mount area. Use an all purpose cleaner or a baking soda and water solution, then rinse with clean water.

Battery Mount Area

❑ Carefully put the battery back into the vehicle.
❑ Install the battery hold-down bracket. Lubricate bracket threads with penetrating oil. Make sure battery is secure.

❑ Connect the positive (+) battery cable.
❑ Connect the negative (-) battery cable.
❑ Coat terminals with anti-corrosion spray. Be careful not to spray the vehicle's finish.

❑ Use the owner's manual to identify electronic modules, security systems, radios, and other accessories that require reinitialization or code entry after reconnecting vehicle battery.

## Clean Up

❑ Clean and put away all tools and supplies.
❑ Wash your hands thoroughly.

## ✍ Activity Journal

1. What is the volt reading on the battery?

_____

2. What information did the battery capacity test reveal?

_____

3. Indicate the specific gravity reading for each cell in the boxes below.

|  |  |  |  |  |  |
|--|--|--|--|--|--|
|  |  |  |  |  |  |

4. What is the typical surface voltage of a fully charged battery?

_____

5. Why is it important to avoid getting baking soda inside the battery? Why do you think a baking soda solution works to clean a battery?

_____

6. What is the typical specific gravity reading of a fully charged battery?

_____

7. How many volts does each cell produce in an automotive battery?

_____

8. Why is it important not to create a spark when connecting and disconnecting a battery?

_____

# Charging Activity

## Objective

Upon completion of this activity, you will be able to safely test the alternator and replace a drive belt.

## NATEF Connections

**Engine – Lubrication and Cooling Systems**
- Inspect, replace, and adjust drive belts, tensioners, and pulleys; check pulley and belt alignment.

**Electrical/Electronic Systems – General**
- Research applicable vehicle and service information, vehicle service history, service precautions, and technical service bulletins.
- Demonstrate proper use of a digital multimeter (DMM) when measuring source voltage, voltage drop (including grounds), current flow, and resistance.

**Electrical/Electronic Systems – Charging System**
- Perform charging system output test; determine necessary action.
- Inspect, adjust, or replace generator (alternator) drive belts; check pulleys and tensioners for wear; check pulley and belt alignment.
- Perform charging circuit voltage drop tests; determine necessary action.

## Tools

Safety glasses, basic hand tools, VOM (volt-ohm meter/multimeter), current clamp, fender cover

## Supplies

Shop rags

## Cautions

Keep your hands away from moving components. Follow all procedures and safety guidelines specified by your instructor.

## Directions

Check off the boxes ❑ when completed. When you see a hand ☚ next to the task, write the information in the activity journal. If you have any questions during the duration of this activity, stop and ask the instructor for assistance.

## Pre-Service

❑ Use the vehicle's maintenance records, the owner's manual, a service manual, and the Internet to research applicable vehicle and service information, vehicle service history, service precautions, and technical service bulletins.

❑ Connect the vehicle's exhaust to the shop exhaust evacuation system or park outside.

❑ Apply the parking brake.

❑ Remove the key from the ignition. *Warning: On a push button keyless ignition refer to the owner's manual for specific safety procedures to prevent an unintended engine startup.*

❑ Put on your safety glasses.

❑ Pop open the hood.

❑ Use a fender cover to protect the vehicle's finish.

## Procedure 1 - Alternator Test

❑ Identify the battery, alternator, voltage regulator (may be inside the alternator or controlled by the PCM), and alternator drive belt.

✍ Set the VOM to Volts DC. Place the red lead on the positive battery post and the black lead on the negative battery post. With the vehicle not running, note the battery voltage. (Typical is between 12.5 to 12.8 volts.)

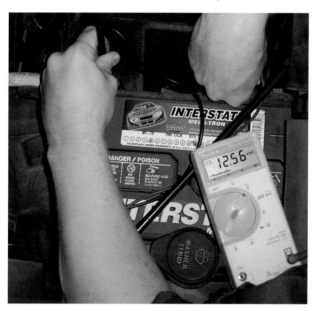

✍ While the VOM is still connected, start the engine. Keep away from moving parts. After the engine is running, note the volts. (Typical is between 13.8 to 14.8).

✍ While the engine is running, turn on the headlights. Note what happens to the volt reading.

✍ While the engine is running (and the headlights still on), turn on the blower (heater) to HI. Note what happens to the volt reading.

❑ Turn off the engine and disconnect the VOM.

❑ Use a current clamp with an induction lead to record alternator amperage output. Put the induction lead over the main positive alternator wire (usually the largest diameter). Follow the directions that come with the induction lead.

✍ Start the engine. While the engine is running, note the amps.

✍ With the engine running, turn on the headlights. Note what happens to the amps reading.

✍ While the engine is running (and the headlights still on), turn on the blower (heater) to HI. Note what happens to the amps reading.

❑ Turn off the engine.

❑ Remove the ignition key.

## Procedure 2 - Belt Replacement

✍ Inspect your vehicle to identify whether your alternator uses a Serpentine or V-belt. Note the type.

Serpentine Belt

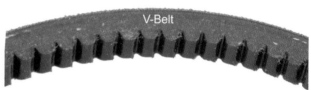

V-Belt

✍ Check the belt for wear (oil soaked, cracked, frayed, pieces missing, or glazed). Neoprene belts crack and lose rib pieces when worn. EPDM wears similar to a tire, losing rubber, but not necessarily cracking. An EPDM belt that isn't cracked or visibly damaged, could still be worn out and need replacing. To inspect EPDM belts, use a belt wear gauge. Follow the instructions that come with the gauge. The belt wear gauge gives an approximation of belt wear from material loss. You also need to consider the mileage, the condition of accessory drive belt components, and vehicle operating conditions. You can obtain a belt wear gauge from Gates Corporation by visiting www.gatesbeltwear.com. Note its condition. Replace if necessary.

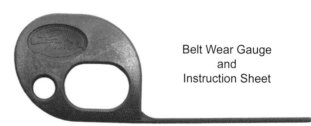

Belt Wear Gauge
and
Instruction Sheet

❏ Remove the negative battery cable.
❏ Review the belt routing diagram, which is commonly on an engine compartment label.
❏ If no diagram exists, sketch the belt routing on a piece of paper.

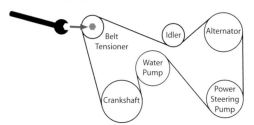

❏ Use a wrench or ratchet on the belt tensioner to release the belt tension.

Belt Tensioner          Wrench Releasing Belt Tension

❏ Slip the belt off.

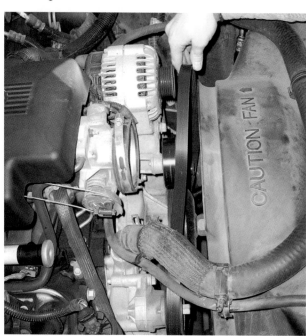

❏ Check the tensioner bearing and spring mechanism for wear.

❏ Make sure all of the accessory pulleys rotate freely.
❏ Route the new belt according to the belt routing diagram, lining up the ribs in the grooves.

❏ Use a wrench to relieve tension on the belt tensioner and position the belt.
❏ Carefully release the belt tensioner.
❏ Double check to make sure the belt is positioned correctly.

❏ Check the alternator drive belt tension. If loose, tighten it. *Note: Many automotive drive belts have automatic belt tensioners – refer to the owner's manual specific to the vehicle to see if the tensioner is adjustable.*

❏ Check the alternator terminals for burn marks or cracked connections.

Alternator Terminals

❏ Reconnect the negative battery cable.
❏ Check both battery cables for tightness on the battery mounts. Tighten if necessary. When using a wrench to tighten battery cables, make certain that the wrench does not touch any metal on the vehicle.
❏ Use the owner's manual to identify electronic modules, security systems, radios, and other accessories that require reinitialization or code entry after reconnecting vehicle battery.
❏ Disconnect shop exhaust evacuation system (if applicable).

## Clean Up
❏ Clean and put away all tools and supplies.
❏ Wash your hands thoroughly.

## ✎ Activity Journal

1. How many volts were present at the battery with the vehicle off?

_____

2. How many volts were present when the engine was running with no accessories on?

_____

3. What was the initial change to the voltage reading when the headlights were turned on?

_____

4. What was the initial change to the voltage reading when the blower motor was turned on?

_____

5. How many amperes were present when the engine was running with no accessories on?

_____

6. What change occurred when the headlights were turned on?

_____

7. What change occurred when the blower motor was turned on?

_____

8. What type of belt was used?

_____

9. What was the condition of the belt?

_____

Name _____ Class _____ Date __/__/__ Score _____

# Starting Activity

## Objective

Upon completion of this activity, you will be able to safely test the starter.

## NATEF Connections

**Electrical/Electronic Systems – General**
- Research applicable vehicle and service information, vehicle service history, service precautions, and technical service bulletins.
- Demonstrate proper use of a digital multimeter (DMM) when measuring source voltage, voltage drop (including grounds), current flow, and resistance.

**Electrical/Electronic Systems – Starting System**
- Perform starter current draw test; determine necessary action.
- Perform starter circuit voltage drop tests; determine necessary action.
- Inspect and test switches, connectors, and wires of starter control circuits; determine necessary action.

## Tools

Safety glasses, basic hand tools, VOM (volt-ohm meter/multimeter), current clamp, fender cover, wheel chocks, jack with jack stands, or drive-on ramps with jack stands, or an automotive lift

## Supplies

Shop rags

## Cautions

Keep your hands away from moving components. Follow all procedures and safety guidelines specified by your instructor.

## Directions

Check off the boxes ❑ when completed. When you see a hand ✍ next to the task, write the information in the activity journal. If you have any questions during the duration of this activity, stop and ask the instructor for assistance.

## Pre-Service

❑ Use the vehicle's maintenance records, the owner's manual, a service manual, and the Internet to research applicable vehicle and service information, vehicle service history, service precautions, and technical service bulletins.

❑ Connect the vehicle's exhaust to the shop exhaust evacuation system or park outside.

❑ Raise the end of the vehicle where the engine is located with a jack and support with jack stands (or use an automotive lift or drive-on ramps with jack stands).

❑ Chock the wheels on the opposite end of the vehicle.

❑ Apply the parking brake.

❑ Remove the key from the ignition. ***Warning: On a push button keyless ignition refer to the owner's manual for specific safety procedures to prevent an unintended engine startup.***

❑ Put on your safety glasses.

❑ Pop open the hood.

❑ Use a fender cover to protect the vehicle's finish.

## Procedure

❑ Identify the starter, solenoid, ignition switch, battery, positive battery cable, negative battery cable, and fuse panel.

❑ Inspect wires and connections. Look for corrosion, fraying, or missing insulation on wires.

❑ Lower vehicle after identification.

✍ Set the VOM to Volts DC. Connect the red lead to the positive post (+) and the black lead to the negative post (-) on the battery. At this time the vehicle should not be running. Note the battery voltage. (Typical is between 12.5 and 12.8 volts.)

❑ This step disables the vehicle's engine so it should not start. If you are in a school lab, obtain approval before proceeding. Disable the ignition system or fuel system by removing the coil wire (if distributor type ignition system), fuel injection wires (throttle body fuel injection only), inertia switch (Ford), fuel pump cutoff switch, or pull a fuse to disable the ignition system or fuel system. Do not guess. If unsure, refer to a service manual specific to your vehicle.

✍ Crank the engine over for 5 seconds and note the volts while the engine is turning over. Keep away from moving parts. The engine should not start. (Typically, the voltage may drop to 9.5 volts.) Always refer to a manual specific to the vehicle being testing for exact acceptable readings. If voltage drop exceeds acceptable readings, the starter may have too much resistance. Refer to a service manual to perform other voltage drop tests between cable leads.

❑ Use a current clamp with an induction lead to read the current draw on the starter. While the ignition or fuel is still disconnected, put the current clamp induction lead over the main positive starter wire (usually the largest diameter one going to the starter). Follow the instructions with the induction lead/VOM or a manual specific for the vehicle.

✍ Crank the engine over for 5 seconds and note the amperes. Keep away from moving parts. (Typically, the amps will read between 150 and 350, but always refer to a manual specific to the vehicle for exact acceptable readings.) Too much current draw may indicate a faulty starter.

❑ Reconnect the coil wire, fuel injection wires, or other method that was used to disable the fuel or ignition system.

❑ Check battery cable tightness on battery mounts. Tighten if necessary. When using a wrench to tighten battery cables, make certain that the wrench does not touch any metal on the vehicle.

❑ Disconnect shop exhaust evacuation system (if applicable).

## Clean Up

❑ Clean and put away all tools and supplies.
❑ Wash your hands thoroughly.

## ✍ Activity Journal

1. How many volts were present at the battery with the vehicle off?

_____

2. What did you do to disable the fuel or ignition system on the vehicle being tested?

_____

3. What did the battery voltage drop to when cranking over the engine?

_____

4. How many amperes were drawn to the starter while cranking?

_____

5. Were all your readings acceptable according to the manual specific to your vehicle?

_____

QR

# 10

# LUBRICATION SYSTEM

## Think Safety

Prolonged exposure to used oil has been shown to cause cancer in laboratory animals. Wear disposable gloves when changing oil so your skin will not be exposed to this hazard.

## Objectives

After reading the *Auto Upkeep* text and completing the following activities, you will be able to:
- Define the purpose of engine oil.
- Explain oil service and viscosity ratings.
- Discuss the advantages and disadvantages of synthetic oils.
- Discuss the importance of oil filters.
- Change the oil and filter on a vehicle.

## Summary

Engine oil lubricates, cools, cleans, and seals engine components. While engine oil is a vital component to the longevity of an engine and may seem extremely complex, it is not very difficult to service. When purchasing oil look for the SAE, API, and other ratings that meet the manufacturer's recommended requirements. Oil filters are used to remove contaminants from the engine oil and should be changed at oil change intervals. Synthetic oils are becoming more popular and accepted due to stringent engine tolerances. Always check the owner's manual for oil recommendations and change intervals.

## Web Exploring

### Key Terms/Internet Search Words
Visit www.google.com to investigate any of the following terms or phrases. Summarize your findings in a research paper.
- AC Delco Oil Filters
- American Petroleum Institute
- Castrol
- Champ Filters
- European Automotive Manufacturer's Association
- Exxon-Mobil
- Fram Oil Filters
- Hastings Oil Filters
- Havoline
- How to Change Oil on an Automobile
- International Lubrication Standardization Approval Committee
- Motorcraft Oil Filters
- Oil Recycling
- Oil Viscosity
- Society of Automotive Engineers
- Valvoline
- Wix Oil Filters

| Name | Class | Date _/ _/ | Score |
|------|-------|------------|-------|

## 📖 Study Questions - Lubrication System

1. What does oil do within an engine?

2. How does engine oil get dirty?

3. What does API stand for and what does it rate?

4. What does SAE stand for and what does it rate?

5. What is a common price for a quart of conventional oil?

6. Why is it not recommended to overfill the engine with oil?

7. What is one advantage and one disadvantage of synthetic oils?

8. How often should the oil and filter be changed?

9. What does an oil filter do?

10. Which oil is more viscous, 5W30 or 20W50?

| Name | | Class | Date | / / | Score | |
|------|--|-------|------|-----|-------|--|

# Oil and Filter Change Activity

## Objective

Upon completion of this activity, you will be able to safely change the oil and filter on a vehicle.

## NATEF Connections

**Engine Repair – General**
- Research applicable vehicle and service information, vehicle service history, service precautions, and technical service bulletins.

**Engine Repair – Lubrication and Cooling Systems**
- Perform engine oil and filter change.

## Tools

Safety glasses, basic hand tools, wrench for oil plug, oil filter wrench, oil drain pan, funnel, fender cover, wheel chocks, jack with jack stands, or drive-on ramps with jack stands, or an automotive lift

## Supplies

Shop rags, disposable gloves, correct type and amount of oil, oil filter

## Cautions

Hot oil can cause burns. Prolonged contact with used oil may cause skin cancer. Follow all procedures and safety guidelines specified by your instructor.

## Directions

Check off the boxes ❑ when completed. When you see a hand ✍ next to the task, write the information in the activity journal. If you have any questions during the duration of this activity, stop and ask the instructor for assistance.

## Pre-Service

❑ Use the vehicle's maintenance records, the owner's manual, a service manual, and the Internet to research applicable vehicle and service information, vehicle service history, service precautions, and technical service bulletins.

❑ Connect the vehicle's exhaust to the shop exhaust evacuation system or park outside.

❑ Warm the engine 5 to 10 minutes to loosen the contaminants and to thin the oil for draining.

❑ Raise the end of the vehicle where the engine is located with a jack and support with jack stands (or use an automotive lift or drive-on ramps with jack stands).

❑ Chock the wheels on the opposite end of the vehicle.

❑ Apply the parking brake.

❑ Remove the key from the ignition. *Warning: On a push button keyless ignition refer to the owner's manual for specific safety procedures to prevent an unintended engine startup.*

❑ Put on chemical resistant gloves.

❑ Put on your safety glasses.

❑ Pop open the hood.

❑ Use a fender cover to protect the vehicle's finish.

## Procedure

✍ Identify the oil viscosity and quantity needed for the vehicle.

❑ Locate and remove the oil filler cap. It is usually located on the valve cover. Removing the filler cap makes the oil flow easier once the drain plug is removed.

❑ Locate the drain plug on the vehicle's oil pan and position the oil drain pan to catch the oil.

❑ Use the correct size wrench to loosen the oil drain plug. Turn counter-clockwise.

❑ Keep a steady inward pressure on the plug to avoid the hot oil from running down your arm. Use a shop rag to protect your hand if the oil is extremely hot or allow it to cool some.

Drain Plug

❑ Make sure the oil will hit the oil drain pan.

❑ While the oil is draining, use an oil filter wrench to loosen the oil filter.

❑ Finish removing the oil filter by hand. Set the oil filter in the oil drain pan so the oil can drain out of it.

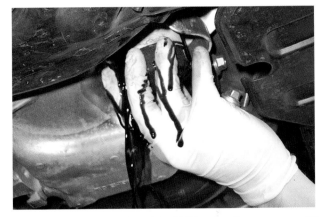

❑ Make certain the old oil filter gasket comes off with the old filter. If it is stuck on the oil filter mounting base, remove and discard it.

❑ Wipe off the oil filter mounting base and the area around the oil drain plug.

Oil Filter Mounting Base

❑ Put a thin film of clean oil on the new oil filter-mounting gasket. This oil helps to seal the gasket. A dry gasket may tear when the filter is installed causing leaks.

❑ Read the instructions on the filter. Install the oil filter by rotating it clockwise by hand. Once the gasket contacts the engine, tighten it according to the instructions - usually 1/2 to 1 full turn. A filter wrench may be necessary. *Note: Do not over-tighten.*

❑ Prior to reinstalling the drain plug, wipe off its threads and the sealing surface with a shop rag. Make certain that the plug's threads and gasket are in good condition before reinstalling. Replace if necessary.

Gasket

Threads

❑ Install the drain plug by hand and temporarily tighten finger tight. Do not cross-thread the plug. Tighten the plug with the correct size of wrench until it is snug. If unsure how tight to get the plug, refer to the owner's or service manual for torque specifications. *Note: Do not over-tighten. Over-tightening can cause thread damage, while under-tightening may result in oil leakage.*

❑ If you are in a school laboratory setting, have the instructor inspect the oil plug and filter.
❑ Lower the vehicle if you used a jack and jack stands method or an automotive lift.

❑ Using a funnel, pour the correct amount and type of oil into the filler opening. *Note: Make sure the API and SAE ratings meet what is required in the owner's manual.*

❑ Start the engine and check for leaks. Extra attention should be given to the oil filter gasket and drain plug gasket. The oil pressure warning light may stay on for up to 5 seconds. If the light stays on longer than 5 seconds, shut the engine off and check for leaks. After about a minute, shut off the engine. This amount of time is ample to circulate the oil throughout the engine and to fill the oil filter. If you used drive-on ramps, remove the safety jack stands and chocks, and then carefully back down the ramps.
❑ Let the engine sit for a couple of minutes to ensure a proper reading. Be sure the vehicle is on level ground.
❑ Check the oil level on the dipstick and correct if necessary. *Note: Some vehicles do not have an oil dipstick. They use an electronic oil level monitor. Check the owner's manual. Do not overfill.*

❑ Recycle your old oil and filter. Do not throw them away in the garbage. Take them to the proper recycling facilities.

❑ If you are in a school laboratory setting, have the instructor check the oil level before closing the hood.

❑ Disconnect shop exhaust evacuation system (if applicable).

## Clean Up
❑ Clean and put away all tools and supplies.
❑ Clean up any oil spills with floor dry.
❑ Wash your hands thoroughly.
❑ Fill out and place an oil change sticker in the vehicle.
❑ Update the vehicle's maintenance record log book.

## ✎ Activity Journal

1.  What oil viscosity rating is required for your vehicle's engine?

_____

2.  What is the oil capacity for your vehicle's engine?

_____

3.  What SAE rating did the owner's manual recommend?

_____

4.  What API rating did the owner's manual recommend?

_____

5.  Why should the engine be warm when changing the oil?

_____

6.  Why did you put a thin film of oil on the new oil filter gasket?

_____

7.  What is the oil change maintenance interval recommended by the vehicle manufacturer?

_____

8.  What was the condition of the old oil?

_____

9.  Name two locations that recycle used oil.

_____

# FUEL SYSTEM

## Think Safety

Fuel injection systems have high pressure fuel systems. Follow the manufacturer's procedure to safely relieve fuel pressure before changing the fuel filter.

## Objectives

After reading the *Auto Upkeep* text and completing the following activities, you will be able to:
- Explain the purpose of the fuel system.
- Describe the parts of the fuel system.
- Remove and replace an air filter.
- Remove and replace a fuel filter.
- State gasoline and diesel properties.
- Explain how fuel is priced.
- Identify ways to improve fuel economy.

## Summary

The purpose of the fuel system is to store, transfer, and then mix the fuel with air. Gasoline engines are spark ignition engines. Diesel engines are compression ignition engines. Various parts of the fuel system work together to supply clean fuel and air to the engine. Technological advancements like GDI and turbocharging are making it possible to build smaller engines that use less fuel and lower emissions, without compromising performance or torque. Fuel economy can also be increased through tune-ups, correct tire pressure, regular oil changes, and moderating your driving habits.

## Web Exploring

### Key Terms/Internet Search Words

Visit www.google.com to investigate any of the following terms or phrases. Summarize your findings in a research paper.
- Alternative Fueled Vehicles
- British Petroleum
- Cetane Ratings
- Cheap Fuel
- Cylinder Deactivation
- Fram Air Filters
- Fuel System Additives
- Gasoline Direct Injection
- Hastings Air Filters
- How to Change a Fuel Filter
- Increasing Fuel Economy
- Octane Ratings
- Positive Crankcase Ventilation
- Shell Oil Company
- Turbocharging
- Ultra-Low Sulfur Diesel
- United States Department of Energy
- Unleaded Fuel
- Wix Air Filters

Name _____   Class _____   Date __ / __ / __   Score _____

## 📖 Study Questions - Fuel System

1.   What is the purpose of the fuel system?

_____

_____

2.   What does the fuel pump do and where might it be found on an automobile?

_____

_____

3.   What do the letters PCV represent?

_____

_____

4.   What do the letters CCV represent?

_____

_____

5.   How often should air filters be changed?

_____

_____

6.   What are common octane ratings of gasoline sold at the pump?

_____

_____

7.   What causes an engine to knock or ping?

_____

_____

8.   What are oxygenates?

_____

_____

9.   What is ultra-low sulfur diesel?

_____

_____

10. How can you improve the fuel economy of your automobile?

_____

_____

| Name | Class | Date / / | Score |
|---|---|---|---|

# Fuel System Activity

## Objective

Upon completion of this activity, you will be able to identify the components of the fuel system and change the air filter, CCV filter, PCV valve, and fuel filter on a vehicle.

## NATEF Connections

**Engine Performance – General**
- Research applicable vehicle and service information, vehicle service history, service precautions, and technical service bulletins.

**Engine Performance – Fuel, Air Induction, and Exhaust Systems**
- Replace fuel filter(s)
- Inspect, service, or replace air filters, filter housings, and intake duct work.

**Engine Performance – Emissions Control Systems**
- Inspect, test, and service positive crankcase ventilation (PCV) filter/breather cap, valve, tubes, orifices, and hoses; perform necessary action.

## Tools

Safety glasses, basic hand tools, vacuum, drain pan, fender cover, wheel chocks, jack with jack stands, or drive-on ramps with jack stands, or an automotive lift

## Supplies

Shop rags, replacement parts (e.g., air filter, CCV filter, PCV valve, fuel filter) specific to your vehicle

## Cautions

Have a fire extinguisher handy when working on the fuel system. Follow all procedures and safety guidelines specified by your instructor.

## Directions

Check off the boxes ❑ when completed. When you see a hand ✍ next to the task, write the information in the activity journal. If you have any questions during the duration of this activity, stop and ask the instructor for assistance. Due to the variations in locations of components, a manual specific to the vehicle would assist you in identifying component locations.

## Pre-Service

❑ Use the vehicle's maintenance records, the owner's manual, a service manual, and the Internet to research applicable vehicle and service information, vehicle service history, service precautions, and technical service bulletins.

❑ Apply the parking brake.

❑ Remove the key from the ignition. *Warning: On a push button keyless ignition refer to the owner's manual for specific safety procedures to prevent an unintended engine startup.*

❑ Put on your safety glasses.

❑ Pop open the hood.

❑ Use a fender cover to protect the vehicle's finish.

✍ Determine and note if the engine has gasoline direct injection (GDI), multi-port fuel injection (MFI), throttle body fuel injection (TBI), or a carburetor.

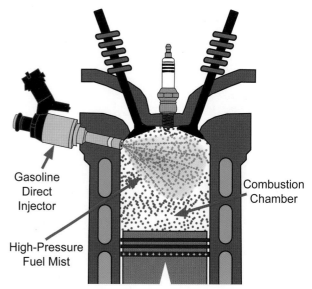

Gasoline Direct Injector

Combustion Chamber

High-Pressure Fuel Mist

✍ Look in the owner's manual and note the octane rating suggested for the vehicle.

✍ Refer to a service manual to identify and note the location of the fuel pump.

## Procedure 1 - Air Filter Change

✍ Identify and note the location of the air filter. On carbureted vehicles, the air filter housing usually sits on top of the engine directly over the carburetor. On fuel-injected vehicles, the air filter may be mounted on the engine or near the inner fender of the vehicle.

❑ Loosen the cover by removing the clips, screws, or wing nuts.

❑ Remove the cover.

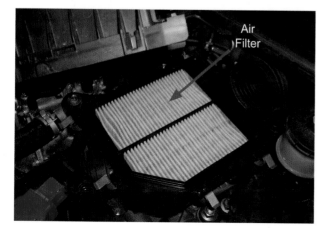

✍ Note how the air filter is positioned in the housing.

❑ Remove the old filter and compare to the replacement. It is not recommended to blow out the filter with air pressure. The air pressure can tear the filter element allowing dirt to enter the engine.

❑ Wipe out or vacuum the housing. Do not get dirt in the throttle body or air intake housing.

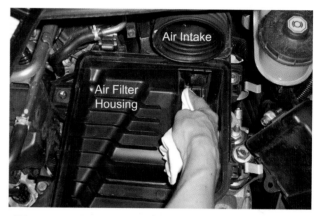

❑ Install the new air filter.

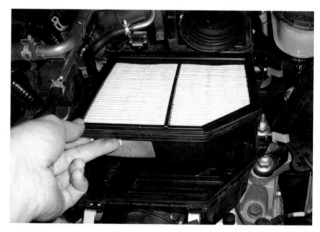

❑ Reinstall the air filter housing cover.

## Procedure 2 - CCV Filter Change

- ❑ Locate the air filter housing. On carbureted vehicles, the air filter housing usually sits on top of the engine directly over the carburetor. On fuel-injected vehicles, the air filter may be mounted on the engine or near the inner fender of the vehicle.
- ❑ Loosen the cover by removing the clips, screws, or wing nuts.
- ❑ Remove the cover.
- ❑ Identify the location of the CCV filter. It is commonly located inside the air filter housing. *Note: Not all vehicles have a CCV filter (also called PCV inlet filter).*
- ❑ Remove the hose that attaches to the CCV filter.
- ❑ Remove the retaining clip.
- ❑ Remove the CCV filter.
- ❑ Install the new CCV filter.

- ❑ Reinstall the air filter housing cover.

## Procedure 3 - PCV Valve Change

- ❑ Identify the location of the PCV valve. It is usually located at the end of a hose and pushed into the valve cover.
- ❑ Remove the old PCV valve. It is usually just a push in connection.

- ❑ Compare the old valve to the new one.

- ❑ Install a new PCV valve.

## Procedure 4 - Fuel Filter Change

- ❑ Connect the vehicle's exhaust to the shop exhaust evacuation system or park outside.
- ❑ Raise the end of the vehicle where the engine is located with a jack and support with jack stands (or use an automotive lift or drive-on ramps with jack stands).
- ❑ Chock the wheels on the opposite end of the vehicle.
- ❑ Apply the parking brake.
- ❑ Remove the key from the ignition. *Warning: On a push button keyless ignition refer to the owner's manual for specific safety procedures to prevent an unintended engine startup.*
- ❑ Put on chemical resistant gloves.
- ❑ Put on your safety goggles.
- ❑ Remove the fuel cap and clean the sealing surface. Replace the fuel cap after cleaning.
- ❑ Identify the location of the fuel tank.

- ❏ Identify the location of the fuel lines.
- ✎ Identify and note the location of the fuel filter. *Warning: The vehicle and exhaust should be cool when changing the fuel filter.*
- ❏ Place a drain pan under the fuel filter.
- ❏ Relieve the fuel pressure. *Warning: Fuel injection vehicles use high fuel pressure. Check a manual specific to your vehicle for the procedure.*
- ❏ Remove the fuel filter. Some fuel filters need special tools to remove clips. If the fuel filter is threaded, use two line wrenches to prevent damage to the fuel lines.

Fuel Filter

- ❏ Clean the connections and threads.
- ❏ Install the new filter with flow arrow in the direction of the engine.

Engine in this Direction

Flow Arrow

- ❏ Start the engine and check for leaks. It may take a couple of cranks to fill the lines and new filter.
- ❏ Disconnect shop exhaust evacuation system (if applicable).

## Clean Up
- ❏ Clean and put away all tools.
- ❏ Wash your hands thoroughly.

## ✎ Activity Journal

1. Does your engine have gasoline direct injectors, multi-port fuel injectors, throttle body fuel injectors, or a carburetor?

   _____

2. Where is your vehicle's air filter located?

   _____

3. Where is your vehicle's fuel filter located?

   _____

4. Where is the fuel pump located on your vehicle?

   _____

5. What is the octane rating suggested for your vehicle?

   _____

6. Why is it not recommended to blow out air filters with compressed air?

   _____

7. If fuel filters are threaded, why should you use two wrenches to loosen the connection?

   _____

# 12

# COOLING SYSTEM AND CLIMATE CONTROL

## Think Safety

Do not loosen or remove a radiator cap when the cooling system is hot. Coolant is under pressure and can actually be above water's boiling point (212°F/100°C).

## Objectives

After reading the *Auto Upkeep* text and completing the following activities, you will be able to:
- Identify the purpose of the cooling system.
- Describe the cooling system's components.
- Define coolant properties.
- Explain how coolant flows in an engine.
- Test and service the cooling system.
- Change a passenger cabin air filter.

## Summary

The cooling system is extremely important to the operation of the engine. It maintains efficient engine-operating temperature, removes excess heat, brings the engine up to operating temperature as quickly as possible, and provides warmth to the passenger compartment. Antifreeze prevents the coolant from freezing, increases the boiling temperature, lubricates components within the engine, and reduces the likelihood of corrosion. The heater core transfers heat from the engine to warm the passenger cabin. A cabin air filter cleans the air that blows through the cabin vent system. If your A/C doesn't work, take it to an ASE certified technician that has the proper equipment to find, repair, and recycle the refrigerant if necessary.

## Web Exploring

### Key Terms/Internet Search Words

Visit **www.google.com** to investigate any of the following terms or phrases. Summarize your findings in a research paper.
- Antifreeze/Water Mixture
- Coolant Colors
- Coolant Test Strips
- Dex-Cool Antifreeze
- Ethylene Glycol Antifreeze
- Extended Life Antifreeze
- Evaporator Drain Tube
- Gates Hoses and Belts
- Goodyear Hoses and Belts
- How Air Conditioning Works
- How to Change a Cabin Air Filter
- How to Change a Radiator Hose
- How to Change a Thermostat
- How to Change a Water Pump
- Peak Antifreeze
- Prestone Antifreeze
- Reconditioned Radiators
- Remanufactured Water Pumps
- Stant Radiator Caps
- Thermostats for Automobiles

## 📖 Study Questions - Cooling System and Climate Control

1. What does the cooling system do within an engine?

   _____

   _____

2. What is the purpose of the radiator?

   _____

   _____

3. What is the purpose of the thermostat?

   _____

   _____

4. Why do automobiles have coolant recovery tanks?

   _____

   _____

5. Why should you mix a 50/50 blend of water and antifreeze?

   _____

   _____

6. How do you get heat in your automobile when it is cold outside?

   _____

   _____

7. What is the purpose of a cabin air filter?

   _____

   _____

8. How are drive belts part of the cooling system?

   _____

   _____

9. How often should antifreeze be serviced?

   _____

   _____

10. What should you do if water is dripping on the interior floorboards when the A/C is on?

    _____

    _____

| Name | Class | Date / / | Score |
|---|---|---|---|

# Air Conditioning Activity

## Objective

Upon completion of this activity, you will be able to inspect and identify components within the air conditioning system.

## NATEF Connections

**Heating and Air Conditioning – General**
- Research applicable vehicle and service information, vehicle service history, service precautions, and technical service bulletins.
- Identify vehicle's A/C components.

**Heating and Air Conditioning – Refrigeration System Components**
- Inspect and replace A/C compressor drive belts, pulleys, and tensioners; determine necessary action.
- Inspect A/C condenser for airflow restrictions; determine necessary action.

**Heating and Air Conditioning – Operating Systems and Related Controls**
- Identify the source of A/C system odors.

## Tools

Safety glasses, garden hose, dull object for probe, fender cover

## Supplies

Water

## Cautions

Keep your hands away from moving components. Follow all procedures and safety guidelines specified by your instructor.

## Directions

Check off the boxes ❏ when completed. When you see a hand ✍ next to the task, write the information in the activity journal. If you have any questions during the duration of this activity, stop and ask the instructor for assistance.

## Pre-Service

❏ Use the vehicle's maintenance records, the owner's manual, a service manual, and the Internet to research applicable vehicle and service information, vehicle service history, service precautions, and technical service bulletins.
❏ Connect the vehicle's exhaust to the shop exhaust evacuation system or park outside.
❏ Apply the parking brake.
❏ Remove the key from the ignition. *Warning: On a push button keyless ignition refer to the owner's manual for specific safety procedures to prevent an unintended engine startup.*
❏ Put on your safety glasses.
❏ Pop open the hood.
❏ Use a fender cover to protect the vehicle's finish.

## Procedure

✍ Locate the refrigerant certification label in the engine compartment. Note refrigerant type.
❏ Identify and locate the accumulator/receiver-drier.

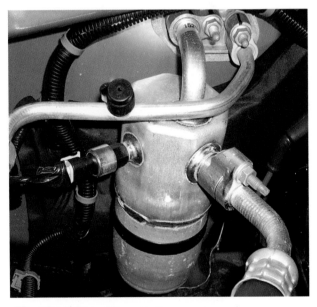

❏ Identify and locate the compressor.
❏ Identify and locate the condenser.
❏ Identify and locate the evaporator.
❏ Turn the A/C controls to high and start the engine. *Warning: Keep your hands away from moving components.*

❑ Inspect the front of the compressor. The clutch on the front of the pulley should be turning.

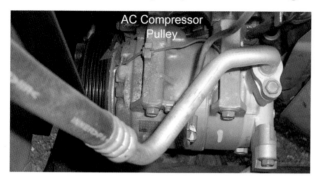

❑ Smell inside the vehicle as the A/C is blowing air. If the blower vents are releasing unpleasant odors, fungi/mold may be present in the ducts. This commonly indicates that the evaporative drain tube may be clogged.

❑ Shut off the engine.

❑ Remove the key from the ignition. *Warning: On a push button keyless ignition refer to the owner's manual for specific safety procedures to prevent an unintended engine startup.*

❑ Inspect the evaporator drain tube. This drain tube is located between the engine compartment and passenger compartment (this area is also known as the firewall). Water should be dripping from the tube to the underside of the vehicle. If water is dripping inside the vehicle, the evaporator drain tube may be clogged. The drain tube can be cleaned by probing a long dull object into it. *Note: Some drain tubes need to be removed to be cleaned.*

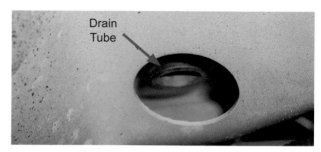

❑ To learn how to neutralize odor after cleaning the drain tube go to www.airsept.com. To stop the odor from returning you will need to use an anti-microbial product to kill any mold.

❑ Inspect the condenser and radiator fins. If debris is found, rinse free with a garden hose.

❑ Check the belt for wear. Follow the inspection techniques for Neoprene and EPDM belts as described in the Belt Replacement Procedure in Chapter 9 Charging System Activity. Replace if necessary.

❑ Inspect the drive belt tension. Tighten if necessary/applicable.

❑ Inspect the A/C hoses. Look for any signs of refrigerant oil leakage around fittings. If the fittings look wet, your system may be losing refrigerant. If it is, have it inspected by a qualified technician.

❑ Disconnect shop exhaust evacuation system (if applicable).

## Clean Up

❑ Clean and put away all tools.

❑ Wash your hands thoroughly.

## ✍ Activity Journal

1. What type of refrigerant is used in your vehicle?

_____

2. Why is it necessary to use an anti-microbial product when working to eliminate A/C odors?

_____

3. How would debris in the condenser fins impact the performance of the A/C system?

_____

4. What would wet areas around A/C hose fittings indicate?

_____

| Name | Class | Date / / | Score |
|------|-------|----------|-------|

## Cabin Air Filter Activity

### Objective

Upon completion of this activity, you will be able to replace the cabin air filter on a vehicle.

### NATEF Connections

**Heating and Air Conditioning – General**
- Research applicable vehicle and service information, vehicle service history, service precautions, and technical service bulletins.

**Heating and Air Conditioning – Operating Systems and Related Controls**
- Inspect A/C-heater ducts, doors, hoses, cabin filters, and outlets; perform necessary action.

### Tools

Safety glasses, vacuum, basic hand tools

### Supplies

Replacement cabin air filter(s) specific to your vehicle, shop rag, towel

### Cautions

Follow all procedures and safety guidelines specified by your instructor.

### Directions

Check off the boxes ❑ when completed. When you see a hand ✍ next to the task, write the information in the activity journal. If you have any questions during the duration of this activity, stop and ask the instructor for assistance.

### Pre-Service

❑ Use the vehicle's maintenance records, the owner's manual, a service manual, and the Internet to research applicable vehicle and service information, vehicle service history, service precautions, and technical service bulletins.
❑ Apply the parking brake.
❑ Remove the key from the ignition. *Warning: On a push button keyless ignition refer to the owner's manual for specific safety procedures to prevent an unintended engine startup.*

❑ Put on your safety glasses.
❑ Pop open the hood.

### Procedure

❑ Check the owner's manual or vehicle specific service manual to see if your vehicle has a cabin air filter.

❑ Cabin air filters are located in the HVAC duct. The filter may be accessible from under the hood or more commonly inside the passenger's compartment under the dash and behind the glove compartment. Some vehicles have more than one filter in the duct.

Glove Box

Cabin Air Filter Housing

✍ Locate and note the cabin air filter location using the owner's or service manual. If you cannot determine how to replace the filter, go to your local auto parts store and look at the replacement. Sometimes instructions are included inside the package.
❑ Identify how the filter is secured in place and remove the housing cover.

Remove Screws

❑ Make a mental note of the arrow direction on the old filter as you remove it.

✍ Compare the old and new filters.

Old                                       New

❑ If accessible, use a vacuum to remove any debris.

Vacuum with Attachment

❑ Wipe the area with a slightly damp shop rag. Then use a dry towel to remove any moisture.

❑ Install new filter. Make sure the arrows on the filter are in the correct air flow direction.

❑ Reverse the procedure for reassembly of the housing cover.

## Clean Up
❑ Clean and put away all tools.
❑ Wash your hands thoroughly.

## ✍ Activity Journal

1. Where was your vehicle's cabin air filter?

_____

2. What is the purpose of a cabin air filter?

_____

3. What types of tools were necessary to remove your cabin air filter?

_____

4. How many cabin air filters did your vehicle require?

_____

5. After comparing the old and new filters, should you replace the filter more often?

_____

| Name | Class | Date / / | Score |
|------|-------|----------|-------|

# Cooling System Activity

## Objective

Upon completion of this activity, you will be able to safely test, inspect, and service the cooling system and observe thermostat operation.

## NATEF Connections

**Heating and Air Conditioning – General**
- Research applicable vehicle and service information, vehicle service history, service precautions, and technical service bulletins.
- Inspect engine cooling and heater systems hoses; perform necessary action.

**Engine Repair – Lubrication and Cooling Systems**
- Check coolant condition and level; inspect and test radiator, pressure cap, coolant recovery tank, and heater core; determine necessary action.

## Tools

Safety glasses, basic hand tools, funnel, garden hose, coolant tester, candy thermometer, portable electric burner, pan, piece of wire, fender cover

## Supplies

Shop rags, correct type and amount of antifreeze, test thermostat, water, coolant test strips

## Cautions

Hot engine coolant can cause severe burns. Never remove a hot radiator cap. Follow all procedures and safety guidelines specified by your instructor.

## Directions

Check off the boxes ❏ when completed. When you see a hand ✍ next to the task, write the information in the activity journal. If you have any questions during the duration of this activity, stop and ask the instructor for assistance.

## Pre-Service

❏ Use the vehicle's maintenance records, the owner's manual, a service manual, and the Internet to research applicable vehicle and service information, vehicle service history, service precautions, and technical service bulletins.
❏ Apply the parking brake.
❏ Remove the key from the ignition. *Warning: On a push button keyless ignition refer to the owner's manual for specific safety procedures to prevent an unintended engine startup.*
❏ Put on your safety glasses.
❏ Pop open the hood.
❏ Use a fender cover to protect the vehicle's finish.

## Procedure 1 - Inspection and Testing the Cooling System

❏ Let the engine cool. *Warning: Never open a hot cooling system, it could spray pressurized coolant over 200°F.* Coolant can actually be above water's boiling point (212°F/100°C). System pressure and antifreeze mixed with water raises the boiling point of the coolant.
❏ Identify and locate the radiator.
❏ Identify and locate the upper radiator hose.
❏ Identify and locate the lower radiator hose.
❏ Identify and locate the thermostat housing.

Lower Radiator Hose   Thermostat Housing   Upper Radiator Hose

Radiator Cap

Example of Reverse-Flow Cooling System

❏ Identify and locate the heater hoses.

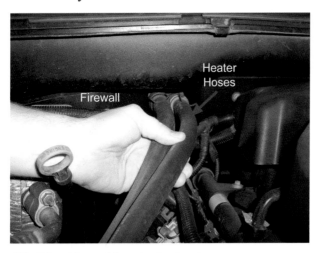

❏ Identify and locate the heater core.
❏ Identify and locate the water pump.
❏ Identify and locate the radiator petcock (drain).

❏ Identify and locate the radiator cap.
❏ Be certain that the cooling system is cool and pressure is relieved. Remove the radiator cap by twisting it while pushing down.

❏ Inspect and clean the radiator cap.
❏ Look for cracks in the rubber gasket.

✍ Note the pressure rating on the cap.
❏ Look inside the radiator. Carefully clean the neck where the cap is installed.

❏ Before using the coolant tester, rinse it out with clean water.
❏ Use the coolant tester to test the coolant's freezing and boiling points. Squeeze the bulb, insert the tube into the radiator neck, then release the bulb to pull antifreeze/coolant into the tester.

✍ Hold the tester up straight to get an accurate reading. Use the gauge on the tester to note the coolant's freezing and boiling points.

🖎 Look at the coolant in the tester. Note whether the coolant is clean or dirty.

❏ Use coolant test strips to analyze the condition of the coolant. Follow the manufacturer's instructions.

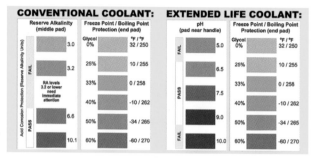

| CONVENTIONAL COOLANT: | | | | EXTENDED LIFE COOLANT: | | | |
|---|---|---|---|---|---|---|---|
| Reserve Alkalinity (middle pad) | | Freeze Point / Boiling Point Protection (end pad) | | pH (pad near handle) | | Freeze Point / Boiling Point Protection (end pad) | |
| | 3.0 | Glycol 0% | °F / °F 32 / 250 | FAIL | 5.0 | Glycol 0% | °F / °F 32 / 250 |
| FAIL | 3.2 | 25% | 10 / 255 | | 6.5 | 25% | 10 / 255 |
| RA levels 3.2 or lower need immediate attention | | 33% | 0 / 258 | PASS | 7.5 | 33% | 0 / 258 |
| | | 40% | -10 / 262 | | | 40% | -10 / 262 |
| PASS | 6.6 | 50% | -34 / 265 | | 9.0 | 50% | -34 / 265 |
| | 10.1 | 60% | -60 / 270 | FAIL | 10.0 | 60% | -60 / 270 |

❏ Top off the coolant in the radiator if low. Use the type and mixture of antifreeze recommended by the manufacturer. ***Note: The coolant added may be a different color***.

❏ Replace the radiator cap. Make sure it is on all the way. There is sometimes an arrow to line it up with the overflow hose.

❏ Check the coolant level in the coolant recovery tank.

❏ Add as necessary. Use the type and mixture of antifreeze recommended by the manufacturer.

❏ Inspect the radiator fins. They should be clean and straight. If debris is found, rinse free with a garden hose.

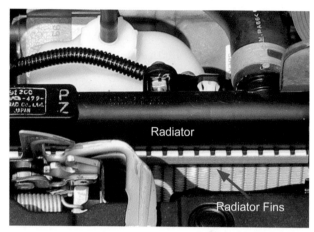

Radiator

Radiator Fins

❏ Check the belt for wear. Follow the inspection techniques for Neoprene and EPDM belts as described in the Belt Replacement Procedure in Chapter 9 Charging System Activity. Replace if necessary.

❏ Inspect the drive belt tension. Tighten if necessary or replace the belt tensioner.

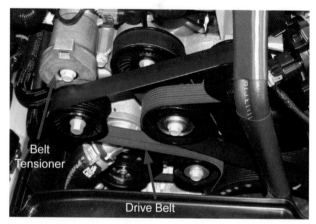

Belt Tensioner

Drive Belt

❏ Inspect the radiator hoses. Worn hoses will be excessively stiff or real spongy.

❏ Look for signs of coolant loss on hose connections, under the water pump, and in the radiator fins.

## Procedure 2 - Thermostat Operation

This lab procedure uses a test thermostat to view thermostat operation.

❑ Fill a pan about 3/4 full with warm water.
❑ Put a candy thermometer in the pan.
❑ Suspend the test thermostat in the pan with a piece of wire.

❑ Put pan on the electric burner and turn on high.
❑ Observe the thermostat as the water is heated.
✍ Note the temperature of the water when the thermostat starts to open. Note the temperature of the water when the thermostat fully opens.

❑ Turn off the electric burner.
❑ Let the water cool and observe the thermostat closing.
❑ Remove the thermostat.
✍ Note the rating stamped on the bottom of the thermostat.

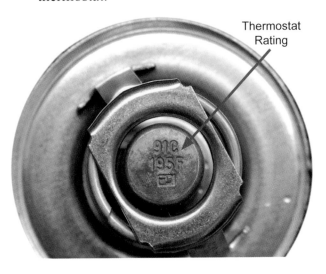

Thermostat Rating

## Clean Up

❑ Clean and put away all tools and supplies.
❑ Wash your hands thoroughly.

## ✍ Activity Journal

1. What is the purpose of the heater core?

_____

2. Why is it necessary to let the antifreeze cool before removing the radiator cap?

_____

3. What is the pressure rating on your vehicle's radiator cap?

_____

4. What are the freezing and boiling points of your vehicle's coolant?

_____

5. What is the condition of the coolant?

_____

6. How would debris in the radiator fins impact the cooling of the engine?

_____

7. When you completed the test thermostat procedure, at what temperature did the test thermostat fully open? What is the rating stamped on the bottom of the test thermostat?

_____

# 13

# IGNITION SYSTEM

## Think Safety

Ignition system components carry very high voltages. On a push button keyless ignition refer to the owner's manual for specific safety procedures to prevent an unintended engine startup.

## Objectives

After reading the *Auto Upkeep* text and completing the following activities, you will be able to:
- Define the purpose of the ignition system.
- Identify ignition system generations.
- Define and discuss the importance of the ignition system components while relating them to their respective generation.
- Test and perform basic service procedures on the ignition system.

## Summary

The ignition system is designed to ignite the air-fuel mixture in the combustion chamber. Ignition systems have gone through three main generations: conventional, distributor, and electronic, and will continue to evolve. The electronic ignition system allows cylinders to be controlled individually, providing reliability, lowering emissions, improving performance, and increasing fuel efficiency. Even though the ignition system may seem complex with sensors and control modules, there are things that the do-it-yourselfer can do to maintain and tune-up the engine to make it run smoothly.

## Web Exploring

### Key Terms/Internet Search Words
Visit **www.google.com** to investigate any of the following terms or phrases. Summarize your findings in a research paper.
- AC Delco Spark Plugs
- Accel Wires
- Autolite Spark Plugs
- Camshaft Position Sensor
- Champion Spark Plugs
- Coil-On-Plug
- Conventional Ignition Systems
- Crankshaft Position Sensor
- Distributor Ignition Systems
- Electronic Ignition Systems
- How to Change Spark Plugs on an Engine
- Ignition Control Modules
- MSD Ignition
- NGK Spark Plugs
- Powertrain Control Module
- Spark Plugs
- Splitfire Spark Plugs
- Standard Ignition Products

Name _____ Class _____ Date __/__/__ Score _____

## 📚 Study Questions - Ignition System

1. What is the purpose of the ignition system?

   _____

   _____

2. How has the ignition system evolved over time?

   _____

   _____

3. What is the purpose of an ignition coil?

   _____

   _____

4. What do spark plugs do?

   _____

   _____

5. How is the battery part of the ignition system?

   _____

   _____

6. What is an advantage of having an electronic (distributorless) ignition system?

   _____

   _____

7. What is the purpose of an ignition module?

   _____

   _____

8. How often should spark plugs be changed?

   _____

   _____

9. What is anti-seize compound and where can it be used?

   _____

   _____

10. Why do some engines use crankshaft and camshaft sensors?

   _____

   _____

| Name | Class | Date / / | Score |
|------|-------|----------|-------|

# Ignition System Activity

## Objective

Upon completion of this activity, you will be able to install spark plugs; inspect, test, and install spark plug wires; and inspect and install distributor cap and rotor on distributor and conventional ignition systems.

## NATEF Connections

**Engine Performance – General**

- Research applicable vehicle and service information, vehicle service history, service precautions, and technical service bulletins.
- Remove and replace spark plugs; inspect secondary ignition components for wear and damage.

## Tools

Safety glasses, basic hand tools, ratchet, spark plug socket, spark plug gap gauge, spark plug wire removing tool, fender cover, VOM, vacuum

## Supplies

Shop rags, spark plugs, distributor cap and rotor (if applicable), spark plug wires (if desired to change), anti-seize compound, dielectric grease

## Cautions

Let the engine cool. Hot engine components can cause burns. Follow all procedures and safety guidelines specified by your instructor.

## Directions

Check off the boxes ❑ when completed. When you see a hand ✍ next to the task, write the information in the activity journal. If you have any questions during the duration of this activity, stop and ask the instructor for assistance.

## Pre-Service

❑ Use the vehicle's maintenance records, the owner's manual, a service manual, and the Internet to research applicable vehicle and service information, vehicle service history, service precautions, and technical service bulletins.
❑ Apply the parking brake.
❑ Remove the key from the ignition. ***Warning: On a push button keyless ignition refer to the owner's manual for specific safety procedures to prevent an unintended engine startup.***
❑ Let the engine cool.
❑ Put on your safety glasses.
❑ Pop open the hood.
❑ Use a fender cover to protect the vehicle's finish.

## Procedure 1 - Installing Spark Plugs

❑ Disconnect one spark plug wire at the spark plug by firmly grasping the boot and turning back and forth to loosen (or use a spark plug wire boot puller). Never pull on the cable - you could break the fragile wire inside. Only remove and replace one wire at a time to avoid mixing up the engine's firing order. On systems with coil-on-plug (COP) technology, remove the COP.

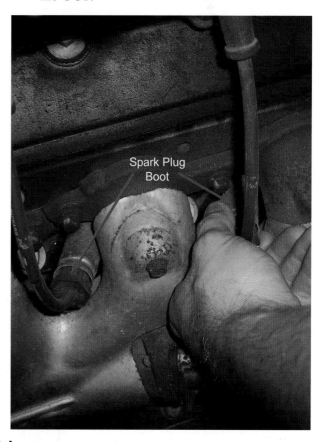

Spark Plug Boot

❑ Loosen the spark plug one complete turn with the ratchet and spark plug socket.

❑ Vacuum around the spark plug with a shop vacuum to minimize the possibility of dirt and rust getting inside the cylinder.

❑ Remove the spark plug the rest of the way.

❑ Inspect the spark plug's condition. Note whether the insulator is cracked, oil deposits are present, electrode is worn, blow-by is on ceramic, or carbon deposits are present.

❑ Use a service manual or refer to the vehicle emission control information sticker under the hood of the vehicle for gap specifications.

❑ Make sure you are using the correct replacement spark plug. Double check your numbers and compare to the old plug. Different brands will use different numbers. The plug and electrode length should look similar to the old plug.

❑ Check the new spark plug's gap to see if it is at specification. If it is at the correct gap the gauge will just fit in the gap.

❑ If the gauge is too tight or loose in the gap use the bender on the spark plug gauge tool to make an adjustment.

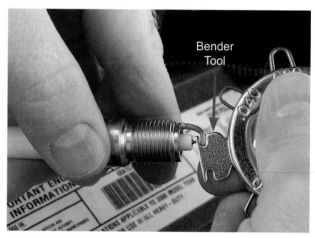

❑ Recheck the gap and adjust until the gauge just fills the gap. *Note: The distance between the two electrodes has to be exact for the spark to fire correctly; otherwise the engine will not run efficiently.*

❑ Some vehicles use a spark plug that has an O-ring washer. If your engine uses this type, make certain that the ring is placed over the threads. Other engines commonly use a tapered seat, where no ring is necessary.

❑ Put a small dab of anti-seize compound on the upper threads of the spark plug if recommended by the manufacturer.

❑ Thread the spark plug in by hand. Finish tightening the spark plug using manufacturer's torque specifications. (A common rule of thumb is to tighten O-ring style plugs 1/4th turn pass finger tight and tighten tapered style plugs 1/16th of a turn past finger tight.) *Note: Do not over-tighten.*

❑ Put a dab of dielectric grease in the boot of the spark plug wire.

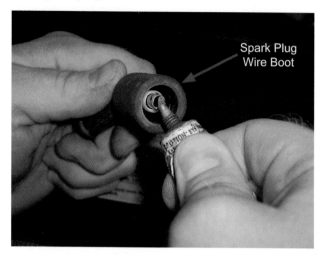

Spark Plug
Wire Boot

❑ Replace the spark plug wire or COP unit. A snap/click should be felt.

❑ Repeat the procedure for remaining spark plugs.

## Procedure 2 - Inspecting and Installing Spark Plug Wires

❑ Disconnect one spark plug wire at the spark plug by firmly grasping the boot and turning back and forth to loosen (or use a spark plug boot puller). Never pull on the cable - you could break the fragile wire inside. Remove and replace one wire at a time to avoid mixing up the engine's firing order.

Spark
Plug
Wires

❑ Disconnect the other end of the same spark plug wire at the distributor cap on distributor ignition vehicles or on the coil pack on electronic (distributorless) vehicles.

Coil

❑ Use the VOM to test the resistance of the spark plug wire. As a general rule, spark plug wires should have no more than 7,000 ohms of resistance per foot.

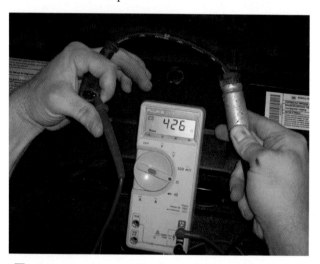

❑ Inspect the spark plug wire's condition for cracks, punctures, or burn marks. Note its condition.

❑ If replacing, remove the spark plug wire from the vehicle - noting the routing.

❑ Compare the old wire to the new one.

❑ Route the new wire, using the original clips or brackets.

❑ Put a dab of dielectric grease in the boot at both of the ends.

❑ Reinstall the spark plug wire on both ends. A snap/click should be felt.

❑ Repeat procedure for remaining spark plug wires, replacing one at a time.

## Procedure 3 - Inspecting and Installing a Distributor Cap and Rotor

❏ Locate the distributor cap. Do not remove the spark plug wires at this time.

Distributor Cap

❏ Remove the distributor cap by the screws or clips.

❏ Turn cap upside down and inspect it for cracks and burns.

❏ Inspect the terminals inside the cap for corrosion.

❏ Remove the rotor from the distributor. Screws are used to attach some rotors, while others just pull off.

❏ Inspect the rotor's terminal for corrosion.

❏ If replacing the distributor cap, remove one spark plug wire on the old cap and replace it in the same place on the new cap. Use dielectric grease in each boot end. Continue until all wires have been transferred.

❏ Reinstall rotor (or replace with new one if needed). *Note: Replace the cap and rotor as a set.*

❏ Replace the cap and secure by the screws or clips.

## Clean Up

❏ Clean and put away all tools.
❏ Wash your hands thoroughly.

## ✍ Activity Journal

1. Why should you grasp the boot of the spark plug wire and not the cable itself when removing the wire?

_____

2. Why should you vacuum around a spark plug before removing it?

_____

3. What is commonly put on the upper threads of the spark plug? Why?

_____

4. What did you put in the boot of the spark plug wire? Why?

_____

5. What is the gap on your engine's spark plugs?

_____

# SUSPENSION, STEERING, AND TIRES

## Think Safety

Tires are the only connection your vehicle has with the road. They provide traction (adhesive friction) for driver control. A severely worn tire is more likely to lose traction.

## Objectives

After reading the *Auto Upkeep* text and completing the following activities, you will be able to:

- Define the purpose and identify the functions of the suspension system.
- Define the purpose and identify the functions of the steering system.
- Discuss the importance of tires and explain their ratings.
- Inspect suspension and steering components.
- Inspect and rotate tires.

## Summary

The suspension system absorbs bumps in the road to give a smooth ride. The steering system allows the operator to control left and right motions of the vehicle. Tires provide the traction (adhesive friction) necessary for maneuvering. Knowing tire specifications can be beneficial when buying new tires. UTQG ratings make it easier for you to compare different tires. Abnormal tire wear patterns show possible problems with the vehicle. Suspension and steering components work in conjunction to provide a safe ride.

## Web Exploring

### Key Terms/Internet Search Words

Visit www.google.com to investigate any of the following terms or phrases. Summarize your findings in a research paper.

- Bridgestone/Firestone Tires
- BFGoodrich Tires
- Cooper Tires
- Directional Tires
- Dunlop Tires
- Goodyear Tires
- How to Rotate Tires
- Kelly-Springfield Tires
- Michelin Tires
- Monroe Shocks and Struts
- Parallelogram Steering System
- Passenger and Light Truck Tires
- Rack and Pinion Steering System
- Run Flat Tires
- Tire Load Ranges
- Tire Plugs and Patches
- Tire Pressure Monitoring System
- Toyo Tires
- Uniform Tire Quality Grading Ratings

Name _____ Class _____ Date ___/___/___ Score _____

# ⌘ Study Questions - Suspension, Steering, and Tires

1. What is the purpose of the steering system?

   _____

   _____

2. What is the purpose of the suspension system?

   _____

   _____

3. What do shocks do?

   _____

   _____

4. How are shocks different than struts?

   _____

   _____

5. What is used to reduce the effort needed to steer an automobile?

   _____

   _____

6. What do the letters UTQG represent? What are the three UTQG ratings?

   _____

   _____

7. Why is it important to torque lug nuts?

   _____

   _____

8. How often should tires be rotated?

   _____

   _____

9. Why is it not recommended to fix a tire's sidewall?

   _____

   _____

10. What can cause a tire to wear excessively?

    _____

    _____

# Suspension and Steering Activity

## Objective

Upon completion of this activity, you will be able to safely inspect and perform basic service procedures on suspension and steering components.

## NATEF Connections

**Suspension and Steering Systems – General**
- Research applicable vehicle and service information, vehicle service history, service precautions, and technical service bulletins.

**Suspension and Steering Systems – Related Suspension and Steering Service**
- Inspect rack and pinion steering gear inner tie rod ends (sockets) and bellows boots.
- Determine proper power steering fluid type; inspect fluid level and condition.
- Inspect power steering hoses and fittings.
- Inspect pitman arm, relay (centerlink/intermediate) rod, idler arm and mountings, and steering linkage damper.
- Inspect tie rod ends (sockets), tie rod sleeves, and clamps.
- Inspect upper and lower control arms, bushings, and shafts.
- Inspect track bar, strut rods/radius arms, and related mounts and bushings.
- Inspect upper and lower ball joints.
- Inspect suspension system coil springs and spring insulators (silencers).
- Inspect suspension system torsion bars and mounts.
- Inspect front stabilizer bar (sway bar) bushings, brackets, and links.
- Inspect strut cartridge or assembly.
- Inspect rear suspension system lateral links/arms (track bars), control (trailing) arms.
- Inspect rear suspension system leaf spring(s), spring insulators (silencers), shackles, brackets, bushings, center pins/bolts, and mounts.
- Inspect shock absorbers; inspect mounts and bushings.
- Inspect electric power-assisted steering.

## Tools

Safety glasses, grease gun, fender cover, wheel chocks, jack and jack stands (or an automotive lift)

## Supplies

Shop rags, chassis grease

## Cautions

Be sure to chock wheels and use jack stands before going under a vehicle. Follow all procedures and safety guidelines specified by your instructor.

## Directions

Check off the boxes ❏ when completed. When you see a hand ✍ next to the task, write the information in the activity journal. If you have any questions during the duration of this activity, stop and ask the instructor for assistance.

## Pre-Service

❏ Use the vehicle's maintenance records, the owner's manual, a service manual, and the Internet to research applicable vehicle and service information, vehicle service history, service precautions, and technical service bulletins.

❏ Apply the parking brake.

❏ Remove the key from the ignition. ***Warning: On a push button keyless ignition refer to the owner's manual for specific safety procedures to prevent an unintended engine startup.***

❏ Put on your safety glasses.

## Procedure 1 - Bounce Test

❏ Perform a bounce test. To test the shocks and/or struts on a vehicle push down as hard as you can on the end that you want to test and then let go. The vehicle should come to a rest after one cycle. If it cycles more than once, the shocks, struts, or springs could be worn.

## Procedure 2 - Inspect Suspension and Steering Components

☐ Raise the end of the vehicle where the engine is located with a jack and support with jack stands (or use an automotive lift or drive-on ramps with jack stands).

☐ Chock the wheels on the opposite end of the vehicle.

☐ Apply the parking brake.

☐ Remove the key from the ignition. *Warning: On a push button keyless ignition refer to the owner's manual for specific safety procedures to prevent an unintended engine startup.*

☐ Inspect the shocks/struts for signs of leakage. Inspect the mounts and bushings.

✎ Note the condition of shocks/struts.

☐ Inspect the upper (if applicable) and low control arms. Inspect the mounts and bushings.

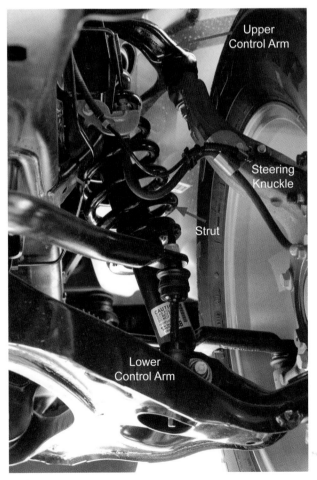

☐ Inspect suspension system tracking bars, trailing arms, torsion bars, and related mounts and bushings.

☐ Identify if the vehicle has springs (leaf or coil).

☐ Inspect the springs, spring insulators, shackles, brackets, bushings, pins/bolts, and mounts for cracks or breaks.

✎ Note the condition of the suspension system.

✎ Note whether the vehicle uses a parallelogram or a rack and pinion steering system.

**If a Parallelogram Steering System**

Locate, identify, and inspect the following parts.

☐ Steering Knuckles    ☐ Idler Arm
☐ Outer Tie Rods    ☐ Pitman Arm
☐ Inner Tie Rods    ☐ Sway Bar
☐ Adjustment Sleeve    ☐ Sway Bar Links
☐ Upper Ball Joints    ☐ Steering Box
☐ Lower Ball Joints    ☐ Grease Zerks

✎ Note the condition of the parallelogram steering system.

**If a Rack and Pinion Steering System**

Locate, identify, and inspect the following parts.

☐ Steering Knuckles    ☐ Sway Bar Links
☐ Outer Tie Rods    ☐ Upper Ball Joints
☐ Inner Tie Rods      (if applicable)
☐ Tie Rod Locknuts    ☐ Lower Ball Joints
☐ Bellows Boots    ☐ Rack and Pinion
☐ Sway Bar    ☐ Grease Zerks

✎ Note the condition of the rack and pinion steering system.

☐ On rack and pinion systems, identify if the vehicle uses a hydraulic power steering pump or an electric power steering unit.

☐ On hydraulic systems, inspect power steering hoses and fittings for wear and leakage.

## Parallelogram Steering Linkage and Suspension Components

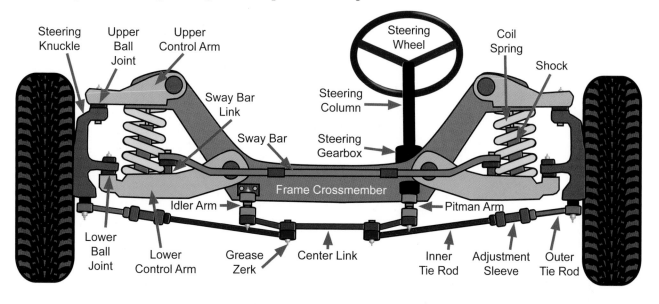

## Rack and Pinion Steering Linkage and Suspension Components

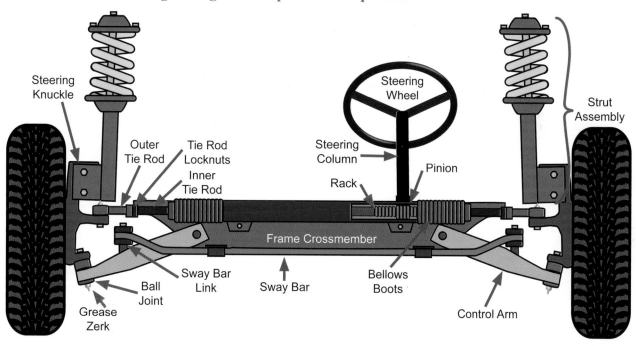

## Rack and Pinion Electric Power Steering

## Procedure 3 - Grease Zerks

❏ Identify, locate, and grease the suspension and steering grease fittings. Look for points that pivot.

✍ Note the number of fittings.

❏ Place the grease gun on the grease zerk. Just pump the grease gun enough to fill the cavity. Excess grease can drop on the inside of the wheel and throw the wheel off balance. Wipe off all excess grease with a shop rag. Be sure to use the correct type of grease for your vehicle.

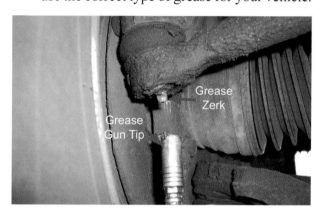

❏ Do not oil or grease rubber components. Grease can cause rubber to swell and crack prematurely.

❏ Lower the vehicle.

## Procedure 4 - Power Steering Fluid (Hydraulic Power Steering)

❏ Use the procedure in the Chapter 8 Fluid Level Check to inspect the power steering fluid level. When checking the power steering fluid, analyze its condition.

## Clean Up

❏ Clean and put away all tools.

❏ Wash your hands thoroughly.

## ✍ Activity Journal

1. What was the condition of the suspension system?

_____

2. Does the vehicle utilize a parallelogram steering system or a rack and pinion steering system?

_____

3. What was the condition of the steering system?

_____

4. How many grease fittings did your vehicle have?

_____

5. Why should you wipe off excess grease?

_____

6. Did all the pivoting points have grease fittings? Why or why not?

_____

# Tire Inspection and Rotation Activity

## Objective

Upon completion of this activity, you will be able to safely check the air pressure, inspect tires for wear, and rotate tires.

## NATEF Connections

**Suspension and Steering Systems – General**

- Research applicable vehicle and service information, vehicle service history, service precautions, and technical service bulletins.

**Suspension and Steering – Wheels and Tires**

- Inspect tire condition; identify tire wear patterns; check for correct size and application (load and speed ratings) and adjust air pressure; determine necessary action.
- Rotate tires according to manufacturer's recommendations.

## Tools

Safety glasses, tread depth gauge, tire pressure gauge, lug wrench (manual or pneumatic), torque wrench, basic hand tools, air compressor, jack and jack stands (or automotive lift)

## Supplies

Shop rags, anti-seize compound

## Cautions

Never use only a jack to support a vehicle. Use approved jack stands for safety. Follow all procedures and safety guidelines specified by your instructor.

## Directions

Check off the boxes ❑ when completed. When you see a hand ✍ next to the task, write the information in the activity journal. If you have any questions during the duration of this activity, stop and ask the instructor for assistance.

## Pre-Service

- ❑ Use the vehicle's maintenance records, the owner's manual, a service manual, and the Internet to research applicable vehicle and service information, vehicle service history, service precautions, and technical service bulletins.
- ❑ Apply the parking brake.
- ❑ Remove the key from the ignition. *Warning: On a push button keyless ignition refer to the owner's manual for specific safety procedures to prevent an unintended engine startup.*
- ❑ Put on your safety glasses.
- ❑ Use the tire placard (commonly inside driver's door) to check tires for the correct size and application (load and speed ratings).

## Procedure 1 - Tire Air Pressure

- ❑ Check the owner's manual, tire placard, or tire sidewall for correct tire pressure. It should be noted that the pressure rating on the tire sidewall is the maximum pressure. The recommended tire pressure is calculated according to type of tire, weight of vehicle, and the desired ride. Tire inflation changes with temperature. For every 10°F drop in temperature, tire pressure is lowered by 1 psi.

| TIRE AND LOADING INFORMATION | | | |
|---|---|---|---|
| SEATING CAPACITY – TOTAL 5   FRONT   2   REAR   3 | | | |
| THE COMBINED WEIGHT OF OCCUPANTS AND CARGO SHOULD NEVER EXCEED 392 KG OR 865 LB | | | |
| TIRE | FRONT | REAR | SPARE |
| ORIGINAL TIRE SIZE | P195/65R15 | P195/65R15 | T125/70D15 |
| COLD TIRE INFLATION PRESSURE | 240 kPa, 35 PSI | 240 kPa, 35 PSI | 420 kPa, 60 PSI |
| SEE OWNERS MANUAL FOR ADDITIONAL INFORMATION | | | 6T316309 |

- ✍ Note the recommended tire pressure for the front, rear, and spare tires.
- ❑ Check the tire pressure when the tires are cold and when you have access to an air compressor.
- ❑ Remove the valve stem cap.

❑ Use a tire pressure gauge to check the tire pressure of each tire. Push the tire gauge firmly onto the valve stem. Your should hear air rush into the gauge. Note the reading.

❑ Use an air compressor to add air if the reading is below the recommended pressure. ***Note: Do not overinflate.***

❑ If too much air is added, bleed some air from the tire. Many air gauges have a special tip for pressing in the valve to release air pressure.

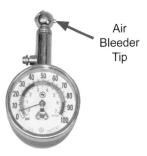

Air Bleeder Tip

❑ Recheck the pressure.
❑ Once the tire is at the correct pressure, replace the valve stem cap and check the other tires.
❑ Do not forget to check the air pressure in the spare tire (if applicable).

❑ Make sure all emergency tools (e.g., lug wrench, jack, inflator kit) are properly stowed.

## Procedure 2 - Tread Inspection

✍ Check the tread depth on each tire using the tread depth gauge. Note the readings in 1/32nds (industry standard) of an inch.

Tread Depth Reading

Check all tires for the following wear patterns.
❑ Both Edges Worn (Underinflation)
❑ Wear on One Edge (Camber Incorrect)
❑ Wear in the Center (Overinflation)
❑ Bald Spots (Wheel out of Balance)
❑ Cupped (Worn Parts)
❑ Feathering (Toe Incorrect)

Edge Wear (Underinflation)    One Edge Wear (Camber Incorrect)    Center Wear (Overinflation)

Bald Spots (Out of Balance)    Cupped (Worn Parts)    Feathered (Toe Incorrect)

✍ Identify and note the current UTQG ratings (treadwear, traction, temperature) on each tire.

TREADWEAR 500 TRACTION A TEMPERATURE B

## Procedure 3 - Tire Rotation

❑ Check the owner's manual for recommended tire rotation patterns. ***Note: Some tires are directional, designed to roll in only one direction and should not be moved to the other side of the vehicle unless they are dismounted from the wheel, flipped, and remounted. An arrow on the sidewall indicates their forward rotation.***

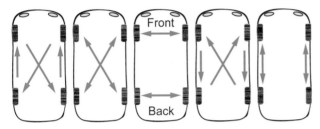

❑ Remove wheel covers if applicable. Check the owner's manual for procedure. Some covers (hubcaps) have locking mechanisms that need to be removed first.

❑ Loosen lug nuts 1/2 turn counterclockwise with a lug wrench.

4-Way Lug Wrench

❑ Your vehicle may have one locking lug nut on each wheel. A special coded key tool is needed to remove locking lug nuts.

Locking Lug Nut

Locking Lug Nut Key Tool

❑ Use a jack and jack stands (or an automotive lift) to raise and support the vehicle.

❑ Identify each tire's location before rotation.

❑ Remove the lug nuts on each tire. Inspect lug nuts and wheel studs for damage.

❑ Remove each tire and move it to the new location according to the owner's manual rotation pattern recommendation.

❑ Apply anti-seize compound to the wheel stud threads.

❑ Start all lug nuts by hand. Do not cross-thread nuts.

❑ Spin the nuts on with a lug wrench and snug. Use a star pattern when tightening lug nuts. Do not use a pneumatic wrench at this time.
❑ Remove the jack stands and lower the vehicle just until the tires touch the ground.
❑ Check the owner's manual or specification's chart for torque recommendations.
❑ Use a torque wrench or color-coded torque sticks with an impact wrench to tighten the lug nuts on each wheel. When tightening, use a star

pattern. Failure to torque wheels may result in warped brake rotors. Under torqued wheels may allow the wheel to work loose and come off when driving, causing a hazardous situation.

Torque Wrench

❑ Completely lower the vehicle.
❑ Recheck all lug nuts with the torque wrench.
❑ Replace wheel covers.
❑ Check and adjust the tire pressure according to the tire placard on the vehicle.

## Clean Up

❑ Clean and put away all tools.
❑ Wash your hands thoroughly.

## ✍ Activity Journal

1. What were the recommended pressure ratings for your vehicle's tires?

| Front | Rear | Spare |
|---|---|---|
| | | |

2. Most new passenger tires are manufactured with 11/32nds of an inch of tread (truck and SUV tires may differ). How much tread did each of your tires have?

| Front Right | Front Left | Rear Right | Rear Left |
|---|---|---|---|
| | | | |

3. What were the UTQG ratings on your vehicle's tires?

_____

4. How tight did you tighten your wheels in lb-ft?

_____

5. Why is it necessary to torque wheels?

_____

6. Why is it important to rotate tires?

_____

# BRAKING SYSTEM

## Think Safety

Brakes are critical to safely slowing and stopping a vehicle. If the brake pedal is really easy to depress and/or required braking distance increases, have the vehicle towed in for repair.

## Objectives

After reading the *Auto Upkeep* text and completing the following activities, you will be able to:
- Define the purpose and principles of the braking system.
- Identify the different types of brakes and their components.
- Identify brake fluid properties.
- Discuss the advantages of antilock brakes.
- Explain how the parking brake works.
- Safely perform basic inspections on the braking system.

## Summary

Hydraulic brake systems use friction to slow and stop a vehicle. Regenerative braking captures kinetic energy to slow down a vehicle. Disc brakes use rotors, pads, and calipers. Drum brakes use drums, shoes, and wheel cylinders. Antilock brakes assist in preventing wheel lockup and provide the operator with maximum directional control. Advanced technological systems such as ABS, TCS, and ESC have been installed on vehicles to maximize driver control. The parking brake uses a mechanical linkage (cable) or motor instead of a fluid linkage (brake fluid).

## Web Exploring

### Key Terms/Internet Search Words
Visit www.google.com to investigate any of the following terms or phrases. Summarize your findings in a research paper.
- Antilock Brake Systems
- Bendix Brakes
- Brake Caliper Lube
- Brake Drums
- Brake Fluid
- Brake Fluid Test Strips
- Brake Rotors
- Disc Brake Systems
- Drum Brake Systems
- Electronic Parking Brake
- Electronic Stability Control
- How Do Brake Systems Work
- How to Bleed Brakes
- How to Inspect Disc Brakes
- Midas International Corporation
- Raybestos Brakes
- Regenerative Braking
- Traction Control System
- Wagner Brake Products

| Name | Class | Date / / | Score |
|------|-------|----------|-------|

## 📚 Study Questions - Braking System

1. What is the purpose of the braking system?

   _____

   _____

2. How is a disc brake system different than a drum brake system?

   _____

   _____

3. What does brake fluid do?

   _____

   _____

4. What do the letters ABS represent?

   _____

   _____

5. What are benefits of antilock brakes?

   _____

   _____

6. Why does the parking brake use a mechanical linkage instead of a fluid linkage?

   _____

   _____

7. What can cause brake rotors to warp?

   _____

   _____

8. If you hear a high pitch squeal that goes away every time you apply your brakes, what might this indicate?

   _____

   _____

9. What happens if the wheels lockup when braking?

   _____

   _____

10. What is electronic stability control?

    _____

    _____

| Name | Class | Date / / | Score |
|---|---|---|---|

# Brake Inspection Activity

## Objective

Upon completion of this activity, you will be able to safely inspect the disc brakes on a vehicle.

## NATEF Connections

**Brakes – General**
- Research applicable vehicle and service information, vehicle service history, service precautions, and technical service bulletins.

**Brakes – Hydraulic System**
- Check master cylinder for external leaks and proper operation.
- Inspect brake lines, flexible hoses, and fittings for leaks, dents, kinks, rust, cracks, bulging, wear, loose fittings and supports; determine necessary action.
- Select, handle, store, and fill brake fluids to proper level.
- Test brake fluid for contamination.

## Tools

Safety glasses, basic hand tools, torque wrench, ruler, fender cover, wheel chocks, jack and jack stands (or an automotive lift)

## Supplies

Shop rags, anti-seize compound, correct type and amount of brake fluid, brake fluid test strips

## Cautions

Brake fluid will harm eyes. Wear safety glasses and know the location of the eyewash station. Brake fluid will strip paint. Avoid dripping brake fluid on a vehicle's finish. Do not mix different types (DOT 3, 4, 5, 5.1) of brake fluid. Follow all procedures and safety guidelines specified by your instructor.

## Directions

Check off the boxes ❑ when completed. When you see a hand ✍ next to the task, write the information in the activity journal. If you have any questions during the duration of this activity, stop and ask the instructor for assistance.

## Pre-Service

❑ Use the vehicle's maintenance records, the owner's manual, a service manual, and the Internet to research applicable vehicle and service information, vehicle service history, service precautions, and technical service bulletins.

❑ Apply the parking brake.

❑ Remove the key from the ignition. *Warning: On a push button keyless ignition refer to the owner's manual for specific safety procedures to prevent an unintended engine startup.*

❑ Put on your safety glasses.

❑ Pop open the hood.

❑ Use a fender cover to protect the vehicle's finish.

## Procedure 1 - Inspecting and Testing Brake Fluid

❑ Inspect the brake master cylinder and reservoir for brake fluid leaks.

Brake Fluid Reservoir

Master Cylinder

❑ Use a shop rag to clean the brake fluid cap and reservoir.

❑ Check the fluid level in the brake fluid reservoir. On some reservoirs, the fluid level can be checked by simply looking at the clear reservoir. On others, the cap may need to be removed. Some master cylinder caps screw off, others have clips, while others snap off. The fluid should be about 1/4th of an inch from the top (or at the full line on a clear reservoir). Read the owner's or service manual if unsure.

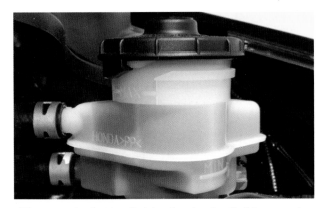

❑ Test the brake fluid using brake fluid test strips or a brake fluid tester to analyze the condition of the brake fluid. Follow the manufacturer's instructions.

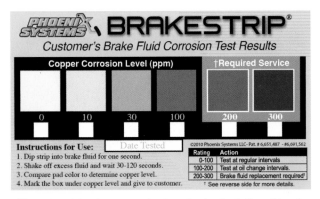

❑ Identify the type (DOT 3, 4, 5, 5.1) of brake fluid that is recommended for your braking system. The type may be identified on the brake fluid reservoir cap.

❑ If low, carefully add the correct type of brake fluid from a fresh sealed container. Do not overfill the reservoir. Brake fluid needs room to expand as it heats up. *Note: Do not spill fluid on the vehicle's finish - it will strip paint.*

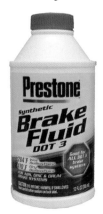

❑ Reinstall the cap. Make sure the rubber gasket seats properly and the cap is secure.

## Procedure 2 - Inspecting Disc Brakes

❑ Remove the front wheel covers.
❑ Loosen front wheel lug nuts 1/2 turn.
❑ Jack up the front of the vehicle and support with jack stands (or use an automotive lift).
❑ Chock the tires on the vehicle's opposite end.
❑ Remove the lug nuts and the front wheels.
❑ Identify brake system components: caliper, inner and outer brake pads, brake rotor, rubber brake lines, steel lines, and bleeder. Use a manual specific to your vehicle if you are unsure of component locations.

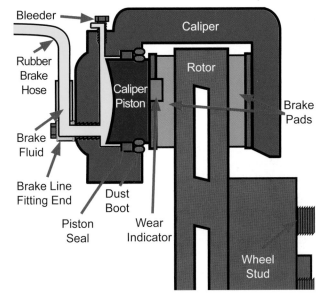

❑ Inspect the calipers for leaks. Uneven brake pad wear indicates a problem with the caliper.

❑ Inspect the bleeder and dust cap.

✍ Inspect the rubber brake lines for cracks, leaks, kinks, budges, and wear. Rubber lines are used to allow for turning and suspension travel (up and down movements). Note the condition of rubber brake lines.

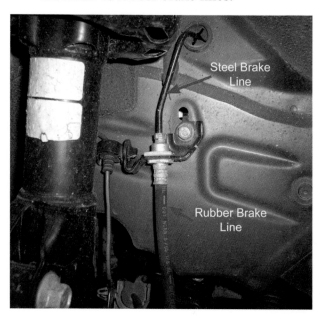

✍ Inspect the steel brake lines and fittings for cracks, leaks, dents, kinks, rust, wear, and loose connections. Note the condition of steel brake lines and fittings.

✍ Use a ruler to measure the brake pad thickness. Measure only the pad, not the metal backing. Brake pads with less than 1/8th of an inch are usually considered worn out. Measure both inner and outer pad on disc brakes.

❑ The inner pad thickness can be inspected through the caliper inspection hole.

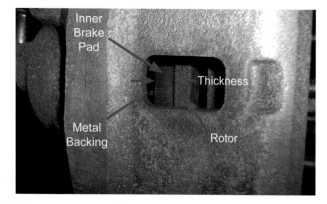

❑ Inspect rotors for grooves. Large grooves indicate brake pads are completely worn. When brake pads are replaced the grooved rotors will need to be resurfaced or replaced. Worn brake pads create an unsafe driving condition, so get them serviced right way.

Rotor Surface

❑ Replace the wheels.
❑ Start all lug nuts by hand. Snug up lug nuts in a star pattern.
❑ Lower vehicle just until the tires are touching the ground.
❑ Tighten lug nuts in a star pattern to manufacturer's torque specifications.
❑ Lower the vehicle completely.
❑ Double check lug nut torque tightness.
❑ Replace wheel covers.

## Clean Up

❑ Clean and put away all tools.
❑ Wash your hands thoroughly.

## ✍ Activity Journal

1. What should you be aware of when handling brake fluid?

_____

2. What was the brake fluid's condition?

_____

3. What is the condition of your brake pads and rotors?

_____

4. What is the condition of your steel brake lines and fittings?

_____

5. What is the condition of your rubber brake lines?

_____

6. Why do auto manufacturers use rubber hoses to connect to brake calipers?

_____

7. How thick were the inner and outer disc brake pads?

_____

8. What are some visual signs of a worn brake rotor?

_____

# DRIVETRAIN

## Think Safety

There are usually warning signs or noises before a component of a vehicle's drivetrain leaves you stranded. Check and change fluids as recommended and have service performed as needed.

## Objectives

After reading the *Auto Upkeep* text and completing the following activities, you will be able to:
- Define the purpose of the drivetrain.
- Identify drivetrain components.
- Identify and describe different drivetrain systems.
- Inspect drivetrain systems.

## Summary

Drivetrains transfer power from the engine to the wheels. Gears, transmissions, drive shafts, and differentials are used to transmit the power. Vehicles can be front-, rear-, four-, or all-wheel drive. All-wheel drive vehicles have become popular because they have superior traction on all types of road conditions.

## Web Exploring

### Key Terms/Internet Search Words
Visit **www.google.com** to investigate any of the following terms or phrases. Summarize your findings in a research paper.
- Automatic Transmission Fluid
- Clutch Alignment Tool
- Clutch Kits
- Constant Velocity Shafts
- Continuously Variable Transmission
- CV Boots
- CVT Fluid
- Differential Fluid
- Drivetrain Systems
- How All-Wheel Drive Works
- How to Change a Clutch and Pressure Plate
- How to Change a CV Boot
- How to Change a U-Joint
- How Transmissions Work
- Manual Transmission Fluid
- Pressure Plate
- Throw Out Bearing
- U-Joints

Name _____ Class _____ Date __ / __ / __ Score _____

## 📚 Study Questions - Drivetrain

1. What is the purpose of the drivetrain system?

   _____

   _____

2. What are gears?

   _____

   _____

3. What does a drive shaft do?

   _____

   _____

4. What does a clutch do in a manual transmission?

   _____

   _____

5. What are four drivetrain systems (configurations)?

   _____

   _____

6. What would be a symptom of a worn CV joint?

   _____

   _____

7. How is an all-wheel drive vehicle different from a four-wheel drive vehicle?

   _____

   _____

8. What causes a front-wheel drive vehicle to have better traction than a rear-wheel drive vehicle?

   _____

   _____

9. What color is automatic transmission fluid?

   _____

   _____

10. What are benefits of a continuously variable transmission when compared to an automatic transmission?

    _____

    _____

Name _____    Class _____    Date ___/___/___    Score _____

# Drivetrain Activity

## Objective

Upon completion of this activity, you will be able to safely inspect drivetrain components.

## NATEF Connections

**Automatic Transmission and Transaxle – General**

- Research applicable vehicle and service information, fluid type, vehicle service history, service precautions, and technical service bulletins.
- Check fluid level in a transmission or a transaxle equipped with a dipstick.
- Check fluid level in a transmission or a transaxle not equipped with a dipstick.
- Check transmission fluid condition; check for leaks.

**Automatic Transmission and Transaxle – In-Vehicle Transmission/Transaxle**

- Inspect for leakage at external seals, gaskets, and bushings.
- Inspect power train mounts.

**Manual Drivetrain and Axles – General**

- Research applicable vehicle and service information, fluid type, vehicle service history, service precautions, and technical service bulletins.
- Check fluid condition; check for leaks.

**Manual Drivetrain and Axles – Clutch**

- Check and adjust clutch master cylinder fluid level.
- Check for system leaks.

**Manual Drivetrain and Axles – Drive Shaft, Half Shafts, Universal and Constant-Velocity (CV) Joints**

- Inspect shafts, yokes, boots, and universal/CV joints

**Manual Drivetrain and Axles – Differential Case Assembly**

- Clean and inspect differential housing; check for leaks; inspect housing vent.
- Check and adjust differential housing fluid level.

**Manual Drivetrain and Axles – 4-Wheel Drive/All-Wheel Drive**

- Check for leaks at drive assembly seals; check vents; check lube level.

## Tools

Safety glasses, basic hand tools, grease gun, fender cover, wheel chocks, jack with jack stands, drive-on ramps with jack stands, or an automotive lift

## Supplies

Shop rags, grease, transmission fluid (if needed), differential fluid (if needed)

## Cautions

Be sure to chock wheels and use jack stands before going under a vehicle. Follow all procedures and safety guidelines specified by your instructor.

## Directions

Check off the boxes ❑ when completed. When you see a hand ✍ next to the task, write the information in the activity journal. If you have any questions during the duration of this activity, stop and ask the instructor for assistance. A manual specific to your vehicle can assist you in component identification and specific service procedures. Whenever adding fluids, refer to the owner's manual for correct fluid specifications.

## Pre-Service

- ❑ Use the vehicle's maintenance records, the owner's manual, a service manual, and the Internet to research applicable vehicle and service information, fluid type, vehicle service history, service precautions, and technical service bulletins.
- ❑ Raise the vehicle with a jack and support with jack stands (or use an automotive lift or drive-on ramps with jack stands).
- ❑ Chock the wheels on the opposite end of the vehicle.

❑ Apply the parking brake.

❑ Remove the key from the ignition. *Warning: On a push button keyless ignition refer to the owner's manual for specific safety procedures to prevent an unintended engine startup.*

❑ Put on your safety glasses.

❑ Pop open the hood.

❑ Use a fender cover to protect the vehicle's finish.

## Procedure 1 - Drivetrain Components

❑ When inspecting the drivetrain and transmission components, check for signs of leaks at external seals and gaskets.

✎ Identify and note whether your vehicle is front-wheel drive, four-wheel drive, all-wheel drive, or rear-wheel drive.

❑ Identify the location of the transmission.

✎ Note whether your transmission is manual, automatic, or continuously variable.

❑ Identify the location of the drive shaft, constant velocity shafts, and/or U-joints.

❑ Some U-joints can be greased. Look for a grease zerk. If applicable, use the grease gun to lube the joint. U-joints do not hold much grease, so pump the gun slowly. Some four-wheel drive vehicles have front drive shafts with slip joints with a grease zerk.

Drive Shaft   Slip Joint
U-Joints

❑ If your vehicle has CV joints, check the rubber boots for cracks. If cracks are present, the boots should be replaced by a qualified technician.

Rubber Boots

## Procedure 2 - Fluid Check

❑ Use the procedures in the Chapter 8 Fluid Level Check to inspect the transmission, differential, and clutch (if applicable) fluid levels. When checking fluids, analyze the fluid conditions.

❑ Lower the vehicle.

## Clean Up

❑ Clean and put away all tools.

❑ Wash your hands thoroughly.

## ✎ Activity Journal

1. What is your vehicle's drivetrain system?

2. What type of transmission does your vehicle have? How do you know?

3. Why do you think that an engine in a front-wheel drive vehicle is positioned differently than a rear-wheel drive vehicle?

4. What type of transmission fluid is recommended for your vehicle?

5. Why do you think cracks in CV boots could harm the joint?

# 17

# EXHAUST AND EMISSION SYSTEM

## Think Safety

Exhaust components remove hot exhaust gases from the engine. To avoid burns, allow the exhaust system to cool before working near exhaust components.

## Objectives

After reading the *Auto Upkeep* text and completing the following activities, you will be able to:

- Define the purpose of the exhaust and emission system.
- Identify and explain the components in an exhaust and emission system.
- Inspect exhaust and emission system components.

## Summary

As technology advances, the internal combustion engine will become more efficient and pollute less. Over time, exhaust system components have been added to lower noise, while emission system components have been added to convert harmful gases into more environmentally friendly by-products. I/M testing helps to keep in-use vehicle emission levels regulated, minimizing pollution released into the environment. Consumers can reduce pollution by upgrading to a more efficient vehicle and by driving less.

## Web Exploring

### Key Terms/Internet Search Words

Visit **www.google.com** to investigate any of the following terms or phrases. Summarize your findings in a research paper.

- Carbon Monoxide Poisoning
- Clean Air Act
- Components of Smog
- Dynomax Exhaust
- Emission Performance Warranty
- EPA Emission Standards
- Evaporative Emission Control Canister
- Exhaust Gas Recirculation
- How Catalytic Converters Work
- How Mufflers Work
- How Oxygen Sensors Work
- How to Replace a Muffler
- How to Replace an Oxygen Sensor
- Positive Crankcase Ventilation
- Smog
- Stainless Steel Exhaust Systems
- Tenneco Automotive
- Tomco Inc.
- Walker Exhaust Systems

Name _____  Class _____  Date ___/___/___  Score _____

## 📚 Study Questions - Exhaust and Emission System

1. What is the purpose of the exhaust system?

   _____

   _____

2. What is the purpose of the emission system?

   _____

   _____

3. What do the exhaust manifolds do?

   _____

   _____

4. What is the purpose of the muffler?

   _____

   _____

5. What do the letters EGR represent and what does the EGR do?

   _____

   _____

6. What does an oxygen sensor do?

   _____

   _____

7. What is the purpose of an evaporative emissions control canister?

   _____

   _____

8. What causes smog?

   _____

   _____

9. What may be the problem if your vehicle is excessively loud?

   _____

   _____

10. What is the purpose of an exhaust hanger?

   _____

   _____

| Name | Class | Date / / | Score |
|------|-------|----------|-------|

# Exhaust and Emission Activity

## Objective

Upon completion of this activity, you will be able to safely inspect exhaust and emission components.

## NATEF Connections

**Engine Performance – General**

- Research applicable vehicle and service information, vehicle service history, service precautions, and technical service bulletins.

**Engine Performance – Fuel, Air Induction, and Exhaust Systems**

- Inspect integrity of the exhaust manifold, exhaust pipes, muffler(s), catalytic converter(s), resonator(s), tailpipe(s), and heat shields; determine necessary action.
- Inspect condition of exhaust system hangers, brackets, clamps, and heat shields; repair or replace as needed.

## Tools

Safety glasses, hammer, fender cover, wheel chocks, jack with jack stands, drive-on ramps with jack stands, or an automotive lift

## Supplies

Shop rags

## Cautions

Let the exhaust system and engine components cool. Follow all procedures and safety guidelines specified by your instructor.

## Directions

Check off the boxes ❑ when completed. When you see a hand ✍ next to the task, write the information in the activity journal. If you have any questions during the duration of this activity, stop and ask the instructor for assistance. A manual specific to your vehicle can assist you in component identification and specific service procedures.

## Pre-Service

- ❑ Use the vehicle's maintenance records, the owner's manual, a service manual, and the Internet to research applicable vehicle and service information, vehicle service history, service precautions, and technical service bulletins.
- ❑ Raise the vehicle with a jack and support with jack stands (or use an automotive lift or drive-on ramps with jack stands).
- ❑ Chock the wheels on the opposite end of the vehicle.
- ❑ Apply the parking brake.
- ❑ Remove the key from the ignition. *Warning: On a push button keyless ignition refer to the owner's manual for specific safety procedures to prevent an unintended engine startup.*
- ❑ Put on your safety glasses.

## Procedure

- ❑ Identify the tailpipe. Inspect for holes, corrosion, and loose or broken hangers.
- ❑ Identify the muffler. Inspect for holes, corrosion, and loose or broken hangers.
- ❑ Take a hammer and lightly tap on the muffler. If it sounds like there is loose material inside, the muffler might be worn.
- ❑ Identify the intermediate exhaust pipe. Inspect for holes, corrosion, and loose or broken hangers. Inspect the connection to the catalytic converter.
- ❑ Identify the catalytic converter. Inspect the heat shield. It should be secure. Use large steel hose clamps to secure the heat shield if a weld is broken.

❑ Identify the exhaust pipe in front of the catalytic converter. Inspect for holes, corrosion, and loose or broken hangers. Inspect the connection at the exhaust manifold(s). The pipe should be secure. Look for cracks or black marks on the exhaust manifold(s). A black carbon mark identifies a leak.

❑ Repair or replace broken or loose hangers, clamps, brackets, and heat shields.

❑ Identify the oxygen sensor(s). Often oxygen sensors are placed between the catalytic converter and the exhaust manifold. Some vehicles also have oxygen sensors in or after the catalytic converter. Oxygen sensors have wires going to them. Inspect the connection and wire insulation.

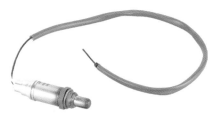

❑ Identify the evaporative emissions canister. It is commonly located near the fuel tank. Inspect the rubber lines that are attached to it.

❑ Lower the vehicle.

❑ Pop the hood open.

❑ Identify the exhaust manifold(s) from inside the engine compartment. Look for black carbon deposits.

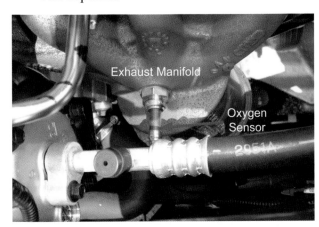

❑ Identify the PCV valve. It is usually located on the valve cover or between the valve cover and the air filter housing. Inspect the hoses for cracks.

❑ Identify the EGR valve.

❑ Connect the vehicle's exhaust to the shop exhaust evacuation system or park outside.

❑ Start the vehicle.

❑ Listen for and locate any exhaust leaks.

✍ In the activity journal draw a picture of your exhaust system. On your drawing label all exhaust components, clamps, and hangers. Identify any holes or corrosion on your drawing.

### Clean Up

❑ Clean and put away all tools.

❑ Wash your hands thoroughly.

## ✍ Activity Journal

1. Why might tapping on the muffler with a hammer identify whether or not the muffler is worn?

_____

2. Were the exhaust system components on your vehicle connected by welds or clamps?

_____

3. Overall, how would you rate the condition of your vehicle's exhaust system?

_____

4. Sketch a picture of your exhaust system on a blank sheet of paper.

# 18

# ALTERNATIVE FUELS AND DESIGNS

## Think Safety

Hybrid and electric vehicles have a separate high voltage battery pack. To avoid shock, injury, burn, or death always follow manufacturer recommended precautions and warning labels.

## Objectives

After reading the *Auto Upkeep* text and completing the following activities, you will be able to:
- Identify differences in automotive design, depending on the fuel source.
- Compare and contrast advantages and disadvantages between vehicles types.
- Compare petrobased and biobased fuels.
- Calculate the payback period on an alternative fueled vehicle.

## Summary

The exponential growth of technology, crude oil prices, and consumer acceptance of new technology will drive the marketplace. From E85 ethanol burning to hybrids to 100% electric vehicles, changes are being made to make personal transportation more efficient and environmentally friendly. The two alternative energy technologies with the most promise for protecting the environment are solar and hydrogen fuel cells, however they are very cost prohibitive to mass-produce at this time. Continued technological advancements will help us work towards implementing better alternatives in the future.

## Web Exploring

### Key Terms/Internet Search Words
Visit www.google.com to investigate any of the following terms or phrases. Summarize your findings in a research paper.
- Bi-fuel Vehicles
- Biodiesel
- Electric Vehicles
- Ethanol
- Extended Range Electric Vehicles
- Flex-fuel Vehicles
- How Hybrid Vehicles Work
- Hybrid Electric Vehicles
- Hydrogen Fuel Cells
- Integrated Starter/Generator
- Mild Hybrids
- Natural Gas Vehicles
- Plug-in Hybrid Electric Vehicles
- Photovoltaic Cells
- Propane Vehicles
- Proton Exchange Membrane
- Regenerative Braking
- Solar Powered Vehicles
- Start-Stop Technology

## 📖 Study Questions - Alternative Fuels and Designs

1.  Why are alternative fueled vehicles necessary?

    _____

    _____

2.  What is biodiesel?

    _____

    _____

3.  What is a flex-fuel vehicle? How is a flex-fuel vehicle different from a bi-fuel vehicle?

    _____

    _____

4.  What is a hybrid vehicle?

    _____

    _____

5.  What is the benefit of a plug-in hybrid?

    _____

    _____

6.  Why are some hybrids classified as mild hybrids?

    _____

    _____

7.  Why are pure all-electric vehicles more practical for short range driving?

    _____

    _____

8.  How is hydrogen used in a fuel cell to power an electric motor?

    _____

    _____

9.  What is the difference between a renewable and non-renewable resource?

    _____

    _____

10. What factors are commonly considered when choosing alternatives?

    _____

    _____

Name _____ Class _____ Date __ / __ / __ Score _____

# Payback Period Activity

## Objective

Upon completion of this activity, you will be able to calculate payback period on an alternative fueled vehicle.

## NATEF Connections

None

## Tools

Computer with Internet access, calculator (or use the calculator on the computer)

## Supplies

None

## Cautions

Follow all procedures and safety guidelines specified by your instructor.

## Directions

Check off the boxes ❑ when completed. When you see a hand ✍ next to the task, write the information in the activity journal. If you have any questions during the duration of this activity, stop and ask the instructor for assistance.

## Note

Internet addresses were accurate at the time of printing. If the webmasters of these domains change links or home pages, please look for similar navigational items to complete this activity.

## Procedure

❑ Log on to your computer and open up an Internet browser.

❑ Type in the following Internet address - **www.kbb.com**.

❑ Click on *New Car Pricing*.

❑ Follow the instructions on the website to price out two similar vehicles. Choose one that is gasoline powered and one that an alternative design (hybrid, all-electric, or plug-in hybrid electric vehicle). For example, the 2013 Ford

Fusion was available with gasoline, hybrid, or plug-in hybrid electric powertrains.

✍ Note the manufacturer, make, model, year, and highway MPG of both vehicles. For this activity, use MSRP as the comparable price. Use the table in the activity journal to organize your data.

✍ Calculate the MSRP difference.

**Example**

| **$24,000** | **-** | **$18,000** | **=** | **$6,000** |
|:---:|:---:|:---:|:---:|:---:|
| Hybrid MSRP | | Conventional MSRP | | MSRP Difference |

✍ Note the current cost of fuel.

✍ Calculate the fuel cost per mile for each vehicle.

**Example**

| **$3.60** | **÷** | **30** | **=** | **$0.12** |
|:---:|:---:|:---:|:---:|:---:|
| Cost Per Gallon | | MPG Conventional | | Cost Per Mile |

| **$3.60** | **÷** | **60** | **=** | **$0.06** |
|:---:|:---:|:---:|:---:|:---:|
| Cost Per Gallon | | MPG Hybrid | | Cost Per Mile |

✍ Calculate the cost per mile difference.

**Example**

| **$0.12** | **-** | **$0.06** | **=** | **$0.06** |
|:---:|:---:|:---:|:---:|:---:|
| Conventional Cost Per Mile | | Hybrid Cost Per Mile | | Cost Per Mile Difference |

✍ Calculate the number of miles to break even.

**Example**

| **$6,000** | **÷** | **$0.06** | **=** | **100,000** |
|:---:|:---:|:---:|:---:|:---:|
| MSRP Difference | | Cost Per Mile Difference | | Miles to Break Even with MSRP Difference |

| **100,000** | **÷** | **15,000** | **=** | **6.7** |
|:---:|:---:|:---:|:---:|:---:|
| Miles | | Miles Per Year | | Years |

*Note: This number only takes into consideration the cost of fuel and no other maintenance costs or environmental benefits.*

❑ Log off your computer.

## ✎ Activity Journal

1. Organize data in the table below for conventional (gasoline) and hybrid powered vehicles.

| | Manufacturer | Make | Model | Year | Highway MPG | MSRP |
|---|---|---|---|---|---|---|
| Conventional | | | | | | |
| Hybrid | | | | | | |

2. What is the MSRP difference between the two vehicles?

_____

3. What is the current cost of fuel?

_____

4. What is the fuel cost per mile on each vehicle?

_____

5. What is the cost per mile difference between the two vehicles?

_____

6. How many miles are needed to break even?

_____

7. What other factors could increase or decrease the payback period?

_____

8. What are environmental benefits of choosing a hybrid?

_____

9. How would negotiating a better deal on the hybrid impact the payback period?

_____

10. How would tax credits or other incentives on the hybrid impact the payback period?

_____

11. What would happen to the payback period if fuel price doubled?

_____

# AUTOMOTIVE ACCESSORIES

## Think Safety

Do not use a remote starter to warm up your vehicle and leave it running in a garage. Carbon monoxide is an odorless, colorless, and poisonous gas.

## Objectives

After reading the *Auto Upkeep* text and completing the following activities, you will be able to:
- Identify automotive accessories.
- Explain different accessory functions.
- Estimate the cost of selected accessories for your vehicle.

## Summary

Vehicle accessories can be for function or aesthetics. Be sure the accessories you add are designed specifically for your vehicle.

## Web Exploring

### Key Terms/Internet Search Words

Visit **www.google.com** to investigate any of the following terms or phrases. Summarize your findings in a research paper.
- Automotive Accessories
- Automotive Smartphone Apps
- Automotive Gauges
- Bug Shields
- Car Alarms
- Car Entertainment Systems
- Custom Wheels
- Electric Vehicle Charging Dock
- Engine Heaters
- Global Positioning System (GPS)
- How to Tint Car Windows
- Navigation Systems
- OnStar
- Towing Supplies
- Trailer Brake Controller
- Trailer Hitch Classifications
- Trilateration in GPS
- Undercoating and Rustproofing
- Winch Accessories

**Name** _____  **Class** _____  **Date** ___ / ___ / ___  **Score** _____

## 📖 Study Questions - Automotive Accessories

1. What is the benefit to using floor mats?

   _____

   _____

2. When are engine heaters necessary?

   _____

   _____

3. What is an electronic key fob?

   _____

   _____

4. What is a GPS receiver?

   _____

   _____

5. What is OnStar?

   _____

   _____

6. When are wheel lock lug nuts commonly used?

   _____

   _____

7. Why are towing mirrors sometimes necessary?

   _____

   _____

8. What is a trailer brake controller?

   _____

   _____

9. How are trailer hitches classified?

   _____

   _____

10. Why is it important to use trailer safety chains?

   _____

   _____

| Name | Class | Date / / | Score |
| --- | --- | --- | --- |

# Automotive Accessories Activity

## Objective

Upon completion of this activity, you will be able to estimate the cost of accessories for a vehicle.

## NATEF Connections

None

## Tools

Computer with Internet access, calculator (or use the calculator on the computer)

## Supplies

None

## Cautions

Follow all procedures and safety guidelines specified by your instructor.

## Directions

Check off the boxes ❑ when completed. When you see a hand ✍ next to the task, write the information in the activity journal. If you have any questions during the duration of this activity, stop and ask the instructor for assistance.

## Note

Internet addresses were accurate at the time of printing. If the webmasters of these domains change links or home pages, please look for similar navigational items to complete this activity.

## Procedure

❑ Identify a vehicle of your choice.

✍ Note the manufacturer, make, model, and year.

✍ Make a list of accessories that you would like to add to the vehicle. Examples include anything from mud guards to car covers to rear spoilers to a trailer hitch.

❑ Log on to your computer and open up an Internet browser.

❑ Type in the following Internet address - www.autoanything.com.

*Screen Capture from* www.autoanything.com

✍ Use this Internet site to estimate the cost of the accessories. If you choose accessories that need professional installation or finishing (e.g., parts that need to be painted by a body shop), call local service centers for estimates.

❑ Use a search engine (e.g., www.google.com) to find other suppliers of automotive accessories.

*Screen Capture from* www.google.com

❑ Compare prices from multiple sources.

✍ Organize your information in the activity journal table or use a spreadsheet program such as Microsoft Excel.

❑ Log off your computer.

## ✍ Activity Journal

1. What is the manufacturer, make, model, and year of your vehicle?

   _____

2. List accessories and estimated cost (including installation or finishing if needed). Find multiple sources.

| Accessory Name | Estimate Cost Source 1 | Estimate Cost Source 2 | Estimate Cost Source 3 |
|---|---|---|---|
|  |  |  |  |
|  |  |  |  |
|  |  |  |  |
|  |  |  |  |
|  |  |  |  |
|  |  |  |  |
|  |  |  |  |
|  |  |  |  |
|  |  |  |  |

3. What types of accessories did you choose and why?

   _____

4. What factors contribute to the overall cost of adding accessories?

   _____

5. Were all the accessories that you wanted available for your vehicle? If not, explain why.

   _____

6. How much did the price of a similar accessory vary from one vendor to another?

   _____

# COMMON PROBLEMS AND ROADSIDE EMERGENCIES

## Think Safety

When performing roadside emergencies, use caution. If your vehicle is in a hazardous location call a tow truck for emergency assistance.

## Objectives

After reading the *Auto Upkeep* text and completing the following activities, you will be able to:

- Identify common automobile problems.
- Analyze basic automotive problems and make a decision about a solution.
- Replace a headlight.
- Clean a battery.
- Replace wiper blades.
- Prepare for a road trip.
- Prepare for roadside emergencies.
- Jump-start a vehicle safely.
- Change a flat tire.

## Summary

Common problems and roadside emergencies can range from minor mechanical issues to serious accidents. The key to getting through these often difficult and stressful situations is to be prepared and stay calm. Analyze the situation and find an appropriate solution. Keep in mind that vehicles can be replaced. Human safety needs to be the number one priority.

## Web Exploring

### Key Terms/Internet Search Words

Visit www.google.com to investigate any of the following terms or phrases. Summarize your findings in a research paper.

- Automotive Emergency Roadside Kit
- Automotive Winter Survival Kit
- Car Accident Check List
- Check Engine Light
- Cleaning Battery Cables
- Diagnostic Trouble Code Scanner
- Finding a Vehicle Fluid Leak
- How to Change a Flat Tire
- How to Jump-Start a Battery
- Malfunction Indicator Lights
- OBD II
- Replacing a Headlight
- Replacing a Serpentine Belt
- Replacing Wiper Blades
- Road Trip Checklist
- Technical Service Bulletin (TSB)
- Temporary Spare Tire Speed
- Tire Chains
- TPMS Safe Liquid Tire Spray

Name _____   Class _____   Date ___ / ___ / ___   Score _____

## 📚 Study Questions - Common Problems and Roadside Emergencies

1. What is OBD and how can it be helpful?

   _____

   _____

2. What does it mean if your vehicle's check engine light comes on?

   _____

   _____

3. What does black smoke from the tailpipe usually indicate?

   _____

   _____

4. What does white smoke from the tailpipe usually indicate?

   _____

   _____

5. What might be the problem if you smell a rotten egg/sulfur odor?

   _____

   _____

6. How can you find a leak in a tire?

   _____

   _____

7. What should you do if you get in a car accident?

   _____

   _____

8. What is the proper procedure to hook up jumper cables?

   _____

   _____

9. Why shouldn't you drive your vehicle if the engine's drive belt breaks?

   _____

   _____

10. What types of items are handy to have in an emergency roadside kit?

   _____

   _____

| Name | Class | Date / / | Score |
|---|---|---|---|

# Changing a Flat Tire Activity

## Objective

Upon completion of this activity, you will be able to safely change a spare tire. The purpose of this lab is to simulate changing a flat tire on the side of the road.

## NATEF Connections

**Suspension and Steering – General**
- Research applicable vehicle and service information, vehicle service history, service precautions, and technical service bulletins.

**Suspension and Steering – Wheels and Tires**
- Inspect tire condition; identify tire wear patterns; check for correct size and application (load and speed ratings) and adjust air pressure; determine necessary action.

## Tools

Torque wrench, wheel chocks, tools in the vehicle (e.g., jack, lug wrench), work gloves

## Supplies

Shop rags, anti-seize compound

## Cautions

Watch out for steel cords poking out of a blown out or worn tire. Follow all procedures and safety guidelines specified by your instructor.

## Directions

Check off the boxes ❑ when completed. When you see a hand ✍ next to the task, write the information in the activity journal. If you have any questions during the duration of this activity, stop and ask the instructor for assistance.

## Pre-Service

❑ Use the vehicle's maintenance records, the owner's manual, a service manual, and the Internet to research applicable vehicle and service information, vehicle service history, service precautions, and technical service bulletins.

❑ Park where the ground is flat, solid, and level.
❑ Apply the parking brake.
❑ Remove the key from the ignition. *Warning: On a push button keyless ignition refer to the owner's manual for specific safety procedures to prevent an unintended engine startup.*
❑ Put on your safety glasses.
❑ Check tires for the correct size and application (load and speed ratings).

## Procedure

❑ Read the owner's manual to find the location of the spare tire, jack, lug wrench, and jacking location.
❑ Remove the jack, lug wrench, and spare tire from vehicle.
❑ Chock at least one wheel at the opposite end of the vehicle.

❑ If your wheel has a wheel cover, remove it. Read the owner's manual if you can't determine how it comes off.
❑ Using the lug wrench provided with the vehicle or a 4-way lug wrench, loosen lug nuts about 1/2 turn counterclockwise.

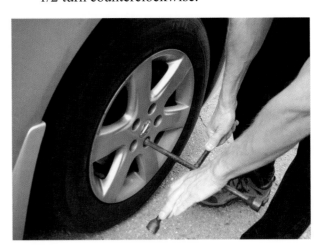

❑ Read the owner's manual to determine where to place the jack under the vehicle. Scissor and bottle jacks are less stable than large floor jacks - so make sure you put the jack where the manufacturer recommends.

❑ Turn the handle to lift the vehicle until the flat tire is off the ground.

❑ Remove the lug nuts.
❑ Put on work gloves if the tires are excessively worn or have cords showing.
❑ Using your legs (not your back), remove the flat tire (watch out for dangerous cords that might be sticking out from a blown tire).
❑ Lay the flat tire on the ground under the vehicle. If the jack failed, it could help to keep the vehicle from crushing you.

❑ Carefully lift the spare tire into place.
❑ Start all lug nuts by hand (cone end towards wheel) and snug with the lug wrench using a star pattern. Move the flat tire out from under the vehicle.
❑ Slowly lower the vehicle just until the tire touches the ground.
❑ Finish tightening up the spare with a lug wrench. Completely lower the vehicle.
❑ If you are in a school laboratory, have the instructor check the spare.
❑ If you were completing this activity for practice, replace your original tire by repeating the procedure. Use a torque wrench to correctly torque the original wheel's lug nuts.
❑ Check the tire pressure in all the tires, including your vehicle's spare tire. Tire pressure information is found on the tire placard located on the driver's door jamb. Adjust as necessary.

## Clean Up
❑ Put the spare, jack, and lug wrench neatly back into the vehicle.
❑ Wash your hands thoroughly.

## ✍ Activity Journal

1. Where is the spare tire located on your vehicle?

_____

2. Is the spare tire different than the rest of your vehicle's tires?

_____

3. What are some precautions you should take when lifting a tire?

_____

4. Why did you chock at least one tire on the opposite end of the vehicle while changing a flat tire?

_____

5. What is the recommended torque specification for your vehicle's wheels?

_____

| Name | Class | Date / / | Score |
|------|-------|----------|-------|

# Jump-Starting Activity

## Objective

Upon completion of this activity, you will be able to safely jump-start a vehicle.

## NATEF Connections

**Electrical/Electronic Systems – General**

- Research applicable vehicle and service information, vehicle service history, service precautions, and technical service bulletins.

**Electrical/Electronic Systems – Battery Service**

- Jump-start vehicle using jumper cables and a booster battery or an auxiliary power supply.

## Tools

Safety goggles, chemical resistant gloves, fender cover, jumper cables

## Supplies

Shop rags

## Cautions

Wear safety goggles while performing this activity. Know where the eyewash station is and how to use it. Do not allow flame or sparks near battery gases. Battery gases can explode. Make sure you follow the correct procedure for hooking up the cables. Never try to jump-start a frozen battery. Keep your hands away from moving engine components. Follow all procedures and safety guidelines specified by your instructor.

## Directions

Check off the boxes ❑ when completed. When you see a hand ✍ next to the task, write the information in the activity journal. If you have any questions during the duration of this activity, stop and ask the instructor for assistance.

## Pre-Service

❑ Use the vehicle's maintenance records, the owner's manual, a service manual, and the Internet to research applicable vehicle and service information, vehicle service history, service precautions, and technical service bulletins.

❑ Remove rings and watch.

❑ Put on your safety goggles.

## Procedure

❑ Maneuver the booster vehicle near the vehicle with the discharged battery. Do not let the two vehicles touch.

❑ Turn off the ignition switch, lights, and accessories in both vehicles. Place both vehicles in Park (automatic transmission) or Neutral (manual transmission) and engage the parking brake.

❑ Pop open the hood on each vehicle.

❑ Use a fender cover to protect the vehicle's finish.

❑ Complete a visual inspection on the battery. Check for loose battery cables, corroded terminals, deposits on connections, cracks or leaks in the case, and frayed or broken cables. Correct problems if necessary.

❑ Identify the positive (+) and negative (-) posts on both batteries. Do not assume the color of the battery cable reflects if the post is positive (+) or negative (-). Look for the positive (+) or negative (-) on each battery.

❑ You should wear chemical resistant gloves anytime you are working around electrolyte. Open the vent caps, if possible, to check the electrolyte level. The fluid in each cell should be even with the bottom of the filler ring. *Note: Do not remove vent caps on sealed batteries.*

❏ If the electrolyte is low, add distilled water. Do not overfill. Once the fluid level has been checked, replace the vent caps. *Warning: Never try to jump-start a battery with low electrolyte or that is frozen.*

❏ Make sure the battery cables are tight on the terminals and vent caps are securely in place.

❏ Connect the positive jumper cable clamp (usually red) to the positive (+) terminal on the discharged battery. *Warning: Do not allow jumper cable ends to touch any other part of the vehicle or each other.* Some vehicles have junction blocks to connect the positive cable to instead of connecting directly to the battery. Always check the owner's manual before proceeding.

❏ Connect the other positive jumper cable clamp to the positive (+) terminal of the booster vehicle.

❏ Connect the negative jumper cable clamp (usually black) to the negative (-) terminal of the booster vehicle.

❏ Put shop rags over both batteries.

❏ Connect the other negative jumper cable clamp to a clean metal part of the discharged vehicle's engine block or frame. Position the clamp as far away from the battery as possible. This connection will usually spark when clamped. This spark indicates a completed circuit. *Warning: Do not make this connection directly to the battery. A spark near the battery could result in an explosion.*

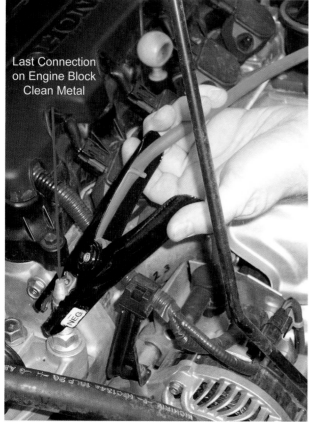

Last Connection on Engine Block Clean Metal

❏ Start the engine on the booster vehicle and rev the engine slightly. Allow the battery to charge for 15 minutes.

❏ Turn off all accessories (e.g., heater, lights). Anyone near should stand clear of the discharged vehicle while you attempt to start.

❏ Do not crank the engine for more than 20 seconds at a time. Starter damage could result.

❏ Allow starter to cool for a minimum of 2 minutes between cranking sessions.

❏ If the discharged vehicle's battery turns over very slow, allow the battery to charge for an additional 15 minutes.

❏ If the engine starts, proceed with the following.

❏ Disconnect the negative (-) jumper cable from the previously discharged vehicle. *Warning: Do not allow jumper cable ends to touch any other part of the vehicle or each other.*

❏ Disconnect the negative (-) jumper cable from the booster vehicle.

❏ Disconnect the positive (+) jumper cable from the booster vehicle.

❏ Disconnect the positive (+) jumper cable from the previously discharged vehicle.

❏ Neatly put away jumper cables for future use.

❏ Allow previously discharged vehicle to idle for 15 to 30 minutes.

❏ Identify what (e.g., lights being left on) caused the battery to go dead on the previously discharged vehicle.

❏ Shut off vehicle and try to restart.

❏ If battery continues to be discharged, test the battery and alternator.

## Clean Up

❏ Clean and put away all tools and supplies.

❏ Wash your hands thoroughly.

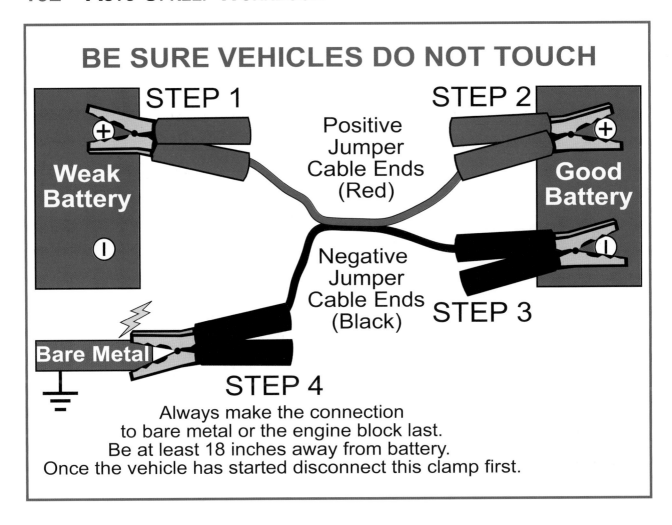

# BE SURE VEHICLES DO NOT TOUCH

**STEP 1**

**STEP 2**

Positive
Jumper
Cable Ends
(Red)

**Weak
Battery**

**Good
Battery**

Negative
Jumper
Cable Ends
(Black)

**STEP 3**

**Bare Metal**

**STEP 4**

Always make the connection
to bare metal or the engine block last.
Be at least 18 inches away from battery.
Once the vehicle has started disconnect this clamp first.

## ✍ Activity Journal

1. What caused the disabled vehicle's battery to be discharged?

_____

2. Why is it important to follow the correct cable hook-up procedure when jump-starting a battery?

_____

3. What and where should the last connection be made when jump-starting a battery?

_____

4. Why do you think you should turn off all of the vehicle's accessories?

_____

5. Why shouldn't you crank the disabled vehicle's engine for more than 20 seconds?

_____

| Name | Class | Date | / / | Score |
| --- | --- | --- | --- | --- |

# Lighting Activity

## Objective

Upon completion of this activity, you will be able to replace various lights on a vehicle.

## NATEF Connections

**Electrical/Electronic Systems – General**
- Research applicable vehicle and service information, vehicle service history, service precautions, and technical service bulletins.

**Electrical/Electronic Systems – Lighting System**
- Inspect interior and exterior lamps and sockets including headlights and auxiliary lights (fog lights/driving lights); replace as needed.

## Tools

Safety glasses, basic hand tools, VOM (volt-ohm meter/multimeter), Phillips screwdriver, flat-head screwdriver, nut drivers, torx screwdrivers

## Supplies

Shop rags, dielectric grease, replacement lights

## Cautions

If your vehicle has composite style headlights, do not touch the bulbs. If you accidentally touch the bulb, clean it off with rubbing alcohol. Follow all procedures and safety guidelines specified by your instructor.

## Directions

Check off the boxes ❑ when completed. When you see a hand ✍ next to the task, write the information in the activity journal. If you have any questions during the duration of this activity, stop and ask the instructor for assistance. Use the following list as a guide. Not all vehicles will have all the lights listed.

## Notes

If any of the lights you check need replacing, a manual specific to the vehicle should have replacement procedures. When removing bulbs try not to force plastic parts, some are fragile and can break easily. If the bulb still doesn't light after replacing the bulb, test the socket for voltage with a light tester or VOM (volt-ohm meter). When replacing bulbs, use dielectric grease in the sockets/connectors to inhibit corrosion.

## Pre-Service

❑ Use the vehicle's maintenance records, the owner's manual, a service manual, and the Internet to research applicable vehicle and service information, vehicle service history, service precautions, and technical service bulletins.

❑ Apply the parking brake.

❑ Remove the key from the ignition. *Warning: On a push button keyless ignition refer to the owner's manual for specific safety procedures to prevent an unintended engine startup.*

❑ Put on your safety glasses.

❑ Pop open the hood.

❑ Use a fender cover to protect the vehicle's finish.

## Procedure 1- Headlight Bulb

❑ Look behind the headlight assembly. You should only have to turn the bulb socket or a retainer clip that holds the bulb in place a quarter turn.

Back of Bulb

Back of Headlight Assembly

Wiring Harness

❑ After the retainer clip is removed or bulb assembly is turned, carefully pull on the bulb. It may seem a little snug. It has a rubber O-ring gasket that keeps it tight.

❑ Once the bulb is removed, lift up on the clips that hold the wiring harness to release the bulb.

❑ Remove and replace the bulb. Do not touch the glass part of the new bulb. It will shorten the life.

❑ Reverse the procedure to install the new bulb and reconnect the wiring harness assembly.

❑ Once the new bulb is installed be sure to test the headlights.

## ✍ Activity Journal

1. List any bulbs that did not work.

_____

2. Why is it important to keep all the lights working on a vehicle?

_____

3. Did your vehicle have any lights not listed in the activity?

_____

4. Why do you think you shouldn't touch composite light bulbs?

_____

5. If you test the socket for voltage, how many volts should be present?

_____

6. Why do you think some bulbs have two wires/filaments in them?

_____

## Procedure 2 - Light Check

✍ Test the following lights and note in the activity journal any lights that do not work.

❑ Headlights - high and low beam.
❑ Front side markers - come on with headlights.
❑ Rear side markers - come on with headlights.
❑ Taillights - come on with headlights.
❑ License plate light - comes on with headlights.
❑ Brake lights - you need to press the brake pedal.
❑ High mount brake light (also known as the 3rd brake light) - you need to press the brake pedal.
❑ Turn key to on position, but do not start engine.
❑ Front turn signals.
❑ Rear turn signals.
❑ Cornering lights - a bright light that comes on that helps to see around a corner. The corresponding turn signal light needs to be on.
❑ Backup lights - key is on, gear in reverse, parking brake on, but engine is not running.
❑ Fog lights.
❑ Inside lights - glove box, storage box, instrument cluster, shift indicator, map.
❑ Engine and trunk compartment lights.
❑ Other lights.

## Clean Up

❑ Wash your hands thoroughly.

Name _____ Class _____ Date __/__/__ Score _____

# Replacing Wipers Activity

## Objective

Upon completion of this activity, you will be able to replace wiper blades on a vehicle.

## NATEF Connections

**Electrical/Electronic Systems – General**

- Research applicable vehicle and service information, vehicle service history, service precautions, and technical service bulletins.

## Tools

Safety glasses, flat-head screwdriver, basic hand tools

## Supplies

New wiper blades

## Cautions

After removing the wiper blade from the wiper arm, do not allow the wiper arm to snap back and hit the windshield. This forceful action could cause the windshield to crack or chip. Follow all procedures and safety guidelines specified by your instructor.

## Directions

Check off the boxes ❑ when completed. When you see a hand ✍ next to the task, write the information in the activity journal. If you have any questions during the duration of this activity, stop and ask the instructor for assistance. Use the following as a guide. Read the instructions that accompany the replacement wiper blades.

## Notes

It is best to replace wipers in pairs and the whole blade, not just the rubber "refill" component. If the metal pivoting points and spring mechanisms have worn out, the blade will apply uneven pressure across the windshield. Skipping, chattering, or streaking wipers can cause a hazardous driving condition.

## Pre-Service

❑ Use the vehicle's maintenance records, the owner's manual, a service manual, and the Internet to research applicable vehicle and service information, vehicle service history, service precautions, and technical service bulletins.

❑ Apply the parking brake.

❑ Remove the key from the ignition. *Warning: On a push button keyless ignition refer to the owner's manual for specific safety procedures to prevent an unintended engine startup.*

❑ Put on your safety glasses.

❑ The following are the three most common types of wiper arm connectors.

## Procedure 1 - Hook Style

❑ Compare the new wiper to the old wiper to ensure you have the correct length.

❑ Read the instructions that accompany the replacement wiper blade.

❑ Raise the wiper blade assembly up from the windshield and locate the lock assembly.

❑ Remove any covers if applicable. A wiper blade may have a little cover over the blade lock assembly. If yours has a cover, push the cover tabs to release the cover.

❑ Grip the blade firmly with your fingers where the wiper arm connects to the wiper blade.

❑ Press the lock tab to release the wiper blade from the wiper arm.

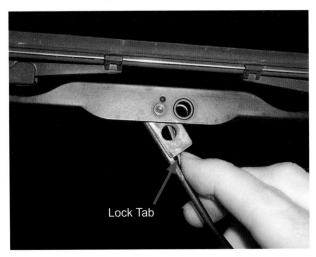

Lock Tab

❑ Move the blade assembly toward the wiper arm to release the wiper arm hook.

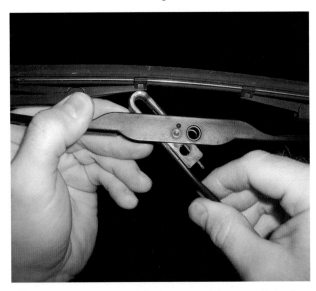

❑ Remove the old blade assembly once it is free from the wiper arm hook.

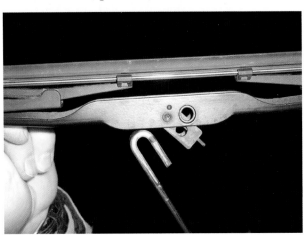

❑ Install the new wiper blade. Position the wiper arm hook in front of the groove on the wiper blade. Slide the wiper blade into the wiper arm by pushing the blade away from the wiper arm hook. You should here a clicking sound when it locks into place.

❑ Repeat the above steps for other wipers on the vehicle. Remember, some vehicles also have rear wipers.

## Procedure 2 - Straight/Bayonet Connector Style

❑ Compare the new wiper to the old wiper to ensure you have the correct length.

❑ Read the instructions that accompany the replacement wiper blade.

❑ Raise the wiper blade assembly up from the windshield and locate the lock assembly.

❑ Grip the blade firmly with your fingers.

❑ Detach the blade by pressing a locking latch. Some types require little screws to be removed.

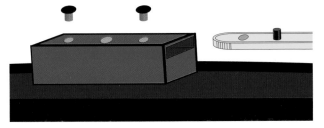

❑ Move the blade assembly away from the wiper arm to remove the old blade assembly.

❑ Install the new wiper blade. Reverse the procedure to reinstall, sliding the wiper blade toward the wiper arm. You should here a clicking sound when it locks into place. ***Note: If the bayonet connector used two little screws and lock washers, be careful not to drop them when reinstalling.***

❑ Repeat the above steps for other wipers on the vehicle. Remember, some vehicles also have rear wipers.

## Procedure 3 - Pin/Side Lock Style

- ❑ Compare the new wiper to the old wiper to ensure you have the correct length.
- ❑ Read the instructions that accompany the replacement wiper blade.
- ❑ Raise the wiper blade assembly up from the windshield and locate the lock assembly.
- ❑ Grip the blade firmly with your fingers.
- ❑ Locate the locking button. Inspect the attachment to determine how to remove the wiper blade. Some pin/side lock wipers have a slot to insert a small screwdriver to release the spring tension or a spring lock that requires being pulled up. Other styles require flexing the blade away from the windshield at the pivoting points to release spring tension.

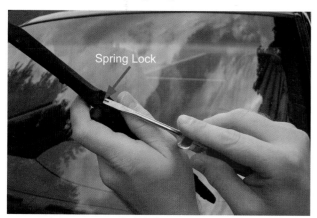

- ❑ Remove the old blade assembly once it is free from the wiper arm pin.

- ❑ Install the new wiper blade. Usually you only need to push the wiper onto the pin. You should here a clicking sound when it locks into place.
- ❑ Repeat the above steps for other wipers on the vehicle. Remember, some vehicles also have rear wipers.

## Procedure 4 - Washer Fluid

- ❑ Check the windshield washer fluid reservoir.

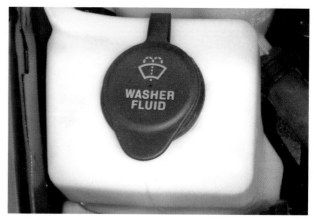

- ❑ Add fluid as needed and test the wipers.
- ❑ Some rear wipers have a separate reservoir in the rear of the vehicle.

## Clean Up

- ❑ Clean and put away all tools and supplies.
- ❑ Wash your hands thoroughly.

✍ **Activity Journal**

1.  Why is it important to replace the wipers when they are worn?

    _____

2.  What type of wiper blade arms (hook, straight/bayonet, or pin/side lock) did your vehicle have?

    _____

3.  What parts of the wipers wear out?

    _____

4.  Were the instructions that accompanied the wipers helpful? Why or why not?

    _____

5.  What difficulties did you encounter when replacing the wipers?

    _____

## On-Board Diagnostics Activity

### Objective

Upon completion of this activity, you will be able to safely retrieve diagnostic trouble codes (DTCs) from an OBD II system using a basic scan tool.

### NATEF Connections

**Engine Performance – General**

- Research applicable vehicle and service information, vehicle service history, service precautions, and technical service bulletins.

**Engine Performance – Computerized Engine Controls**

- Retrieve and record diagnostic trouble codes, OBD monitor status, and freeze frame data; clear codes when applicable.
- Describe the importance of operating all OBD II monitors for repair verification.

### Tools

Safety glasses, OBD II scan tool, computer with Internet access

### Supplies

None

### Cautions

Refer to the OBD II scan tool manual for specific test procedures. Follow all procedures and safety guidelines specified by your instructor.

### Directions

Check off the boxes ❑ when completed. When you see a hand ✍ next to the task, write the information in the activity journal. If you have any questions during the duration of this activity, stop and ask the instructor for assistance. Use the following as a guide.

### Notes

Use a vehicle that has a check engine or service engine soon light illuminated. Your instructor may set a code on a shop vehicle for you to test. *Note: The DTC is a starting point for identifying a problem. Do not rely solely on the DTC to replace parts. The issue may be any component or fault within that system or circuit that is triggering the DTC. It could be something as simple as a loose electrical connection.* Refer to a service manual for in-depth diagnostic procedures.

### Pre-Service

- ❑ Use the vehicle's maintenance records, the owner's manual, a service manual, and the Internet to research applicable vehicle and service information, vehicle service history, service precautions, and technical service bulletins.
- ❑ Apply the parking brake.
- ❑ Put on your safety glasses.
- ❑ Pop open the hood.
- ❑ The following is a general procedure to retrieve OBD II diagnostic trouble codes (DTCs). Always follow the procedures as specified with the scan tool manufacturer.

### Procedure

- ❑ Locate the Vehicle Emission Control Information label. Ensure that the vehicle being tested is OBD II certified.

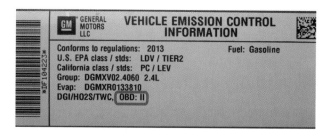

- ❑ Locate the OBD II 16 pin Data Link Connector (DLC). OBD II requires that the DLC be accessible from the driver's seat. This plug will allow the scan tool to communicate with the Powertrain Control Module (PCM).

❑ Reconfirm that the ignition key is OFF. If the vehicle has a keyless ignition system, follow the specific instructions from the vehicle manufacturer and scan tool.

❑ Connect the scan tool using the provided cable connector. The connector is designed to fit in the DLC only one way.

Data Link Connector

❑ Once the cable is plugged in, most scan tools will turn on automatically.

❑ Follow the instructions on the display screen.

❑ Turn the ignition key on, but do not start the engine.

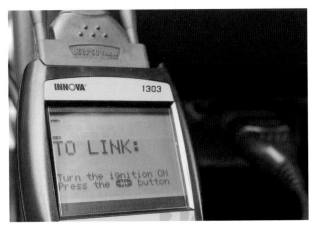

❑ Follow the instructions on the scan tool to display the DTCs and monitor status.

❑ Follow the scan tool instructions to access the freeze frame data retrieved from the PCM.

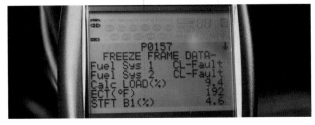

✍ Note the DTCs in the activity journal.

❑ Ask your instructor if you should erase the DTCs using the scan tool. If authorized to erase the DTCs, follow the instructions accompanied with the scan tool. ***Note: Erasing a DTC does not fix the problem.***

❑ Follow the instructions on the scan tool to determine when to turn off the ignition key and unplug the tool.

❑ Use a service manual or the Internet to decode the DTC.

❑ For sites listing generic OBD II DTCs, visit www.3rd.AutoUpkeep.com/resources/ch20.

## Clean Up

❑ Put away the scan tool.

❑ Wash your hands thoroughly.

## ✍ Activity Journal

1. Why isn't it recommended just to replace a part solely on a DTC?

2. Where was the DLC located on the test vehicle?

3. List the DTCs that the scan tool retrieved.

4. What did the DTCs signify? What should be your next course of action?

# SAFETY RULES

**Personal Protection**

- Safety glasses are not optional. Wear them at all times when working on a vehicle. *Warning: Ordinary prescription glasses are not safety glasses.* You can purchase approved prescription safety glasses with sideshields.

- Do not have bare feet or wear open-toed sandals. Wear shoes that protect your feet.

- Loud noises can damage your hearing, so wear ear protection (e.g., earplugs).

- Keep your tools and hands free of grease and oil. Wearing mechanic gloves is smart, but do not wear gloves when moving parts are present. *Warning: Keep your hands away from moving parts.* Never use your hands to stop components that are moving.

- Remove your rings, watch, and other jewelry.

- If you have long hair, tie it back. It could get caught in moving parts.

- Do not wear loose or baggy clothing that could get caught in moving parts.

- Do not work on a hot engine.

- Do not touch spark plug wires while the engine is running. Tens of thousands of volts are present.

- Never put your hands on or near the cooling fan. Many fans are electric and can start at anytime, even if the ignition is off.

- Never open a hot radiator cap.

- Use proper lifting procedures to avoid injury. Use your legs, not your back.

**Shop/Lab Procedures**

- Know the location and operational procedures of fire extinguishers, first-aid kits, eyewash stations, and a telephone. Dial 911 for emergencies.

- Someone must be sitting in the driver's seat whenever a vehicle is started and/or running.

- The exhaust system of a running engine must be connected to a ventilation system if the vehicle is in an enclosed location such as a garage. *Warning: Carbon monoxide is a colorless, odorless, and poisonous gas. Proper ventilation is required.*

- Always engage the parking brake to prevent the vehicle from moving.

- Put oily rags in an approved can for combustible materials.

- Always clean up spilled oil and grease off the floor. Sawdust, kitty litter, and oil dry work well for this.

- Never pour chemicals, solvents, antifreeze, or oil down the sanitary drain. Put them in their proper containers to be recycled.

- Use an approved safety cabinet for flammable materials.

**Equipment Safety**

- Stand creepers up when not in use.

- Place floor jack handles in the up position when not being used.

- If a vehicle is off the ground (except when on an automotive lift) it must be supported by jack stands.

- Use the proper tool for each job.

- Do not put tools on top of a vehicle's battery. Accidentally touching both terminals will cause a spark, which could lead to an explosion.

Name _____    Class _____

# ACTIVITY COMPLETION RECORD

| | Activity | Date | Points | Grade |
|---|---|---|---|---|
| **Chapter 1** | Car Identification Activity | | | |
| **Chapter 2** | Buying a New Automobile Activity | | | |
| | Buying a Used Automobile Activity | | | |
| **Chapter 3** | Automotive Expenses Activity | | | |
| **Chapter 4** | Repair Facilities Activity | | | |
| **Chapter 5** | Automotive Safety Activity | | | |
| **Chapter 6** | Basic Tools Activity | | | |
| **Chapter 7** | Interior Cleaning Activity | | | |
| | Exterior Cleaning Activity | | | |
| | Waxing Activity | | | |
| **Chapter 8** | Fluid Level Check Activity | | | |
| **Chapter 9** | Battery Activity | | | |
| | Charging Activity | | | |
| | Starting Activity | | | |
| **Chapter 10** | Oil and Filter Change Activity | | | |
| **Chapter 11** | Fuel System Activity | | | |
| **Chapter 12** | Air Conditioning Activity | | | |
| | Cabin Air Filter Activity | | | |
| | Cooling System Activity | | | |
| **Chapter 13** | Ignition System Activity | | | |
| **Chapter 14** | Suspension and Steering Activity | | | |
| | Tire Inspection and Rotation Activity | | | |
| **Chapter 15** | Brake Inspection Activity | | | |
| **Chapter 16** | Drivetrain Activity | | | |
| **Chapter 17** | Exhaust and Emission Activity | | | |
| **Chapter 18** | Payback Period Activity | | | |
| **Chapter 19** | Automotive Accessories Activity | | | |
| **Chapter 20** | Changing a Flat Tire Activity | | | |
| | Jump-Starting Activity | | | |
| | Lighting Activity | | | |
| | Replacing Wipers Activity | | | |
| | On-Board Diagnostics Activity | | | |

| | Total Points | Overall Grade |
|---|---|---|
| | | |

| Name | | | | | Class | | pts./154 | = | GPA |

**Score/Mastery**

| A | B | C | D | F |
|---|---|---|---|---|
| Master | Proficient | Apprentice | Novice | No Attempt |

**Grade Scale**

| 4.0 = A | 3.0 = B | 2.0 = C | 1.0 = D |
|---|---|---|---|
| 3.7 = A- | 2.7 = B- | 1.7 = C- | 0.7 = D- |
| 3.3 = B+ | 2.3 = C+ | 1.3 = D+ | 0 = F |

| 4 | 3 | 2 | 1 | 0 | Task/Skill | Domain | Level |
|---|---|---|---|---|---|---|---|
| | | | | | **Chapter 1. Introduction and How Cars Work** | | |
| | | | | | Locate and identify the Vehicle Identification Number (VIN). | Psychomotor | Imitation |
| | | | | | Identify the engine size and configuration. | Cognitive | Knowledge |
| | | | | | Explain the difference between manufacturer, make, and model. | Cognitive | Comprehension |
| | | | | | Classify vehicle types. | Cognitive | Analysis |
| | | | | | Distinguish operational differences between spark ignition and compression ignition engines. | Cognitive | Analysis |
| | | | | | Relate pollutants to gasoline and diesel engines. | Cognitive | Synthesis |
| | | | | | Propose and discuss possible future vehicle designs. | Affective | Valuing |
| | | | | | Practice identifying automobiles by make, model, year, and type. | Psychomotor | Manipulation |
| | | | | | **Chapter 2. Buying an Automobile** | | |
| | | | | | Differentiate between transportation needs and wants. | Cognitive | Analysis |
| | | | | | Develop a budget. | Cognitive | Application |
| | | | | | Identify the steps in purchasing an automobile. | Cognitive | Knowledge |
| | | | | | Compare and contrast different places to purchase an automobile. | Cognitive | Evaluation |
| | | | | | Calculate a reasonable offer for a vehicle. | Cognitive | Application |
| | | | | | Advocate for safety features in an automobile. | Affective | Characterization |
| | | | | | Carry out research on vehicles using available resources. | Psychomotor | Imitation |
| | | | | | **Chapter 3. Automotive Expenses** | | |
| | | | | | Explain how car payments are calculated. | Cognitive | Synthesis |
| | | | | | Describe insurance coverage levels. | Cognitive | Evaluation |
| | | | | | Propose when it may be beneficial to have additional insurance. | Affective | Valuing |
| | | | | | Calculate monthly expenses on a given vehicle. | Cognitive | Application |
| | | | | | Point out differences between routine maintenance and unexpected repairs. | Cognitive | Analysis |
| | | | | | **Chapter 4. Repair Facilities** | | |
| | | | | | Describe how technicians can become certified. | Cognitive | Knowledge |
| | | | | | Communicate effectively with a technician or service writer. | Affective | Responding |
| | | | | | Interpret a repair invoice. | Cognitive | Evaluation |
| | | | | | Conduct research to locate a quality repair facility. | Psychomotor | Manipulation |
| | | | | | Characterize business ethics. | Affective | Characterization |
| | | | | | Summarize differences between warranty types. | Cognitive | Evaluate |
| | | | | | **Chapter 5. Safety Around the Automobile** | | |
| | | | | | Demonstrate safe work practices. | Psychomotor | Precision |
| | | | | | Identify types of fires and explain what types of fire extinguishers to use. | Cognitive | Synthesis |
| | | | | | Evaluate when it is appropriate to wear specific personal protection equipment. | Cognitive | Evaluation |
| | | | | | Describe the purpose of OSHA. | Cognitive | Knowledge |
| | | | | | Use different types of automotive lifts to safely support a vehicle. | Psychomotor | Precision |
| | | | | | Operate a jack and use jack stands to safely support a vehicle. | Psychomotor | Precision |
| | | | | | Judge when it is safe to work on a vehicle with airbag systems. | Affective | Organization |

| 4 | 3 | 2 | 1 | 0 | Task/Skill | Domain | Level |
|---|---|---|---|---|---|---|---|
| | | | | | **Chapter 6. Basic Tools** | | |
| | | | | | Recognize basic hand tools. | Cognitive | Comprehension |
| | | | | | Select the correct tool for the job. | Cognitive | Evaluation |
| | | | | | Use tools properly. | Psychomotor | Precision |
| | | | | | Utilize print and online service manuals. | Psychomotor | Precision |
| | | | | | Classify socket types. | Cognitive | Analysis |
| | | | | | Identify different types of wrenches. | Cognitive | Analysis |
| | | | | | Identify different types of pliers. | Cognitive | Analysis |
| | | | | | List the different types of screwdriver tips. | Cognitive | Knowledge |
| | | | | | Decide when it is justified to invest in a specialty tool. | Affective | Organization |
| | | | | | Categorize units into the metric or English system. | Cognitive | Synthesis |
| | | | | | **Chapter 7. Auto Care and Cleaning** | | |
| | | | | | Identify different automotive finishes. | Cognitive | Knowledge |
| | | | | | Explain the importance of interior and exterior cleaning. | Cognitive | Evaluation |
| | | | | | Clean a vehicle inside and out. | Psychomotor | Articulation |
| | | | | | Wax a vehicle. | Psychomotor | Manipulation |
| | | | | | Differentiate between polishing and waxing. | Cognitive | Synthesis |
| | | | | | Describe why you should not use a hose or pressure washer on an engine. | Cognitive | Comprehension |
| | | | | | Locate and lubricate hinges, latches, and locks. | Psychomotor | Manipulation |
| | | | | | Repair a chip or scratch. | Psychomotor | Manipulation |
| | | | | | **Chapter 8. Fluid Level Check** | | |
| | | | | | Identify different types of fluids used in the automobile. | Cognitive | Knowledge |
| | | | | | Analyze fluid conditions. | Cognitive | Analysis |
| | | | | | Perform basic fluid level checks. | Psychomotor | Articulation |
| | | | | | Add fluids when required. | Psychomotor | Manipulation |
| | | | | | Justify using more environmentally friendly coolants. | Affective | Valuing |
| | | | | | Summarize why it is important to add the correct types of fluids. | Cognitive | Evaluation |
| | | | | | **Chapter 9. Electrical System** | | |
| | | | | | Define electricity in terms of voltage, current, and resistance. | Cognitive | Knowledge |
| | | | | | Identify and locate starting system components. | Psychomotor | Manipulation |
| | | | | | Identify and locate charging system components. | Psychomotor | Manipulation |
| | | | | | Test an alternator. | Psychomotor | Manipulation |
| | | | | | Test a starter. | Psychomotor | Manipulation |
| | | | | | Clean and test a battery. | Psychomotor | Manipulation |
| | | | | | Explain battery performance ratings. | Cognitive | Comprehension |
| | | | | | Inspect drive belts. | Psychomotor | Manipulation |
| | | | | | Locate fuse junction blocks. | Psychomotor | Manipulation |
| | | | | | Remove, inspect, and replace a blade style fuse. | Psychomotor | Imitation |
| | | | | | Describe the difference between a sealed beam and composite headlight. | Cognitive | Comprehension |
| | | | | | **Chapter 10. Lubrication System** | | |
| | | | | | Define the purpose of engine oil. | Cognitive | Knowledge |
| | | | | | Explain oil service and viscosity ratings. | Cognitive | Comprehension |
| | | | | | Discuss the advantages and disadvantages of synthetic oils. | Cognitive | Comprehension |
| | | | | | Discuss the importance of oil filters. | Cognitive | Comprehension |
| | | | | | Change the oil and filter on a vehicle. | Psychomotor | Manipulation |
| | | | | | Advocate the importance of oil recycling. | Affective | Characterization |

| 4 | 3 | 2 | 1 | 0 | TASK/SKILL | DOMAIN | LEVEL |
|---|---|---|---|---|---|---|---|
| | | | | | **Chapter 11. Fuel System** | | |
| | | | | | Explain the purpose of the fuel system. | Cognitive | Comprehension |
| | | | | | Describe the parts of the fuel system. | Cognitive | Comprehension |
| | | | | | Remove, inspect, and replace an air filter. | Psychomotor | Manipulation |
| | | | | | Remove and replace a fuel filter. | Psychomotor | Manipulation |
| | | | | | State gasoline and diesel properties. | Cognitive | Knowledge |
| | | | | | Identify ways to improve fuel economy. | Cognitive | Comprehension |
| | | | | | Explain how fuel is priced. | Cognitive | Evaluation |
| | | | | | Justify the use of clean burning fuels. | Affective | Valuing |
| | | | | | **Chapter 12. Cooling System and Climate Control** | | |
| | | | | | Identify the purpose of the cooling system. | Cognitive | Comprehension |
| | | | | | Describe the components in the cooling system. | Cognitive | Comprehension |
| | | | | | Define coolant properties. | Cognitive | Knowledge |
| | | | | | Explain how coolant flows in an engine. | Cognitive | Comprehension |
| | | | | | Test coolant properties. | Psychomotor | Manipulation |
| | | | | | Change a cabin air filter. | Psychomotor | Manipulation |
| | | | | | List causes of engine overheating. | Cognitive | Knowledge |
| | | | | | Explain how the air conditioning system works. | Cognitive | Comprehension |
| | | | | | **Chapter 13. Ignition System** | | |
| | | | | | Define the purpose of the ignition system. | Cognitive | Knowledge |
| | | | | | Identify ignition system generations. | Cognitive | Analysis |
| | | | | | Categorize ignition system components into respective generations. | Cognitive | Analysis |
| | | | | | Remove, inspect, gap, and replace spark plugs. | Psychomotor | Manipulation |
| | | | | | Test spark plug wire resistance. | Psychomotor | Manipulation |
| | | | | | Remove, inspect, and replace distributor cap and rotor. | Psychomotor | Manipulation |
| | | | | | **Chapter 14. Suspension, Steering, and Tires** | | |
| | | | | | Define the purpose of the suspension system. | Cognitive | Knowledge |
| | | | | | Define the purpose of the steering system. | Cognitive | Knowledge |
| | | | | | Identify components in the suspension system. | Cognitive | Comprehension |
| | | | | | Identify components in the steering system. | Cognitive | Comprehension |
| | | | | | Inspect suspension and steering components. | Psychomotor | Manipulation |
| | | | | | Inspect and rotate tires. | Psychomotor | Manipulation |
| | | | | | Measure tire tread depth. | Psychomotor | Manipulation |
| | | | | | Locate the tire placard on a vehicle. | Psychomotor | Manipulation |
| | | | | | List causes of excessive tire wear. | Cognitive | Knowledge |
| | | | | | Propose reasons for snow tire use vs. all season tires. | Affective | Valuing |
| | | | | | Explain when run flat technology may be beneficial. | Affective | Organization |
| | | | | | **Chapter 15. Braking System** | | |
| | | | | | Define the purpose and principles of the braking system. | Cognitive | Knowledge |
| | | | | | Identify components in the brake system. | Cognitive | Comprehension |
| | | | | | Identify brake fluid properties. | Cognitive | Comprehension |
| | | | | | Discuss the advantage of antilock brakes. | Cognitive | Comprehension |
| | | | | | Explain how the parking brake works. | Cognitive | Comprehension |
| | | | | | Perform brake inspections and measure brake pad thickness. | Psychomotor | Articulation |
| | | | | | Formulate an opinion on the benefits of electronic stability control. | Affective | Organization |

| 4 | 3 | 2 | 1 | 0 | TASK/SKILL | DOMAIN | LEVEL |
|---|---|---|---|---|---|---|---|
| | | | | | **Chapter 16. Drivetrain** | | |
| | | | | | Define the purpose of the drivetrain. | Cognitive | Knowledge |
| | | | | | Identify drivetrain components. | Cognitive | Comprehension |
| | | | | | Describe different drivetrain systems. | Cognitive | Comprehension |
| | | | | | Inspect drivetrain system components. | Psychomotor | Manipulation |
| | | | | | Communicate CVT transmission benefits. | Affective | Responding |
| | | | | | **Chapter 17. Exhaust and Emission System** | | |
| | | | | | Define the purpose of the exhaust and emission system. | Cognitive | Knowledge |
| | | | | | Identify components in the exhaust and emission system. | Cognitive | Comprehension |
| | | | | | Inspect exhaust and emission system components. | Psychomotor | Manipulation |
| | | | | | Explain how the catalytic converter works. | Cognitive | Comprehension |
| | | | | | Locate the vehicle emission control information (VECI) sticker. | Psychomotor | Manipulation |
| | | | | | Describe the benefits of a properly working emission system. | Affective | Valuing |
| | | | | | **Chapter 18. Alternative Fuels and Designs** | | |
| | | | | | Identify differences in automotive design, depending on the fuel source. | Cognitive | Analysis |
| | | | | | Compare and contrast advantages and disadvantages between alternative vehicle types. | Cognitive | Evaluation |
| | | | | | Compare petrobased and biobased fuels. | Cognitive | Evaluation |
| | | | | | Calculate the payback period on an alternative fueled vehicle. | Cognitive | Analysis |
| | | | | | Conduct research to determine if a vehicle is E85 compatible. | Psychomotor | Manipulation |
| | | | | | Explain how regenerative braking works. | Cognitive | Comprehension |
| | | | | | Differentiate between full, plug-in, and mild hybrids. | Cognitive | Analysis |
| | | | | | Illustrate how hydrogen can be used to power an electric motor. | Cognitive | Application |
| | | | | | Participate in a discussion regarding technological issues with alternative fueled vehicles. | Affective | Responding |
| | | | | | **Chapter 19. Automotive Accessories** | | |
| | | | | | Identify available automotive accessories. | Cognitive | Analysis |
| | | | | | Explain different accessory functions. | Cognitive | Comprehension |
| | | | | | Estimate the cost of selected accessories for a specific vehicle. | Cognitive | Application |
| | | | | | Participate in a discussion identifying the issues associated using electronic devices while driving. | Affective | Valuing |
| | | | | | Describe how global positioning systems work. | Cognitive | Comprehension |
| | | | | | Discuss negative impacts of remote starters. | Affective | Organizing |
| | | | | | **Chapter 20. Common Problems and Roadside Emergencies** | | |
| | | | | | Identify common automotive problems. | Cognitive | Analysis |
| | | | | | Analyze basic automotive problems and make a decision about a solution. | Cognitive | Analysis |
| | | | | | Remove and replace a headlight. | Psychomotor | Manipulation |
| | | | | | Explain the different causes of black, blue, and white smoke from the tailpipe. | Cognitive | Comprehension |
| | | | | | Identify unusual sounds and associate a possible problem to that sound. | Cognitive | Analysis |
| | | | | | Identify unusual smells and associate a possible problem to that smell. | Cognitive | Analysis |
| | | | | | Explain what might cause a "no-start" situation. | Cognitive | Comprehension |
| | | | | | Clean a battery. | Psychomotor | Manipulation |
| | | | | | Inspect, remove, and replace wiper blades. | Psychomotor | Manipulation |
| | | | | | Locate a leak on a tire. | Psychomotor | Manipulation |
| | | | | | List items that should be in a emergency roadside kit and a winter safety kit. | Cognitive | Knowledge |
| | | | | | Perform a jump-start safely. | Psychomotor | Manipulation |
| | | | | | Inspect, remove, and replace a drive belt. | Psychomotor | Manipulation |
| | | | | | Remove and replace a flat tire with a spare tire. | Psychomotor | Manipulation |

Name _____    Class _____    Week __ / __ / __    Score _____

## DAILY REFLECTION LOG

Directions - At the end of each day, write a short 3-5 sentence reflection on what you learned.

### MONDAY

_____
_____
_____
_____
_____

### TUESDAY

_____
_____
_____
_____
_____

### WEDNESDAY

_____
_____
_____
_____
_____

### THURSDAY

_____
_____
_____
_____
_____

### FRIDAY

_____
_____
_____
_____
_____

Name _____    Class _____    Date __/__/__    Score _____

# ARTICLE OR WEBSITE REVIEW

## BIBLIOGRAPHY

_____

_____

## SUMMARY

_____

_____

_____

_____

_____

_____

_____

_____

_____

_____

_____

_____

_____

_____

## OPINIONS/CONCLUSIONS/REACTIONS

_____

_____

_____

_____

_____

_____

_____

_____

_____

Name _____  Class _____  Date __/__/__  Score _____

## Career Exploration

Directions - Use the Occupational Outlook Website (www.bls.gov/ooh) to research a career. As you identify the following, write complete sentences in your own words. Do not copy verbatim from the website.

### Career
_____

### Salary Potential
_____

### Education/Training Required
_____
_____
_____

### Job Outlook
_____
_____
_____

### Nature of the Work
_____
_____
_____

### Working Conditions
_____
_____
_____

### Reason You Chose this Career
_____
_____
_____

# REPAIR INVOICE/WORK ORDER

**Repair and Service Facility**
**123 Any Town, USA**
**(555) 555-0100**

Work Order Number: _____
Date & Time Received: ___/___/___ ___:___A.M. P.M.
Promised: ___/___/___ ___:___A.M. P.M.
Order Written By: _____

| Customer Contact Information |
|---|
| Name: |
| Address: |
| City:     State:     Zip: |
| Phone Home: ( ) |
| Work: ( )     Cell: ( ) |

| Vehicle Information | |
|---|---|
| Make and Model | |
| Year/Color | |
| License Number | |
| Odometer Reading | IN      OUT |
| Engine Size | |
| VIN | |

| Description of Customer Concern |
|---|
| |
| |
| |
| |

| Customer Rights | |
|---|---|
| Do you want your parts returned? | Yes ❑ No ❑ |
| If the job exceeds the estimate by 10% or more, do you authorize us in proceeding? | Yes ❑ No ❑ |
| If additional repairs are found necessary, do you authorize us in proceeding? | Yes ❑ No ❑ |
| Do you request a written estimate for repairs with cost in excess of $50.00? | Yes ❑ No ❑ |

| Service History |
|---|
| |
| |

I hereby authorize the above repair work to be done with the necessary material, and hereby grant you and/or your employees permission to operate the vehicle herein described on streets, highways, or elsewhere for the purpose of testing and/or inspection. An express mechanic's lien is hereby acknowledged on above vehicle to secure the amount of repairs thereof.
X _____

| Estimate of Repair | |
|---|---|
| Parts | $ |
| Labor Rate $ ____ Per Hr. x ____ Hrs. | $ |
| Other/Supplies | $ |
| Preliminary Estimate Total | $ |

❑ **Lubricate Chassis**    ❑ **Change Oil**    ❑ **Check All Fluids**    ❑ **Rotate Tires**    ❑ **Wash**

| Parts Required | | | |
|---|---|---|---|
| Qty. | Item No. | Description | Price |
| | | | |
| | | | |
| | | | |
| | | | |
| | | | |
| | | **Total Parts** | |

| Labor Required | | |
|---|---|---|
| Service Description | Hours | Charge |
| | | |
| | | |
| | | |
| | | |
| | | |
| | **Total Labor** | |

| Other/Supplies Required | | | |
|---|---|---|---|
| Qty. | Item No. | Description | Price |
| | | | |
| Towing | | | |
| Environmental Fees | | | |
| Supplies | | | |
| | | **Total Other/Supplies** | |

| Repair Total | |
|---|---|
| Total Parts | $ |
| Total Labor | $ |
| Total Other/Supplies | $ |
| Subtotal | $ |
| Tax | $ |
| **Total Amount Due ▶** | $ |

Name _____  Class _____  Date __ / __ / __  Score _____

# VEHICLE REFERENCE INFORMATION

| | |
|---|---|
| Make | _____ |
| Model | _____ |
| Model Year | _____ |
| Production Date | _____ |
| Drivetrain FWD, RWD, 4WD, or AWD | _____ |
| VIN (Vehicle Identification Number) | _____ |
| Engine Size (L or cu. in.) | _____ |
| Number of Cylinders | _____ |
| Fuel Efficiency (City and Highway) | _____ |
| Fuel Type | _____ |
| Fuel Capacity | _____ |
| Octane or Cetane Number Required | _____ |
| Oil SAE & API Requirements (Summer/Winter) | _____ |
| Oil Capacity | _____ |
| Oil Filter Number | _____ |
| Coolant Type Required | _____ |
| Antifreeze to Water Ratio | _____ |
| Air Filter Number/Brand | _____ |
| Tire Size (Front, Rear, and Spare) | _____ |
| Tire PSI (Front, Rear, and Spare) | _____ |
| Lug Nut Torque Requirement | _____ |
| Brake Fluid Type | _____ |
| Brakes Front and Rear Type (Disc or Drum) | _____ |
| Transmission Fluid Type | _____ |
| Power Steering Fluid Type | _____ |
| Spark Plug Number and Gap | _____ |
| Headlight Number and Style | _____ |
| Wiper Blade Length and Style | _____ |
| Battery Group Number (Size/Terminal Position) | _____ |
| Belt Type (Serpentine or V) | _____ |
| Cabin Air Filter Number | _____ |
| Paint Color and Code | _____ |
| Radio Security Code | _____ |

**EDITION**

# 3RD

QR

# AUTO UPKEEP

## BASIC CAR CARE, MAINTENANCE, AND REPAIR

### MICHAEL E. GRAY AND LINDA E. GRAY

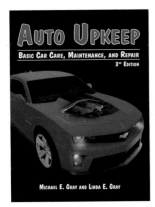

### TEXTBOOK

ISBN: 978-1-62702-001-5
Paperback, 200 Pages

ISBN: 978-1-62702-006-0
Hardcover, 200 Pages

## PAPERBACK SET

ISBN: 978-1-62702-004-6
Includes:
   1 - Paperback Textbook
   1 - Paperback Workbook

## HARDCOVER SET

ISBN: 978-1-62702-007-7
Includes:
   1 - Hardcover Textbook
   1 - Paperback Workbook

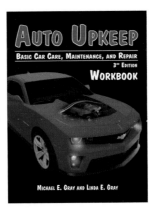

### WORKBOOK

ISBN: 978-1-62702-002-2
Paperback, 152 Pages

### INSTRUCTOR CD

ISBN: 978-1-62702-003-9

CD Includes:
- Course Syllabus Outline
- Competency Profile
- PowerPoint Slides
- Lab Activities
- Study Questions
- Chapter Tests
- Exams & Final
- Answer Keys

## *Auto Upkeep* is excellent for:

- Automotive Programs
- New Drivers
- Boy Scouts - Auto Merit Badge
- Girl Scouts - Car Sense/Car Care Badge
- 4-H Automotive Programs
- Homeschool Students
- After School Programs
- Car Care Clinics

---

Discount pricing and order information available at:

# www.AutoUpkeep.com     (800) 918-READ